Look What You Made Me Do

John Lanchester was born in Hamburg, grew up in Hong Kong and lives in London. He has written six works of fiction and four of non-fiction. His books have won the Hawthornden Prize, the Whitbread First Novel Award, the E. M. Forster Award and the Premi Llibreter, been longlisted for the Booker Prize and translated into twenty-five languages. The television mini-series of his novel *Capital* won an International Emmy Award. He is a contributing editor to the *London Review of Books* and a Fellow of the Royal Society of Literature.

by the same author

THE DEBT TO PLEASURE
MR PHILLIPS
FRAGRANT HARBOUR
FAMILY ROMANCE
CAPITAL
WHOOPS!: WHY EVERYONE OWES EVERYONE AND NO ONE CAN PAY
WHAT WE TALK ABOUT WHEN WE TALK ABOUT THE TUBE
HOW TO SPEAK MONEY
THE WALL
REALITY AND OTHER STORIES

JOHN
LANCHESTER

Look
What
You
Made
Me Do

faber

First published in 2026
by Faber & Faber Limited
The Bindery, 51 Hatton Garden
London EC1N 8HN

This export edition first published in 2026

Typeset by Faber & Faber Ltd
Printed in the UK by CPI Group (UK) Ltd, Croydon, CR0 4YY

All rights reserved
© Orlando Books Limited, 2026

The right of John Lanchester to be identified as author
of this work has been asserted in accordance with Section 77
of the Copyright, Designs and Patents Act 1988

*All characters, names, places and events in this book are fictitious
and any resemblance to persons living or dead, places or events
is entirely coincidental.*

A CIP record for this book
is available from the British Library

ISBN 978–0–571–29867–9

Printed and bound in the UK on FSC® certified paper in line with our continuing
commitment to ethical business practices, sustainability and the environment.
For further information see faber.co.uk/environmental-policy

Our authorised representative in the EU for product safety is
Easy Access System Europe, Mustamäe tee 50, 10621 Tallinn, Estonia
gpsr.requests@easproject.com

2 4 6 8 10 9 7 5 3 1

For Miranda

PART ONE

1
KATE

Every successful marriage has its own private language. I was finishing my make-up in front of the bathroom mirror – the least flattering and therefore the most fit-for-purpose light in the house – when I heard my husband call up the stairs.

'Want your body, disco doll,' said Jack.

This meant: please hurry up, we're going to be late. It was a reference to an old *New Yorker* cartoon. Sad-looking businessman walks past a boom box thumpily blasting the line, 'want your body, disco doll'. He thinks to himself: 'They're singing songs of love, but not for me.'

'Two seconds,' I called back. That meant: less than five minutes, but possibly not by much.

A private language is only part of what a long marriage involves. A marriage has a body of mythology and folklore and anecdote and codes; is its own world, its own ecology, its own system of beliefs and values. And perhaps more than that, its own closed universe of jokes and references, shorthand and nicknames.

These are almost by definition things that are cruel, or mean spirited, or at the very least unfair and inappropriate. The things you wouldn't say in front of anyone else. The people we were going to visit for dinner that evening, a married couple of architects we've known for more than thirty years, are known to us, for reasons lost in the mists of antiquity, as 'the swingers'. (They could not be less likely to be swingers.) My closest girlfriends, the book group who I've been meeting once a month for the last twenty years, would be aghast to know that Jack referred to them as 'the hags', 'your fatties' or 'the enormous great big hairy lesbians'. The prisoners who I've been charity-visiting for almost as long are always referred to simply as 'your axe murderers'. Our well-meaning but irrevocably nosy immediate neighbour, addicted to good works since her husband left her and not coincidentally also addicted to knowing other people's business, was 'the Poisoner'. Jack's notion, or pretend notion, was that her ex had 'ended up under the patio'. So sometimes she was Madame Patio, or Mrs DIY, or Mrs B&Q, or Frau Crippen. And of course it wasn't just – wasn't even mainly – other people who would be the subject of jokes and nicknames and stories. Part of the point is that you call each other things in private that you would never say in public. It goes without saying that these nicknames and tropes and in-jokes are embarrassing, or would be if anyone ever knew about them.

I finished touching up my foundation, checked my teeth for lipstick, and set off downstairs. Jack was waiting for me by the front door, jiggling his car keys in one hand and looking at something on his phone in the other. Our stairwell is brushed concrete, illuminated by uplights set in the floor, and when you come down there is a doubly theatrical effect: the person descending feels as if they are making an entrance (because they are) and the person at the bottom looks as if they are already standing on stage, waiting for their cue. Because of that I had one of those moments when you briefly see the person who you see all day, every day, as if you're looking at a stranger. I saw a tall trim affluent man in middle age, wearing smart clothes negligently, very much at ease with himself – a good person to marry, thriving on no longer being young but not yet being old; the kind of husband who looks like a husband in ads about pension planning, retirement-age cruise holidays, the 'after' character in before-and-after montages about the benefits of taking Viagra.

'We'll be fine,' I said.

'You look nice,' he said, which was true, I did, in my current favourite long emerald-green dress, though it was thoughtful of him to say so. I was wearing gold and amber earrings he had given me on our twentieth wedding anniversary. 'God-Emperor Google says twenty-five minutes,' he said. 'We should be OK.' One of Jack's peculiarities was that when it came to things like traffic and weather, he would always trust technology over his own knowledge and experience. He would look up on his phone to see if it was raining rather than open the door and stick his head out. He had lived in London for all his adult life and must have made this return journey to our friends' house dozens of times – and yet he preferred to look up the transit time on Google rather than consult his memory or, for that matter, me.

'House, lights pattern two,' he said, and the house lights dimmed and the alarm started beeping a warning for us to hurry up and leave. Further evidence of his attitude to technology: Jack had set up a 'smart home' system with lights and the home alarm and connected speakers; pattern two was the lights we left on when we went out, one downstairs in the sitting room and one upstairs in the bedroom. The operating word for the system was 'House'. (This could cause confusion in conversation when people came to visit, and a stray remark about buildings could lead to a disembodied Irish male voice asking if there was anything it could do to help – Jack, by way of 'making his own entertainment', had set up House to have a baritone Irish accent.) House wasn't exactly his pride and joy and he liked complaining about it, but it was typical of his slight addiction to gadgets and men's toys. He claimed it was 'work', which it could, arguably and tangentially, be said to be, since the clients of his architectural practice would sometimes expect him to know and to advise about tech stuff. I think also he liked being a man in his fifties who knew as much about technology and gadgets and the latest new thing as people three or four decades younger. He always told clients he would not advise them to buy any system he wasn't willing and able to use himself.

We were out in the street when the alarm system made its final warning beep and went quiet. It was that point of mid to late spring when you're expecting it to be warm, even when experience should have taught you that it often isn't. That night wasn't objectively cold but there was a dampness in the air that made me glad I had put on a coat. Jack pressed the button on his car key and looked around for the flashing lights. Our street was now full of near-identical small electric SUVs. Sometimes he was the last to park it, sometimes I was, and rather than have a conversation in which we first tried to remember who'd had the car last, and then the person who'd had the car tried to remember where they'd parked it, looking for the lights was the easiest way to find where it had been left. It was straight in front of us, so close we had overlooked it. By custom and practice, Jack drove on the way to dinner and I drove back. I didn't mind: I've never wanted or needed more than a single glass of wine, and for all his apparent extroversion and ease in company, Jack functioned much better with a roomful of people when he had had a few drinks. He is noisier than I am, but I am more of an extrovert. He is the bossy one, I am the controlling one. It takes a while before anyone realises that about us.

'I wish we didn't have an Audi,' Jack said, as we got into the Audi. 'I was cut up twice on the way to work yesterday and it was Audis both times. I thought Mercedes were for dentists, BMWs were for wankers and Audis were for the people who didn't want to be perceived to be wankers. But it turns out that the people who most mind about being perceived as wankers are actually wankers, so now all the wankers are in Audis.'

'But you often cut people up. You're notably a rather aggressive driver. Not a boy racer but you're not Gandhi either.'

'I'm appropriately confident and assertive about my rights on the road. That's different. I don't defer. I drive like a Londoner.'

'Which for a lot of our fellow countrymen is a synonym for wanker.'

He let that pass.

★ ★ ★

God-Emperor Google was wrong about the traffic. We got there in twenty minutes, bang on time.

Michael and Tanya, our old friends, lived in a house near Notting Hill, or rather two houses, or rather what used to be two terrace houses but had been knocked together to make one single very fancy double-sized house, open-plan on the ground floor with a single huge kitchen/living room/dining room, double height on one side, and upstairs a warren of smaller spaces, bedrooms and studies and a nanny flat. Their children left home a while ago – the oldest of them was in his early thirties – and the whole set-up was now wildly too big for them, but the place they had made together was so much part of their identity, and was such an important calling card and marketing tool when they were setting up their practice, that'd I'd be less surprised if they were to divorce or switch genders than if they moved.

The only person I would ever say this to is Jack, but the truth is: there's something vulgar about Michael and Tanya's house. The way I'd put it is to say it's not *Hello!* vulgar, but on the other hand it is *Architectural Digest* vulgar. Which, arguably, is worse, since architects should know better. Everything is too perfect, too designed and tidy and in-its-place. There's also something vulgar about the way they use their home as a showroom, a tool for recruiting new clients. If you're thinking about hiring them, they'll invite you to lunch or dinner at their home, and the none too subtle signal is 'all this could be yours'. The result is that everything is in display condition, squared away and tidied and freshly primped, as if it were a generally accepted rule of life that a house should at all times be ready for a photographer to come through the door and shoot a set of pictures for *World of Interiors*. A bit like that rule about having your underwear clean in case you get knocked down by a bus, but for house-based photo shoots. And the fact is you probably have seen a photo of Michael and Tanya's house, somewhere in a magazine, because apart from using it to tout for work they also lend it out for advertising shoots and never, literally never, turn down an opportunity to have somebody take a picture of it. There might not be a private dwelling in England that has been photographed more often than that house. Jack has been known to speculate about what would happen if you rang them up and asked to rent it for a porn shoot, and if so how far you would have to go to ask for something that made them turn it down ('you'll probably be wanting to wipe down the surfaces afterwards, is that OK?').

I'm a bad person for thinking those thoughts. It is objectively a very nice house and Michael and Tanya are good hosts as well as old friends.

Michael let us into the house through the right-hand front door – the left-hand front door had an ironically repurposed 'Deliveries – Tradesmen Only' sign, which had the effect of stopping anyone from using it, apart from the tenant of what used to be the nanny flat on the top floor. We left our outer layers of clothing in the vestibule. Michael and Jack exchanged some architecty small talk while we sorted ourselves out and then we went through into the open-plan space, still, after all these visits, thrillingly out of scale. We had thought – I had half hoped – that it might just be the four of us, but it turned out Michael and Tanya had invited two new friends as well, neighbours.

'I'm Al,' said the husband, a balding man in his late thirties in a waistcoat. 'And this is Katrina,' he said, gesturing to his wife. She couldn't at that moment speak for herself because the canapé she had just started eating, a decidedly retro chicken and mushroom vol-au-vent, had exploded as she bit into it and was going to spill all over her dress unless her attempts at containment were successful. It made for a spectacle. I forced myself, with some difficulty, not to watch.

Michael did the introductions. The husband, Al, worked in TV; the wife, Katrina, did a job-share at the *Guardian*. There was no way on earth that their salaries could let them afford an address in this part of town so there must be private money somewhere in the background. This was something Jack would complain about when he was in his mode of pretending to be a Marxist but had a convenient tendency to forget when he was dealing with clients.

Tanya came through from the kitchen with another tray of small things on sticks – olives, chunks of pineapple. Our eyes met.

'I'm going through a seventies thing,' she said. 'Prawn cocktail. Coronation chicken. Steak Diane. Black Forest gâteau. Onion soup with croûtons. Quiche Lorraine. Chicken cacciatore. Coq au vin. Veal escalopes. Done properly, they're all delicious. Where's all that kind of food gone?'

'You'll get him started,' I said, but it was too late. Jack had reached for a vol-au-vent, swallowed it whole in one bite, rinsed it down with a glass of champagne, and seized centre stage, all in one action.

'I couldn't agree more. It's like this. Yotam Ottolenghi,' he said. 'Lovely bloke, I'm told. Colleague of yours, yes?' – to Katrina, who gave a complicated half-nod – 'literally the nicest man in the world, everybody says. And yet the fact is that you have to say, objectively, that he has done more damage to this country than the Luftwaffe.'

I had heard this before and – marriage involves compromise – settled down for the ride.

Michael, circling the room topping up champagne glasses, took the bait.

'I'm not sure it is completely true to say that Ottolenghi has caused more damage to Britain than the Luftwaffe.'

'It's to do with the net destruction of competence. You go to someone's house for supper – not here, obviously, Tanya – and you come in the door and you can see from the other side of the room, twenty feet away, that it's Ottolenghi. You see the pomegranate seeds strewn all over everything and you know what's coming. Here we go again. A random assembly of ingredients thrown together by someone who spent ten hours shopping and ten minutes "cooking", i.e. throwing things together, and the crucial point is that they have no idea what it's supposed to taste like because it has no relationship to any food they actually know about or have eaten before, except at the houses of other people who use the same cookbooks in the same way and therefore have exactly the same level of total cluelessness. Sumac – nobody has a clue how to use it. Za'atar – nobody knows what that is. Is it a leaf? Is it a terrorist movement? Is it the main villain in *A Thousand and One Nights*? Pomegranate molasses – what? And they chuck it all together and it looks pretty if you are photographing it and it tastes like God knows what and everybody says ooh yummy Ottolenghi and everybody goes home does the same thing next time and it's all a huge conspiracy to destroy people's ability to cook. Leek tart? People know what that is and what it's supposed to taste like. Roast chicken? People can assess that. Beef and carrots? This one is good, that one less so. Sumac guinea fowl with za'atar beetroot and jewelled cauliflower rice? Nobody's got a fucking clue! What is it? Who's it for? Why would you want to eat jewelled rice? Nobody can tell if it's a disaster because it's already a disaster. It's gone wrong as soon as it's on the plate. Or maybe it hasn't! But even if it hasn't, people don't know, because they don't know what it's supposed to be like. It's like asking blind people to judge a painting competition. Whereas this vol-au-vent is a bloody masterpiece.'

And with that, Jack ate another one. I noticed that Katrina looked amused, whereas her husband looked as if he might be about to burst into tears.

'I cook Ottolenghi all the time,' he eventually and quietly managed to say.

'I'm sure you're the exception who knows exactly how to make it come out right and how it's supposed to taste,' said Jack with manifest insincerity. 'As for me, Kate and I have been thinking about copying Maupassant. Great French short story writer, as I'm sure you know, but the point here is that he hated the Eiffel Tower so much that he used to go there every day for lunch, because it was the only place in Paris from which you couldn't see the Eiffel Tower. On the same principle, Kate and I are planning to go to Tel Aviv on holiday, because as the ground zero of that kind of cooking I reckon it's the only place that's guaranteed to be Ottolenghi-free.'

I said: 'Don't rope me into this, your rant has nothing to do with me and I haven't the faintest intention of going on holiday to Tel Aviv for that or any other reason.'

'Actually, I do know what sumac is,' said Katrina, who I was relieved to see was smiling slightly.

'Thank you, that exactly proves my point,' said Jack. 'If you go to the *Guardian* offices and start asking around you will eventually find somebody who knows what sumac is. You will have found the only place in the United Kingdom where that is true.'

'Shall we go through?' said Tanya.

I remember that evening well, for a number of reasons. Jack was on good form – after the Ottolenghi speech he dialled it down, remembered to listen and to ask questions, flirted lightly in the good-manners-only way he would deploy in company. There was a certain amount of talk about children. Jack and I had always known that we didn't want them, but we hadn't known how much work it would be pretending to take an interest in other people's. Luckily, that part of the evening didn't drag on too long. The three architects talked a little about their current projects, all of them, surprise surprise, being for rich clients who were doing up houses because the rise in stamp duty meant that it made more sense to pimp their current place rather than buy a new one. Michael and Tanya had a Kazakh client, a princeling who was asking them to install a 'boot room' in his Wiltshire mansion because he had heard of them and liked the sound of it. Jack talked about a Thames-side penthouse he was re-renovating – it had already been renovated at least twice, despite being less than ten years old – for a Qatari investor.

'Do you ever have any, you know, British clients?' asked the journalist.

'God, no,' said Jack, to laughter. 'No, I'm joking, of course we do. But it's all foreign money now, because Brexit trashed the value of sterling, so if you're buying in dollars or euros, or whatever, property is about fifteen per cent cheaper. Basically, foreigners are parking chunks of money in the UK because it's cheap and safe.'

'And you don't mind?'

Michael fielded that one.

'You're sitting in it,' he said, gesturing at the house around us, 'you're eating it and drinking it, I'm wearing it. It would be hypocritical to mind. I don't think it's perfect, but I'm not supreme ruler of the universe. I've never voted for the winning party in a general election.'

'That sounds weirdly like a boast,' she said. It was, very gently, a bit of needle. She was probably rather good at her job. Michael was wrong-footed, because of course it was a boast.

'Well no, of course not, it's horrible never having your side in power, I'm a socialist, it's deeply frustrating.'

'Deeply, yes, I can see that,' she said. Tanya, who never said a word about politics, gave a small snort of unsupportive laughter, directed at her husband.

'I'll go and get the chicken Marengo,' she said. 'I've made it in the authentic old-fashioned way, with eggs and crayfish, so your first thought – I'm addressing this to you, Jack – is that the portions are a bit small, but trust me, it's very rich. There's more if you'd like it but take it slow to start with.'

'Duly warned,' said Jack. 'I hope it's brown. Food should be brown. Otherwise it's been prepared with too much attention to how it looks and not enough to how it tastes.' The Ottolenghi-cooking husband was still looking as if he wished he was somewhere else.

I wonder if any men ever feel that they are picking up the burden of social obligation like a huge bag of other people's laundry; laundry that you don't want to do, that in an ideal world you wouldn't have to do, and yet that in this world, somehow, without your ever having volunteered for the task, is your responsibility. What I really wanted to do at this point, with the TV person visibly uncomfortable, with Jack and Michael talking about architecture at the other end of the table and with the journalist wife listening in – what I really wanted to do was sit there in silence and wait for someone to ask me a question, show some interest, engage with me, see me. What I did instead, with a heavy internal sigh, was turn to the TV person and say:

'Have you ever done a cooking show?'

He smiled, with relief as much as anything, I think.

'Sort of. I don't make TV myself, I'm an agent. And that kind of thing has largely gone away, or gone to the internet. All the TV money is in formats these days, as you probably know. What do you do?'

That question, in my experience, is a sign of conversational desperation. I thought, *are we really doing this?*, and had a moment of wishing I was somewhere else.

'These days, not much,' I said. 'According to Jack, most of the nicest people don't do anything much. I used to be an art historian.'

Which was true. Jack had been making enough money for me to give up work, which I was delighted to do, because the part of it I liked – lecturing – was more than outweighed by the parts of it I didn't: administration, and dealing with students. The pay had never been much more than frock money. It was easy to let go. I could have gone into this, but didn't have to, because at that moment Tanya came back to the table with a Le Creuset casserole dish. She began serving up portions of main course, a delicious-smelling but unpretty stew of chicken and tomato with various other bits and pieces in it.

Al said: 'I saw this thing at the weekend about an Italian futurist who banned pasta and thought that all political discussion should be forbidden during meals.'

'Half the women I know don't eat pasta any more, or indeed

carbs of any kinds. And maybe he was on to something with the ban on politics,' I said. I could hear from the other end of the table a series of sentences beginning with the words 'as a socialist, I . . .'

I snuck a glance at them. The body language was clear: Jack and Michael were showing off, Tanya and Katrina were the audience. Or at least, they were supposed to be. There are times in company when you look at someone and catch them with their real face, their real expression, showing what they're really feeling and thinking behind the social facade. It doesn't happen often but it's always memorable when it does. By pure chance, I caught Katrina at one of those moments. Michael and Jack were directing their act towards Tanya, and Katrina had what amounted to five seconds' holiday from observation, when she wasn't expecting to be seen. She didn't have her guard down, not exactly, but her expression was not armoured for the world, and her face was legible – and what was written on it, I saw, was a startling weariness, even a contempt. Perhaps I am projecting, but what I felt I was seeing was an intergenerational dislike, a mid-thirties person looking at people a quarter of a century older than her and seeing a complacent affluence, an unearned self-confidence and assuredness, born of never having had to do anything difficult; of having cruised through life sitting on the great sofa of baby boomer entitlement and economic good fortune, and believing that every good thing that had happened had come so easily and so naturally that we all thought it our due, a tribute to our talents, rather than a huge piece of lucky timing to which we were oblivious – oblivious of other lives, an entire generation driving the metaphorical Volvo of self-awarded entitlement. It was so raw that I felt a jolt of pure dislike both from her and towards her. And then she got her normal conversational face back on, and said something, and the men laughed, and the moment passed.

'It's odd what's happened to politics,' I said to Al. 'How it's become the thing people small-talk about and use to say what kind of person they are. Once it would be the clothes you wore or where you went on holiday or things like that – signifiers, saying you're this or that kind of person. But now it's politics you use to show if you're this or that kind of person. So it's not really about how you want the world to be. No offence to your wife or Michael, or my lovely but sometimes annoying husband, obviously. But it's just ... well, when people say they're this or that, politically, they're not actually talking about the world outside, they're talking about themselves. Which is what they're doing most of the time anyway. So talk about politics is now just more of the same. It's no different from how people cut their hair or what clothes they wear.'

He gave a snort of assent, and lowered his voice a little.

'Personal branding,' he said. 'That's what it's called.'

When the word brand or branding is used, a mental image flashes through my mind: of a burning brand, applied to human flesh. I can almost hear the hiss as it touches the skin; smell the terrible aroma of cooked meat. And then, internally, I flinch. I don't know where that mind-picture comes from, but it happens every time. An intrusive thought, a therapist would call this. A thought like an intruder, breaking into a place you thought you were safe, meaning you ill, meaning you harm. Brand, branding, branded. Fire and metal on bare flesh. I tried to blink away the image.

'One of my clients has written a TV show that has some fun with this kind of talk,' he said, making a discreet small nod at the other end of the table. 'It's basically adultery in Hampstead, only it's not Hampstead. Everybody spends all their time yakking about politics and having steamy affairs. It's coming out in a couple of months and my hunch is it's going to be a hit. It's called *Cheating*. Look out for it.'

'Is that what it's like in your world? Political talk and extra-marital fucking?' I said – his wife not being the only person who knows how to gently needle. He laughed.

'God, no. We have two children under three. I'm running on fumes. As I sit here now it's almost two hours past my bedtime. I'll get ninety minutes' sleep tonight, if we're lucky. When I think about people having affairs I just think, where on earth do they get the time and the energy? I don't envy them the shagging but I do envy them being sufficiently well rested to be able to get up to whatever it is they get up to.'

He sounded as if he meant it.

'And yet you're representing someone whose show is all about the opposite,' I said.

He snorted again. 'Well, absolutely. But it's frank and sexy and it's by a talented young woman writer who's well up for the marketing side of things and with a bit of luck it'll be watched by the kind of people it's about, and also if someone made a show about my own kind of life, by tired parents, for tired parents, the audience would be too tired to watch it. Whereas adultery was good TV when Flaubert and Tolstoy wrote about it, and it's good TV still.'

'Adultery causes pain,' I said. 'I'm old enough and have seen enough to know that's the simple truth about it. I sometimes think it's a point that's not often enough made. But I've noticed that doesn't seem to stop people doing it.'

Jack, at the far end of the table, was raising his voice to make a point, over laughter and protests from the others:

'. . . and the only reason so many women do British Military Fitness is because it has MILF right there in the name.'

Normal conversation in W11, is how I look back on all this talk now. It seems a long time ago and a long way away.

* * *

It was a much quieter version of Jack – the version of him that only I knew – who got into the passenger seat of the car for the drive home. He was decompressing, as introverts do. It had taken me a long time to understand the nature of his appetite for company combined with his need for time to recover from it.

'OK?' he asked.

'Yes, you?'

Jack had been working hard for the previous few weeks, and in that context people, even old friends, could be especially draining. But I could tell from his affect, from the particular texture of his fatigue, that this had been more fun than he had been expecting.

'I'm fine to drive if you need me to,' he lied. I gave him a look that said 'of course you are, darling', and turned on the ignition. I don't remember what we talked about on the drive home. I wish I did. The trip took fifteen minutes, one of those reminders of how nice London would be if only there were no people in it – or rather if the people were something you could toggle on and off at will. Driving somewhere: uninhabited city. Doctor's waiting room: uninhabited city. Anything involving queues: uninhabited city. Theatre: inhabited city. Eating in restaurant: inhabited city. Trying to book restaurant: uninhabited city.

I pulled up in front of the house and went to go straight in. Jack didn't follow me. I turned to look at him.

'I'm just going to go and check on Ken,' he said. It was late and I was tired; I was a tiny bit annoyed at Jack, but also a tiny bit proud. Ken was a rough sleeper who sometimes used a spot in the newly converted block of flats at the end of our road. The developers, crazed with greed as they tend to be, had made a small space for parking, which they had then made so expensive that none of their tenants would rent it from them, and so the covered entrance to the car port was now occasionally used by people like Ken. He slept in hostels when he could but an increasing number of those had rigid bans on drinking and smoking. Jack disapproved of that policy, but I thought it was fair enough: a mentally ill tramp, drunk and smoking in bed in a building with fifty inhabitants, what could possibly go wrong? But the fact was that a rigid ban on drinking and smoking was also, in practice, a ban on Ken. As a result there were many nights, especially when the weather was warmer, when an unsober Ken would be turned away from the hostel and find himself settling down, with his multiple layers of coats, improvised blankets and newspapers, in the car port of the horrible new development at the end of our street.

I didn't stand around and wait – I needed a pee. I went in and told House to turn on the lights to their evening pattern. While I was doing that, I thought about my husband: about the fact that he was the kind of man who would have a mean nickname for his closest and oldest friends, and would say bitchy things about their house, while also performing small acts of kindness for strangers, showing concern and genuine care, about which he would never speak.

This was another side of Jack that was private, and that I was the only person to truly see. To anyone who knew us from the outside, I was the one who was community minded, who did charitable works, who was the doer of good deeds. I signed an open letter as part of a group resigning from the Labour Party over Iraq, and went on the 'not in my name' march. I campaigned for Remain and marched against Brexit. I have been a school governor. I sat on the committee to protest the closure of the local library, and the committee to protest the council's attempt to use a nearby park as a commercialised event space, and the committee objecting to the lack of affordable housing in the big new development nearby.

I co-founded the group that was formed to object to NIMBY objectors to a halfway house for people transitioning back into community life from various sorts of incarceration and inpatient mental health care. I worked with a charity that helped prisoners. I had an old lady who I visited to chat to once a week and spoke to over the phone every third day. I'd even thought about applying to be a magistrate, because I'd more than once been told that 'they need people like you'. But Jack was the one who would do small acts of charity and generosity, gestures of kindness that nobody apart from the recipient would ever know about. Any chugger or charity door knocker who accosted me would get a brisk no, but when I looked over the monthly bank statement I would often find a new charitable direct debit set up, and it was always for the same reason – Jack had been stopped in the street, or Jack had answered the knock on the door. I would remonstrate, he would always promise to listen, and then it would happen again. I was the one who did charity, but Jack was the one who had it in his heart.

My husband returned from his philanthropic exertions.

'I hope Ken's going to be all right, tonight's not as warm as he might have thought,' he said.

'You could ask him if he'd like to stay the night,' I said, and then quickly added 'that was a joke' – because the fact was, that invitation was not unthinkable for Jack after a couple of drinks, once his charitable mindset had taken hold.

'Darling,' he said, meaning: of course not. We had taken strangers in for the night before. We once got home from a dinner party to find a drunk girl on our doorstep, a woman in her late twenties who had over-commemorated the occasion of a break-up (and evidently been abandoned by her friends on their way home). Where others might have given her a cup of tea and waited for her to be sober enough to take a taxi, Jack had asked her in, poured water into her and made her a toasted cheese sandwich, and then set her up on the sofa with pillows, a blanket and a bucket to throw up in, though mercifully she didn't need it. Oh, and he had also given her the spare new toothbrush for emergency overnight guests. In the morning we went downstairs to find that she had let herself out, leaving behind on the kitchen table a penitent and embarrassingly grateful note. Jack spent the whole day basking in his philanthropic glow. But a single woman in her twenties was one thing, a hard-smoking half-mad alcoholic derelict was another. I was relieved that even Jack could see the difference.

'He'll be fine,' I said, a statement for which I had no evidence, but which came out with enough conviction to make Jack nod in agreement or consent or submission – I didn't much care which. I added: 'I'm for my bed.' I headed for the stairs.

'I'll be with you in a few minutes,' said Jack. 'The chicken Marengo is sitting a little heavily.'

'Poor darling,' I said, and smiled to myself as I walked up, the lights coming on ahead of me and turning themselves off behind – one of Jack's technology tricks. While it was true that Tanya's food had been rich, I also thought this was Jack doing something he often did at the end of an evening out, an introvert's recharging: he would sit with a final glass of wine and a newspaper or some rubbish television for half an hour before coming to bed.

'I may take advantage of you while you sleep,' he called after me. 'I'll just stick it in without so much as a by-your-leave.' I didn't break stride. That was one of the filthy things he often said, a private joke from the early years of our marriage, and of course something he never ever did or would dream of doing, because Jack just wasn't that kind of person. And yet he was also the kind of person whom no one would ever imagine saying something like that – which is why it was part of our private language. The public

Jack and the Jack that only I knew were very different, and yet they were the same person, and I loved both of them, and knew both of them better than anyone else ever could or would.

2
KATE

As it turns out, that was what I was thinking the last time I saw Jack alive. I didn't know that those would be the last words I would ever hear him speak. That sentence makes what happened sound dramatic, which of course it was: the worst moment of my life. But it was also so quiet and so lacking in external fuss and noise and – well, I don't quite know how to put it. You want the heavens to rend, the earth to crack, a terrible roaring to come from the air. You want blazing sun at midnight and total dark at noon. You want the external to mark the internal. But it doesn't work like that. We hunger for the outer to match the inner. It usually doesn't. Some of the most terrible things that you will ever experience are also the quietest and most private.

I went up to our bedroom and did all the usual things, a little perfunctorily because I was tired. I got in bed and thought about reading myself to sleep for the next ten minutes, but realised that I didn't need to and turned out the light instead. I sometimes have trouble sleeping, but I never have difficulty getting to sleep; my tricky patch comes towards dawn, when, if I have things on my mind, I can wake and find it impossible to drift off again. That night, I was out quickly. I half heard, or think I heard, Jack come up and quietly get undressed and use the bathroom and get in beside me, but I didn't fully wake. At about three, I must have heard something, maybe a bump or bang. I came awake slowly and realised I was alone in the bed. I thought about whether or not to go to the loo and came to the conclusion it was only a matter of time, either I'd do it now or later, and if it was later I might have problems getting back to sleep – so, now was best.

People say that all architects' houses are the same, and all architects resent that joke. Part of the reason they resent it is because it's a little bit true. One of the reasons I love our house is that downstairs it has that sense of clean and cool and openness, the architect's-house vibe; but upstairs is different. Clean and cool and open are all positives, of course they are – but they're not the same as warm and cosy and comfortable and womb-like, and that is what our bedroom is. There are hangings on the wall in deep engorged reds and purples, and a huge mirror, and a four-poster bed, not one of those modern minimalist four-posters but something that wouldn't have been out of place for Marie Antoinette or King Henry VIII. The drapes are velvet. It is the proverbial tart's boudoir. And then the bathroom is different again. The walls are brushed concrete, and so is the floor, and the bath is free-standing, and the showerhead is powerful, and the lights are bright to the point of harshness, so that objectively you'd have to say it's a very good bathroom, and if it was in a hotel, you'd be thrilled – but it's not a hotel, it's my home, and as such I have to say it's the only place where I feel I'd like things slightly different, slightly softer, slightly warmer, slightly more 'feminine' (a word no architect would be allowed to use, but I'm not one and I don't care).

All that was how I felt about it, before I found my husband dead on the toilet seat at three o'clock in the morning. Jack was naked; he always slept in the nude. He was slumped, his legs apart, his head right back against the cistern. His eyes and mouth were open. His expression was neutral, slack. It is a bathetic and terrible detail, but I remember his flaccid penis and I recollect thinking, Jack would have hated me seeing that. In all our time together, I had never seen him sitting on the toilet. It felt like the most terrible violation – not death, but the loss of dignity.

I have replayed the moment over and over. It was a long time before the intrusive image of Jack lying dead stopped flashing in my head a dozen, a score, a hundred times a day. One of the things I found myself compulsively asking was how I could have known so completely that he had gone. Because the fact was that I did. There was not the tiniest second of doubt: as soon as I saw Jack, I knew that he was dead. I have done a lot of reading and thinking about grief in the time since, and I have come across the idea that this is how people came to believe in the soul: because when you first see a dead person, especially a dead person you love, the thing that hits you immediately and powerfully is this sense of absence. There used to be something there that is not there any more. Death isn't the presence of something, it is the absence of something. And yet everything about the material person is here, and was here until seconds ago. So what is it that isn't here? The essence of the person you love; their deepest being, their self-ness. I can see why people call that thing – the presence that isn't there any more, the being that has now gone, the vital force that has disappeared – the soul. Because that was what happened with Jack. The part of him that made him *him* wasn't there, and I knew it instantly, completely, and finally.

★ ★ ★

A thing people often say, about a difficult time, is 'I don't know how I got through it'. I can say the same about the weeks after Jack's death. The difference is that most people mean it metaphorically. They mean that they called on some resources they didn't know they had, or they were helped by something or somebody they didn't know was there to help them, or they drank and drugged their way through, or they just struggled through it one day at a time, or some combination of all those. In my case, though, it isn't a figure of speech. I don't know how I got through it because I don't remember. There are big blanks in my memory for the time after Jack died. I must have seen Tanya and Michael and they must have said something, but I have no idea when or what. I have flashes of recall from the funeral: the priest reading Jack's favourite passage from Isaiah. The voice said, Cry. And he said, What shall I cry? All flesh is grass, and all the goodliness thereof is as the flower of the field.

I must have done probate, and I must have had people back to the house for drinks after the funeral because I have a stack of cards and notes and emails that refer to it. I have a vague memory of there being lots of work, but I don't remember any of the actual details. I do remember being told that a death involved so much administration and paperwork that it was like running a small business. 'Sadmin', people call it. As for the specifics of that small business – all gone. I suppose I answered people's notes of condolence. Or maybe I didn't. It doesn't feel like it matters much and either way I don't remember. I suppose that's what it boils down to about that whole period: if anything that happened mattered, I would remember it. I don't, so none of it is relevant. The only thing that mattered was that Jack had suddenly died and I felt alone in a way I never had before. I felt alone with a completeness I had never imagined possible.

Feeling alone was not the same as being alone. My friends 'rallied around' – I believe that's the expression. But it was more complicated than that might sound. When my father died, a long time ago, my mother complained that many of her coupled friends, with whom she had thought she was buddies for life, simply dropped her. It was as if by becoming a widow she had contracted an embarrassing disease; not just embarrassing but somehow contagious, and therefore necessary to avoid. 'It can't have been that they were worried I was going to pinch their husbands,' she said, and at the time it struck me as deeply grotesque that anyone would ever think that. Part of my reason for thinking so is that my mother seemed ancient, decades past any thought of her own attractiveness, let alone any prospect of sex – a perspective that seems much less valid now that I'm several years older than she was then. I suppose what I thought, back then, was: poor Mum, of course your life is over, not just the partnered side of it but all the rest too. It seemed so obvious that it was all over for her, and that that was how she must see the situation too.

How cruel we are when we're young. Or to put it differently, how cruel is the perspective of youth, the perspective from which you're certain that none of this will ever happen to you.

That has all changed. I was spared the old-time widow's invisibility, the casting-out. But that didn't help much. What I hadn't expected is that although couples did not drop me, I found I could not bear to see them. The problem was partly to do with the fact that while people did not want to seem like 'smug marrieds', there really was no way of avoiding it. My coupled-up friends were for the most part people who had been together for two decades or more. Just by being together, completely at ease in each other's company, they were taking for granted the very fact of the other person's continuing presence. That was hard to bear. Michael and Tanya were particularly hard to take, though maybe that wasn't entirely their fault; it was impossible for them not to fill my mind with memories of that last happy oblivious terrible evening. I couldn't bear to see them because they reminded me not just of Jack but of the specific moment of his death. And on top of that, I couldn't stand their marriedness. They squabbled when I saw them, but that was no help at all. They squabbled in the way that married people squabble. I wondered if on some level they were doing it to send small signals that were supposed to say, look, here we are arguing, see, being married isn't that great! That was no consolation. Even small acts of pettiness, arguing and eye-rolling and squashing each other's punchlines, were reminders of the deep intimacy that underpinned it and made it possible – the kind of trivial bickering you can only do with someone with whom you're entirely intimate.

The unthinking intimacy and closeness of the couples, and my being invited to witness it, was not the worst of it. In company, I would sink ever deeper into my sense of misery and loss. I hated that I was constantly having to censor myself, gag myself, bite my tongue. I found myself wanting to say, why do you think this isn't going to happen to you? Can't you see that it's just a matter of time, that the clock is ticking down towards your own bereavement, abandonment, loss, grief, madness? That the one who dies first is the lucky one, the one who is spared the worst of the pain?

I'm going to say something that makes me sound awful. I've never been one for conspicuous displays of female solidarity. That thing where something goes wrong, something bad happens, and your girlfriends send you a bunch of flowers. I've always hated it. The idea that there is a solidarity among suffering sisters – no thanks. Women sitting round in a circle, wailing and comforting each other, knowing that life is a series of things done to us, but the pain is eased by the knowledge that we're all there for each other on the journey . . . I can't stand it, the complacent long-suffering sorority masochism.

Because of that, it was with surprise that I found my female friends, singly and collectively, were the greatest comfort in my loss. It wasn't to do with anything specific that anyone said or did – it was just the sense of companionship and not-aloneness and the comfort of being with people with whom I didn't have to perform or act or do anything, I could just be, even if that being was silent and passive. I wondered if they arranged a rota; I didn't want to ask, because I didn't want to put anyone on the spot. But in those first few weeks there wasn't a day that went past without one of my friends checking in on me, dropping off flowers (I didn't say anything) and then staying for a cup of tea, or bringing around a portion of something they'd cooked, or self-inviting to sit and watch TV, or play cribbage, or suggest one of the outings that I wasn't yet feeling strong enough to face, but which I was glad to be reminded still existed as possibilities, in the distant future – theatre, movies, galleries.

If there was a rota, I'm pretty sure who would have been behind it. Daphne, my oldest friend. We've known each other since our first day at university, by the pure chance of being on the same staircase in a college that had only just started accepting women. I wasn't sure I liked Daphne initially, because the first thing I noticed about her was a bossy, imperious, oblivious quality. To be completely honest, that side of her character is still there and it's no more likeable than it was decades ago; but by now we have spent so much time together, and known each other in so many different life stages and circumstances, that liking doesn't really come into it. She is one of the pillars of my life, a witness and companion, and her better qualities – her warmth and kindness and sheer ability to give, especially to give attention and support – were a huge comfort when Jack died.

This does not mean that she was not annoying, and frequently. One-to-one though, when there was an opportunity for her to be quiet and intimate, Daphne was at her best. I felt completely safe with her, and could say anything to her, up to and including the kinds of things I'm saying here – I'm not expressing anything about her that I haven't said to her face. Anything involving organisation brought out her other side. What is there to organise, you might be wondering, in a friendship group of women in late middle age? Answer: more than you might think. Especially if Daphne was anywhere in the vicinity. Interested in bridge? Then you might be especially interested in this week-long bridge cruise along the Danube, organised with a bridge club who did tours (mates' rates negotiated by Daphne, obviously, but only available to people who committed early). Dabble a bit in painting, and casually and momentarily express an interest in taking it up again? Before you can blink you're in a WhatsApp group with Daphne organising a series of classes in flower painting with a teacher in high demand, places available at special rates, obviously, but only to those willing to commit early. She was perfectly well off, Daphne, as a senior civil servant who could easily have afforded to do any of the things she wanted to do and pay full price; for her, getting deals and discounts was part of the fun, part of her personal code. She rationalised the haggling by saying she was being mindful of those among us who couldn't afford the same level of trips and treats. My answer was always that if people couldn't afford it they wouldn't come and there was no need to second-guess.

Much of this side of Daphne, or this side of her relationship with me, was in abeyance in those difficult days. While I was grieving, she did not try to book whale-watching cruises, or arrange National Trust visits, or snap up discounted tickets to West End productions. The only point of irritation with Daphne, in the aftermath of Jack's death, concerned the book group. Daphne would probably call it 'her' book group. And that was part of the problem. The book group had begun twenty years before, when Daphne and a couple of other women had been restarting their social lives after some of them emerged from the tunnel of early motherhood. It had been through multiple changes of personnel in that time. I had been a member from the very beginning – had been to the first meeting, in fact, discussing Mary McCarthy's *The Group*, of all highly appropriate things, at Daphne's terraced house in Balham, while her then husband crashed and galumphed around in the kitchen, clearly annoyed at being excluded from the conversation. I remember his behaviour better than anything else about that evening; the thought crossed my mind that a man so childish, so insecure at his wife's enjoyment of her friends' company and chat, wasn't much of a companion for Daphne. I suddenly thought: they might not make it. And indeed they didn't, and Daphne filed for divorce about eighteen months later. She was the first of my friends to get divorced – the first of a long list, though the divorces came in waves, with the marriages imploding through the strain of early child-rearing being one wave, then the bored people having affairs a few years later, and then, more recently, the postmenopausal empty nesters looking at their partners and concluding that having already put in a couple of decades with this person, they didn't want to put in a couple more. All the divorces in my circle of acquaintance were initiated by the wife. No exceptions.

I don't remember every meeting of the book group as well as that. It would be weird if I did. More than once we've been on the verge of accidentally discussing the same book twice, and once we did deliberately go back and choose a novel we'd already done before to see if it 'held up'. But because Daphne was the one with a mania for organisation, and maybe because the first meeting had been held at her house, and also, perhaps, because she got divorced not long after it began, when she was still in the isolated phase of early parenthood, so the connectedness that came from the group meant so much to her – for all these reasons, in Daphne's head it was her book group, even though for everyone else it was our book group, and had been through cancer, divorces, disasters, illnesses, successes, pregnancies, child-rearing, school choice anxieties, foreign holiday catastrophes and triumphs, house moves, bankruptcies, career changes, failed attempts to relocate to the country, affairs, spousal adulteries – everything.

Daphne's first attempt to get me back to book group was two weeks after Jack's death. She had come over unannounced – something I normally don't like, even in extreme circumstances, but Daphne was Daphne. She brought a Tupperware box containing something casseroled, bath salts, a packet of biscuits. She made a pot of tea and brought it into the sitting room.

'Book group,' said Daphne.

'No,' I said.

'Everyone would love to see you. It will make you feel better.'

'No.'

'Please? For me?'

'It's too soon.'

She left it there.

The next month, in a highly uncharacteristic display of tact, she didn't mention the group's meeting at all. A month later, she tried again. By this point I was still deep in grief, but less numb, and also less busy. The running-a-small-business sadmin stage of bereavement had passed and I was feeling the absence of Jack very thoroughly and completely – his not-thereness, the hole where my life had been. My days were empty and long and the occasions when people came to interact with and distract me, to entertain me and try to take me out of myself, had only momentary success. People came and went and I was left feeling just as flat as before. Daphne could see that, I think, so she returned to the offensive.

Again she came bringing food and distractions – another casserole, some cake, a small handful of magazines with a holiday brochure 'accidentally' slipped into the middle, and a copy of a new novel by an up-and-coming Irish writer, which Daphne told me I was 'certain to love'. After tea and cake she then slyly said:

'By the way, just in case you're interested, we're going to do this in the book group this month. Same as usual, third Thursday of the month. It's at Rachel's place.'

The added attraction of the meeting being at Rachel's place was that she was the only member of the group who would cook dinner. When other group members were hosting, we ate before the meeting, but Rachel had trained at Cordon Bleu and worked professionally as a cook in her youth, and she liked the opportunity to, frankly, show off. She was an unbelievably good cook, the best I know, and Daphne thought that the chance to eat her food might be an incentive in itself. At any other time it would have been. But my appetite hadn't so much disappeared as become entirely erratic and unreliable. I would eat nothing for two days and then wake starving at three in the morning, take half a loaf of sourdough out of the freezer, eat it toasted with most of a pack of butter, then collapse back into bed and either stare at the ceiling until I couldn't bear it any more and get up, or crash into an unconsciousness that felt deeper than mere sleep, and wake ten hours later.

It wasn't just hunger and the need for sleep that came and went. What I found about most feelings, in those weeks of severe, near deranged grief, was that they were intermittent. I would veer between emotions – grief, depression, anger, hunger, manic energy, crushing fatigue, longing for company, longing to be alone, intrusive thoughts about death, sudden moments where I would feel as if I was jolting awake, even though I hadn't been asleep – and realise that an hour, two hours, a whole day, had gone past.

'I'm not ready yet,' is what I said to Daphne, but I knew that a time would come when I did indeed feel ready – and that was in itself a change. Three weeks after that, I went out for the first real recreational outing, to go and look around the National Gallery. It wasn't to a specific exhibition: like Jack, I can't stand 'blockbusters'. But in the early years of our marriage, when Jack was first training and trying to qualify and we didn't have much money, our favourite weekend hobby was to go to the gallery and look at the pictures, one room per visit. We would take our time; look for a while, chat for a while, look again. Then we would head into Chinatown for dim sum, and depending on weather or mood, take the bus or Tube or walk home. Jack would call these gallery visits 'the second-best free entertainment in town', which, like about seventy-five per cent of the things Jack regularly said, was a private joke about sex. What it really was, though, was a slow and thorough education in art history, the thing that eventually encouraged me to go and do a second degree. The National Gallery had stayed with me as a pleasure and resource for all the years since – and it was that trip which I now wanted to take as the first solo expedition after Jack's death.

This was a test, of sorts. In the event, I didn't manage to do an entire room; I only managed a single picture. Masaccio's *Virgin and Child*. The strange combination of 3D and flatness in it, the painful luminosity of the blues and golds, had the effect of collapsing time, of blurring past and present, or rather of intercutting between them: one moment, it was as if Jack was still beside me and both of us were looking at it together for the first time; another, and all I could feel was his absence. My throat closed and my head swam. But I forced myself to stand still and to keep looking. I tried to sink into the world of the painting. I was sure that I was going to faint. I didn't faint, though, and I kept looking at the picture, and then as I did I suddenly and inexplicably began, not to remember Jack and the time all those years ago when we had stood looking at the picture together, but to feel as if Jack was there, right now, beside me, and that he would continue to be beside me as long as I didn't turn my head and sneak a glance to check – that all I had to do to keep him there with me was to keep looking at the painting, staring at it as if there was nothing else in the world to see.

I don't know how long I stood there. I waited for the feeling of Jack's presence to fade, and eventually it did, and then I turned. There was nobody in the gallery except the usual spray of tourists, a group of bored children huddling around a teacher, a docent frowning at a Chinese couple standing too close to a different Masaccio, a few serious art students and painters staring and sketching. I left the gallery and went straight home.

As I came through my front door, the landline was ringing. 'House, cut out answering machine,' I said, this being a trick of Jack's – you could make the system answer the phone or delay the message cutting in, according to preference. I took off my coat and went into the kitchen. I already knew that it would be a friend: they had all stopped calling me on my mobile because they knew that I was keeping it switched off.

It was Daphne.

'Hello, darling,' she said. 'It's that time of the month. Book group? Before you answer: I've got a special deal. You know that influencer thing I was talking about?'

It had been an emotionally overwhelming afternoon, and the fact that my resources were depleted was the only reason I didn't groan audibly. I did indeed know what she was talking about, because she had already gone on about it at length: Daphne had an Instagram account, and had become an influencer, posting photos and comments about new books. Many of them were things we had discussed or were about to discuss in the group. Publishing being a business, this had been noticed, and Daphne was now getting some encouragement in the form of invitations, freebies, and proof copies. It was very much in character for Daphne to have turned this hobby corner of her life into a combination of job and project – which did not make it any the less exhausting to hear about.

I didn't say anything, which didn't deflect her in the slightest.

'. . . well, I've been sent a whole batch of proofs, specifically for the book club, by the lovely publisher, of what I'm told is definitely the hot book this season and a perfect match for us in terms of subject and writing, because he's followed my Insta for ages and he knows exactly the kind of thing we like. All free! So that's what we're going to do. Please say you'll come.'

It was because of the Masaccio, I think, or more accurately the feeling I had had of Jack's presence while I was in its presence; or perhaps, more simply and banally, the fact that I had just had my first successful solo outing since Jack's death. I found that I could face the thought of people.

'I'm not saying I'll read it,' I said.

'Well, of course you don't have to read it, darling, you know perfectly well we only start by talking about the book before we get on to everything else, it will just be lovely to see you and everyone will be so thrilled.'

That was true, that we didn't mainly discuss the book. Jack said that the purpose of the club was to establish definitively who had the worst husband and/or most disappointing children and/or problematic menopause.

'OK, fine,' I said, not very gracefully.

And that was how it happened. I have asked myself many times whether, if I hadn't gone to the National Gallery, or if I hadn't just come through the door at that exact moment, or if I had missed that particular meeting of the book group, I would have got through life without knowing anything about *Cheating*, and if so, whether none of the things that were to happen, would have happened. In other words, I wonder whether if Daphne hadn't called me and asked me to come, I would have avoided having a bigger violation, and bigger horror, than the time I walked in and found my beloved husband dead.

3

INT - HOTEL ROOM - EVENING

It's a standard room in a chain hotel - the kind of hotel room people use if they are having an affair. TINA comes in. She's about thirty, dressed for an evening out. She has a look around and isn't particularly impressed. She chucks her jacket on the bed, then thinks better of it and hangs it up in the cupboard. The TV has a corporate hotel welcome screen and is playing muzak. She turns it off. She sits on the bed and starts looking at her phone.

We hear keycard noises and JERRY comes into the room. He is a good-looking and well-looked-after man in his late fifties. He's doing his best to look sexy and confident. He is carrying a tote bag.

                JERRY
Want your body, disco doll.

Tina isn't buying it. She's genuinely angry.

                TINA
Is that one of the things you say to her?
One of your lines?

Jerry doesn't answer, he just wears a 'nothing can get to me' smile. He takes a bottle of champagne and two glasses out of the tote bag. While they argue, he opens the champagne and pours two glasses.

                    TINA (CONT'D)
I asked you a question.

                    JERRY
And I ignored it.

                    TINA
It's something you say to her, isn't it. It's one of your set pieces. The ones you think are so charming. Is it because of her you think they're cute? Is that something she's told you? Because just so you know, it isn't. It's just irritating.

                    JERRY
Poor you.

Tina stands in front of him, arms crossed.

This is all about sex, of course it is.

                    TINA
You're a bit out of breath. You parked a couple of streets away, didn't you? Just in case somebody recognised your car. An adulterer's trick.

JERRY

You mind, of course you do. But when I'm here with you, I'm here with you. All of me.

TINA

Always in the middle of the afternoon.

JERRY

It has to be this way.

TINA

Well, I'm sick of it.

JERRY

I know. I'm sorry. I'm sorry and I'm married and you knew that. I've never lied to you.

TINA

But you lie to her. All the time.
 (beat)
Answer me.

JERRY

I didn't hear a question.

TINA

Do you lie to her all the time?

JERRY

 (reluctantly)
Yes, I do. I lie to her all the time. I don't lie to you though. Ever.

TINA

You lie to your 'little dumpling'. Your 'cutie pie'. Your 'wife totty'. Your 'darling sex pot'. Nicknames. Puke. How old are you, for fuck's sake?

JERRY

I should never have told you.

TINA

That's right, you shouldn't. And you shouldn't have told me about the kinky little escapades that the two of you—

JERRY

Stop it.

TINA

Stop it? Stop talking about you and your wife and your special kinky treats, birthdays and anniversaries? Or you'll do what?

JERRY

Just stop it.

From now on we don't see Tina, we're looking only at Jerry as he watches her.

TINA
 (slowly)
Stop what? Stop this?

JERRY

No, don't stop that.

                    TINA
Or this? You want me to stop this too?

                    JERRY
No, don't stop that either.

                    TINA
You like that?

                    JERRY
Yes.

                    TINA
Say it again.

                    JERRY
I like that.

                    TINA
How much?

                    JERRY
I like it very much.

                    TINA
And how about this? How do you feel when
I do this?

                    JERRY
Yes. I like that.

He starts to get to his feet - he obviously wants
to come towards her.

                    TINA

Did I say you could get up?
    (beat)
I asked you a question.

                    JERRY

No.

                    TINA

No what?

                    JERRY

No you didn't say I could get up.

                    TINA

That's right. You just sit there. And now
this is going to happen.

We watch Jerry as he watches her. He reaches out
and picks up his glass but seems to lose the thread
of his thought as he keeps watching, and without
realising he hasn't taken a sip he puts the glass
back on the table.

4
PHOEBE

People who want to be liked turn up early. People who want to be needed turn up late. As for me, it varies according to mood. For lunch with my agent, who's always late, I turn up on time and order a glass of whichever is the most expensive champagne they sell. That way, I get a nice glass of champagne and he gets an incentive not to be so late next time.

The restaurant was a fancy place in the middle of town, see and be seen, waiters in aprons, starched tablecloths, people trying not to swivel their heads as they take in the coming and going, very what the French call *m'as-tu-vu* – have you checked me out? All good fun, as long as someone else is paying. I was wearing a scallop-topped pink shirt and red Izzy Marant trousers with printed flowers and felt that I fitted right in. Across the room I could see a reality TV star with one of those made-over faces, orange tan and fake eyelashes and threaded eyebrows and tweakments, done up along the principle that the best thing in life is to look like everybody else who has the same idea about how they want to look. She was having lunch with a significantly older man, also fake-tanned, who had two shirt buttons too many undone and was flashing a colossal gold Rolex. He had a faint but unmistakable air of predation, not necessarily sexual, more likely to do with money. Talent management, I'd say. Or 'talent' management. Each of them had roughly a third of their attention on each other, a third on their phone, and a third on the room. Most of the tables were engaged in business talk of one sort or another, I would guess. There was only one table of tourists, a corner spot taken by a Chinese family of two smartly dressed adults, two children in T-shirts and trainers, and seven huge Hamleys bags, draped on and over two chairs of their own. The grown-ups were concentrating hard on their menus and the children were doing the same on their phones.

How did people kill time before mobiles? I should be old enough to remember but I actually don't. Like right now, sitting here in a restaurant, waiting around like a piece of spare equipment: what would I have done back then? Stared into space? Looked around the room at the scene, people-watching, not a care in the world? Pretended to read a book? Acted like I didn't mind I was being sort-of-stood-up? Done a fucking crossword? Exhausting even to think about it. I did what any normal person would do and took out my phone, but before I had unlocked it I saw Aloysius crossing the room towards me. He was weaving his path between tables, mouthing apologies. He was wearing a pinstriped suit and a bow tie, of all things, which I knew was a sign that he was tired. He had once told me that he dressed up as a form of self-fortification when he was fatigued or facing a difficult day. I didn't need the evidence, I could see he was knackered, in the classic style for a parent of small children. The bow tie, as bow ties always do, made him look like somebody who had to sign the sex offenders register. Still, I was glad that I had dressed up rather than down.

'Sorry sorry sorry,' Al said, and then turning to the accompanying waiter and pointing at my glass, 'one more of those each, please. Tube running late, firestorm at the office, children up all night, haven't slept since Gordon Brown was PM, everything is chaos, sorry again, but how about you?'

'All the better for being a glass of champagne down already, thank you for asking. I know you're supposed never to tell somebody they look tired but in this case you leave me no alternative, you look absolutely fucked.'

'I know. What do you think about the bow tie?'

'It makes you look like a paedo.'

'Thank you.' One of the things I like about Aloysius is that he isn't hard to read. In this case, he was mostly amused and only a little offended.

'Somebody had to tell you.'

'Katrina already did but I thought it might get better reviews from the wider public.'

The waiter arrived with the two further glasses of bubbles. We raised them to each other.

'To *Cheating*,' Aloysius said. He took a sip of the wine, did a double take, took another sip, then drained his glass and signalled to the waiter for another.

'You sure?' I said. He nodded.

'Had a quadruple espresso on the way here, I'll be fine,' he said. 'Look, listen, on the subject of press: we have an amazing early piece coming about the director, and some of those press that I sent links to the screener – you remember I told you about them – are coming back already raving and foaming with excitement and the headline news is that everybody is going mental and it's blowing up, blowing up in a good way, and my assistant is putting together a package of clips and is going to send it over to you this afternoon, and everyone at the shop thinks the news just keeps getting better. I had a polite email from the head of the production company with an x at the end, and that only means one thing, that he's about to claim credit for what's happening and that's excellent news because it means he's confident it's going to be a hit.'

'And he's always right,' I said.

'To hear him tell it, absolutely,' said Aloysius.

He picked up his menu and made a waggling gesture with it, and we both tacitly agreed to decide on our order. While I pretended to do that – I already knew what I wanted, thanks to that fifteen-minute head start – I thought about what Aloysius had said, and what I felt about it. I had been getting good news about the show for some time now, and had on principle refused to believe any of it. But now, it was beginning to feel as if it might come true. And I was pleased, mainly . . . I think? Though there was a good dose of apprehension mixed in too. Writing is all about control. Nothing happens that you don't want to happen: if you want it to rain it rains, if you want the characters to drop dead or burst into flames or emigrate to Mexico or fall in love with a fire hydrant, you can do it in a sentence. You can set the story underwater, you can set it on Mars, you can set it in your neighbour's hot tub. Then there are all the fights you go through to actually get the thing made, which is a completely different story. But I don't think I've ever had such a pure experience of control as I did when I was writing my spec script.

This part, though, dealing with the script's life in the world, was not like that. It wasn't that Aloysius himself was in any way scary to deal with. Watching him with his head down over the menu, his artlessly scruffy bald patch in contrast with the retro cosplay of his fifties suit and bow tie, it would be difficult to feel over-awed, intimidated, or challenged to raise your game. No – there was nothing anxious-making about Al. He was a nice sweet posh boy, a type I had encountered for the first time at university and quickly discovered I could have for breakfast. Which didn't mean that he was stupid or bad at his job. Just that, in a pinch, I knew that I could bulldoze him. My unwelcome new feelings weren't to do with Aloysius but with the evident fact that I wasn't in control of my life any more. I had moved past the phase where anything and everything that happened to my work was up to me. It had been helpful, while I was writing, both to have the feeling that every word in it was there entirely because of my choices and also that if I wanted it not to be made, or even read by another human being, at the end of the process – if I finished it and simply decided that no one would ever see it – that I could just take the manuscript and chuck it into the bin, and there would be nobody to stop me. But now, if there was anything specific I wanted to happen to the show, there wasn't a thing I could do about it. Nothing was up to me. It was out there in the world and whatever would happen would happen, and my actions or lack of them wouldn't have any effect on anything. It was as if I had been cranked up to the top of a very tall, very twisty, very alarming rollercoaster, and the next thing that was going to happen was that I'd be let go and then gravity would be in charge.

The waiter came and we ordered – salad and fish for me, pâté and pie for Al. We agreed that neither of us wanted or needed more to drink. And then, as if he had been following the train of thought that I hadn't expressed out loud, Aloysius said:

'You'll be hearing from the publicity people soon, if you haven't already. I know they've got quite a bit of stuff lined up. It's a good idea to begin thinking about the kinds of things you might say.'

'The kinds of things I might say. Like, watch my show or there will be a curse on your family.'

'No, not that.'

'Watch my show or you will suffer from an untreatable anal fissure.'

'Not that either.'

Our food came. The plates looked pretty and we started eating.

'It doesn't matter anyway, does it?' I said. 'They'll say what they want to say and if you try and shape it you look like you care too much and if you do that they'll skin you alive.'

Aloysius gave a small smile and with a second bite finished his comedy-small starter. He lifted his napkin and wiped his lips.

'I hope you don't mind if I make an observation,' he said. I thought: oh fuck, here we go. Is there a human being on earth, has there ever been a person in all history, who likes being on the receiving end of an 'observation' about their character? 'The thing about you is.' Here is a rule of conduct, true everywhere and always: any sentence or thought, said by one person to another, that can be framed with the words 'the thing about you is', is a bad thing to say. Sometimes I suppose these things need to be said. But it should be done sparingly and carefully and with all attention to the other person's feelings. Which as a policy is easy to say but harder to put into practice, especially as all 'the thing about you' sentences ultimately come from a place of irritation/annoyance/exasperation/anger.

I should say that I very often break that rule for myself. But that doesn't mean I don't know it's a good rule.

'OK, I get it, brace for incoming.'

'You are, you can be, a bit of a bully.'

I thumped my fork down on the table and sat forward. I did my best to radiate pure fury. I could feel the couple at the next table glancing across.

'How dare you!'

It was funny to see how quickly and completely he looked aghast – terrified. I held the pose for a few seconds. Then slumped back and picked my fork up and speared a salad leaf.

'No, just kidding, it's OK, I know,' I said. Aloysius swallowed; it was gratifying to see how relieved he was. 'It's not something I've never been told before.'

He nodded and thought for a moment about what he was going to say next.

'It comes across,' he said, eventually and carefully. 'It's a kind of forcefulness that you have – maybe you know that and maybe you don't, and sometimes I think it veers between the two. So you know when you're doing it a bit, like just now with that joke about "how dare you", but there are also times when you're doing it and I don't think you know you're doing it. It's just how you are. There is, if you don't mind my saying so, an edge to you. Your jokes, like that one, your talk. I'm not criticising it – I'm a fan, obviously, or I wouldn't be representing you. But there's no point pretending it's not there.'

I thought for a moment of simulating offence; the fact was that I didn't really feel any.

'OK, fine, I know what you mean, more or less,' I said. He nodded.

'The thing is, it's in your show too. That dark quality. The nastiness. It's about someone fucking someone else's husband and when you read it part of the point seems to be that she's doing it not because she particularly wants the husband but because she gets a kick out of messing up the wife, without the wife knowing she's being messed up. So it's fucking plus the thrill of secrecy and the thing about the thrill of secrecy is that it's always ultimately about power. You know that question, would you rather have the ability to fly or to be invisible, and how people who say they want to fly say so because they want to do positive things, you know, go travelling and so on, but people who want to be invisible want to know secrets, what's said about them behind their backs, what other people get up to in private, they want to steal things and make money, and how all of that is finally to do with power? Well, you come across totally as that person who wants to be invisible, and it's very much in your show. That edge of voyeurism. Your narrator – she's someone who likes to watch.

It's sexy but it's dark and kinky and there's an edge of something really nasty in it. In her.'

This was sharper than I had expected. I reminded myself that the balding, slightly weak-looking man in the bow tie was no fool.

'And the point of these riveting observations is?' I said. He blinked.

'Well, what I'm saying is, there's no point pretending to be someone you're not. I mean, you could act like you're a big ingénue, it's all meant to be happy-clappy, warm and fuzzy, it's a love story, it's only that it's just a love story about people who are married to other people and there's an age imbalance and a power imbalance but so what, love is love. Except that's not the show you've written. What I like about it, what everyone at work likes about it, is the amorality. The feeling that you, the writer, actually don't give a shit about any of the ways your characters' behaviour crosses lines. It's not that you see them as bad – that's the point. You just don't see it in ethical terms at all. And that's interesting. So when you talk about it, when you frame it, you can lean into that. Not try to tell them what to think, because you're right, they hate that. But actually, as long as you don't give away that you know that's what you're doing, they quite like it too – to have their understanding of it put in a perspective. So you show them what to think but you don't tell them what to think.'

'Cynical. Nice. I thought I was supposed to be the dark one.'

'All I'm saying is, don't pretend to be someone you aren't. Don't act like the great passion of your life is, I don't know, caring about fluffy bunny rabbits and singing around the campfire. Not because it's morally wrong – I couldn't care less about that and neither, I suspect, could you. But just because it doesn't work.'

'It works for some people.'

'Sure, there are people who are natural mask wearers. That's definitely a thing – going through life with one mask after another.

But you aren't that person, I don't think. So you shouldn't pretend to be. I'm not going to ask where it comes from. Sometimes these things don't come from anywhere, they're just who we turn out to be. But it's who you are and you should go with it.'

'So what you're saying is, don't wear a mask of being the kind of person who wears a mask.'

'Precisely. Stay on brand. You're only happy when it rains. You're dark, you're fascinated by amorality. Are you the voice of a generation, the other side of cancellation and virtue signalling? It's not for you to say. Is it possible that in our hearts we all carry a shadow? Do we need the night in order to appreciate the day? Is it part of the point of art to make us seem hideous and chaotic in order for us to appreciate order and beauty all the more? Is kinky cheating sex, quite simply, more fun?'

At exactly that moment, the waiter arrived to clear our plates. He had obviously heard the last thing Aloysius said. He looked startled and Aloysius, I was pleased to see, blushed almost purple. I laughed so much that I thought I was going to cough up my lettuce.

5
PHOEBE

After lunch, I took the bus to my next appointment. It was a Roastmaster, one of the pointless pretend Routemasters where the whole idea of being able to hop on and off has been banned for health and safety reasons and you sit sweltering in what is effectively a greenhouse on wheels. Even in this not especially sunny version of June, the bus was already uncomfortably hot. I normally like the bus – I prefer it to the Tube – because the people-watching is better. Not today, though. The champagne had come and gone and the pleasant glow of lunch and company and praise was turning into the acidic gloom of a medium-strength mid-afternoon hangover. I felt a little bit sleepy, and a little bit angry, and a little bit sad. But then, why wouldn't I? I was on my way to see my mother.

When Aloysius said that he wasn't going to speculate about where my dark side came from, I had a momentary temptation to interrupt and tell him the answer: from my mother. But if I had said that to Aloysius, it would have been as if she had come to the restaurant and pulled a seat up to our table and joined us for lunch. As for what that would have been like: she'd have sucked up all the oxygen, all the time and attention, for the rest of the meal, and then left me feeling drained, used, exploited, tired, sick of her, sick of myself.

It seems to me that generations have different fashions in toxic parental relationships. Once upon a time, difficult parents were all about repression and control. They were the people who told you don't do this, don't do that. Victorian patriarchs and matriarchs and the children they raised. Talking to my friends, I think it's much less like that now. The problem with our parents' generation isn't that they're always trying to tell us what to do, but that they are always and permanently all about themselves. Was there ever a generation so self-centred and so focused on the validity of their own perspective? So oblivious and narcissistic? Not narcissistic in a 'gazing in the mirror' way, but in the sense of narcissistic personality disorder. Constant one-way emotional support, from the child to the parent, is the norm for my generation. And this is for the most part before we've moved into the having-to-wipe-the-bum years, the phone-call-in-the-middle-of-the-night-because-your-dad-is-naked-in-the-petrol-station-and-doesn't-know-who-he-is years, the what-kind-of-care-home-can-you-afford years, the years of they-don't-know-who-you-are-any-more-but-you-have-to-do-everything-for-them-anyway. This isn't that. This is just their emotional default setting. All their lives, everything has been about them. Why would that change now that they're in their fifties/sixties/seventies/eighties/whatever?

Having said that, there is one respect in which my mother is an outlier. With most of my friends' mothers, their generational narcissism expresses itself in one of three basic types. Type one is the bitch. No need explaining what that is: it's someone who is routinely and deliberately unpleasant, who says mean things, makes nasty observations, uses the people around her as a scratching post and punch bag. The closer you are to them familially and emotionally, the nastier they are. Most bitches are very good at the precise calibration of the horribleness, and are able to administer everything from a pinprick of irritation to a relationship-ending insult, via an escalating scale of rudeness, offence, denigration and tirade. They are walking supercomputers of meanness, and will pick up any weapon at hand, from a chance remark deliberately misinterpreted to something said years ago to any detail about your life, relationships, work, socio-economic status, hobbies, postcode, car or other means of transport, clothes, what you had for dinner, that dust allergy you claim to have but which only seems to manifest when you come here.

The second basic type of toxic mother is the vampire. The vampire's key move is simple: she sucks out, she drains, she depletes. Like vampires do in films, but without the fun sexual subtext. The substance she drains can be one of any number of things: energy, joy, life, love, colour, enthusiasm, interest, will to live. When you finish any exchange with a vampire, from the most fleeting encounter to the maximum unspeakable horror of a full family Christmas, there is less of you at the end than there was at the beginning. Not just less energy, joy, life et cetera, but less of your fundamental matter. You are left feeling drained, shrunk, smaller, thinner, stretched out; you begin as your full self and you end something fainter, paler, see-through. When you have that feeling, you know that you have been vampired.

Category number three is the squid. A squid's signature move is to squirt ink: to spread their mood around them as a suffocating emotional cloud. When a squid is in a bad mood, which with squids is most of the time, everyone within their psychic radius knows about it – and squids are good at having a large psychic radius. The ability to project emotions over the biggest possible area is a core skill for the squid. Squids can make everyone in the vicinity know what they are feeling, and in addition can make them feel responsible for the squid's bad mood, and completely in the dark about what they have done to cause it, and therefore entirely unable to do anything to make it better. Do you know someone who makes you aware that they feel terrible, makes you feel that this is your fault, and makes you feel that there's nothing you can do about it? Know then that you are in the presence of a squid.

So those are the three toxic maternal archetypes: bitch, vampire and squid. By and large, they stay in their lane. They know what they're doing and they stick to it. What's so special about my mother is that she is all three. She's a bitch, a vampire and a squid simultaneously, switching between them so rapidly that the types blur into each other like the colours in a spinning top.

The bus was struggling in the traffic, and we passengers were struggling too. The champagne had definitely been a bad idea. My mood was beginning to slip further downwards. I needed to brace myself to see my mother, because the more ragged and fractious I felt, the worse it would be. My idea when I fixed this date was that I would be feeling boosted after seeing my enthusiastic agent, and the surge in confidence and morale would carry me through the time with Mum. I wouldn't be the oppressed, bullied, manipulated daughter – I would be the exciting young TV writer, the world opening up in front of her, being lifted up by the first surging onrush of a huge wave of acclamation, validation, and unconditional love. That had been the plan. But the reality was this postprandial slump, dragging me down as I grew closer and closer to the regular meeting, which was absolutely guaranteed to drag me down even more.

I saw my mother roughly once a fortnight. In an ideal world, it would have been once a month. About fifteen years ago, that had been the schedule agreed between me and my twin brother, Tristan. That version of my life would have been easier. Maybe much easier. But it didn't work out. What happened instead was that my brother moved to Australia and was cut off from all contact by our mother, in retaliation/revenge/acting out/whatever. When he came back and tried to see her, she slammed the door in his face. I think her emotional logic was that his move felt like a rejection, so she rejected him back extra hard. What it meant was that instead of a shared familial burden, I did all the emotional and practical work. I try not to be bitter about the whole thing.

As for these visits, it would have made more sense to have a dedicated date and time, a specific and recurring place in the calendar when I went over to see her or (hardly ever now) she came to me. But my mother wouldn't do that, because if it was a regular arrangement there wouldn't be enough opportunity to create drama and difficulty. Instead, we had an agreement in principle that I would go over a couple of times a month and phone her every couple of days. In practice, this meant a permanent foam of anxiety and plan-changing and diary-juggling. One of my mother's rules of conduct is to never let an arrangement sit where it was first created. If it's lunch on Monday at her flat, written in blood in the diary, she will make at least one attempt to change it to tea on Tuesday, or accompanying her to the doctor on Wednesday, or she'll leave it on Monday but change it so that what she's asking is for me to come round to help her explain what's wrong with her boiler to the man from British Gas at eight in the morning, and then when I get there tell me that the appointment is one of those non-appointments where the man will in fact come at any time between eight in the morning and five in the afternoon.

None of those examples is hypothetical.

The bus got close to her place in Earl's Court, and I pressed the bell to request a stop. I squeezed out of the seat. Across the aisle, a kid was bent forward, nodding energetically along with whatever he was listening to on his colossal headphones. He looked like a boxer psyching himself up to go in the ring. I could relate.

My mother's flat is a gloomy basement in a house next door to a main traffic artery. It is cramped and dark and has no garden except a small square lightless patch of slate slabs surrounded by the brick walls of neighbouring houses. In winter, you can feel the damp seeping into the walls; in summer it is airless and muggy. The boiler gurgles, the pipes rattle, the small fridge-freezer makes as much noise as a municipal leaf blower. The sofas sag, the oven is useless, the furniture is stained, the radio reception is the worst in London, there's no Wi-Fi or mobile signal, the hallway is so narrow two people can't pass each other, the traffic never stops, the front room is overlooked by passers-by. It is a few hundred metres from the nearest amenities – shops – and because it is an arterial road there are no bus stops. The nearest Tube station is almost a kilometre away. For a young able-bodied person all that would be fine, but for my mother it means that the location is completely, definitively unsuitable. Notwithstanding all that, it's in central, or centralish, London, so it's worth roughly a million quid – when I say it's 'worth' a million, I mean that given prevailing prices some idiot would pay that for it. My mother could very easily sell it and buy something a hundred times nicer and a hundred times more adapted to her needs. When I say she could do it very easily, what I mean is that she could open any of the estate agents' letters that come through on to her soggy doormat at least once a week, call them, and they would do everything from there, and she could relocate to a mansion block with a lift, or a cottage in the country, or (God forbid) a one-floor apartment close to me and Tony; she could make any one of a dozen choices that would make her life better, happier, easier. And that of course was why she would never do anything of the sort, because she didn't want her life to be any of those things, when having her life be miserable, worse, *harder* was her most effective technique for torturing me.

I've never found it difficult to understand why Tristan moved to Australia.

I stepped down to her doorway, where the surface underfoot was claggy with leaves from the next-door neighbour's towering, shade-throwing sycamore. I clattered the door knocker and waited. Then I clattered it again, as hard as I could, and waited some more. My mother is intermittently and tactically deaf. It's part of how she acts when she's with me, as if she's twenty or thirty years older than she actually is. There are times when she can't hear anything: if you propose listening to something to help the time go past, for instance a TV programme or radio programme or podcast or piece of music, she will reliably say that she 'can't hear a thing', or doesn't 'understand what's happening', or ask 'has it started yet?' when it's been running for five minutes. The door knocker, if it is a family member, is almost impossible to perceive, but if it's a delivery she's been expecting she will hear it even at the other end of the flat or in the garden past multiple closed doors – and then she will ask you to go and get it. With anything she can interpret as disobliging or offence-causing or provocative or unnecessary, she has the hearing of a bat, a mole, a superhero called Ears.

Something similar happens with her sight. She has, by her account, been partially blind for ten years. She claims that she can't read or watch television. And yet if I wipe something down, or am asked to straighten a picture, or put something in a particular place, just so, at exactly that angle, she has the vision of a spy satellite that can read number plates from space. She hasn't registered as blind, of course, because that might be helpful, might bring state assistance and certain privileges, might get her a parking permit for me to use when ferrying her around, for instance, and that would be convenient to me, so she won't do it. That's a consistent pattern: she can't hear or see or do anything that will cause you convenience. Her brain is the equivalent of a top-of-the-range supercomputer, constantly scanning and assessing data to find out whether something will make life easier or better for anybody else, and if so, instantly vetoing it. That is what is at the heart of her— well, 'difficulty' is far too mild a term for it. Impossibility, nightmarishness, toxicity, narcissism, black hole of human lack and need and rage.

After a third go of knocking, hammering rather, I heard a noise on the other side of the door. From experience – this was my mother at the spy hole. I composed my face with the expression it has when I know someone is looking at me and I can't see them back. Then a key in the lock, then a chain being unlatched – no, first attempt didn't work, here comes another one, success! – then another key in another lock, and then the door scraped open, snagging on a scurf of pizza delivery leaflets and unsolicited mail. And then the door was two-thirds open and there she was.

'There's no need to batter the door down,' she said.

'Hello Mum!' I said, with maximum brightness.

'And there's no need to shout. You'd better come in.' I squeezed past her, just. As she closed the door, she gave a long, disapproving, assessing stare over my shoulder and behind me, the clear implication being that I had tricked her into lowering her defences and a gang of thieves and murderers was about to shoulder past both of us and either ransack her valuables or slake their bestial appetites upon her frail, defenceless form.

'There's just me, Mum,' I said. But *that* she managed not to hear. I went on ahead into the sitting room, which by a small margin is the most depressing place in her terrible flat. There is brown furniture and the room is either nastily bright, if the lights are on, or too dark to read. There are no books. The sofa slumps down low and is set at an angle so that you have a view of the shins of people walking past, interrupted occasionally by urinating dogs.

You are fully visible to anyone going by in vehicular transport. When I mention this to my mother – roughly once a year, when I can't stop myself, knowing that stop myself is exactly what I should do – she says that it doesn't bother her since she can't see, so why should it bother anyone else?

'There's a mark on your shirt, you've evidently spilled oily food on it. I hope you enjoyed your lunch, you were obviously somewhere expensive from the way you're all done up. Not like that awful place we went to for my birthday, I hope. I thought you were never going to come,' said my mother, following me into the room. I looked at my watch: I was seven minutes late. 'I have a list. The oven again. And I need you to find another plumber. That one you found me is awful. Awful. And—'

The list went on. That was fine by me. There are a number of different kinds of visit to my mother, though they broadly speaking divide into the ones where she uses me as an emotional chew toy and the ones where she treats me as a factotum. There is overlap between the categories, of course, but that's the rough distinction. This was to be a factotum slash indentured labour visit, which was OK with me, since that was my preferred type. At least, by doing things, I could feel myself moving through the duration of the visit, the end getting closer, liberation nearing, the exit sign in clearer sight with every passing minute.

First chore: the kitchen. Not feeling very much like the creator of an about-to-be-a-hit TV show, I put a tea towel on the kitchen floor and got down on my knees in front of the oven to try and see why it wasn't working. So much for these Izzy Marants – should have seen this coming. I wouldn't put it past my mother to see what I was wearing and then decide to make me sort the oven out. The problem was that the oven seemed to be grilling on the baking setting and vice versa, and since my mother 'couldn't see' the settings and had to navigate the cooker by touch, the confusion meant she was unable to prepare her own food. My mother can't use technology of any sort – I've tried to set her up with a smartphone and a voice-controlled speaker, but they didn't take. In fact, they turned into complex disasters with extended recriminations that still sometimes flared up. I am tech savvy, indeed very tech savvy – I'm the person friends call when they have problems. I configure people's Wi-Fi for them, they ring me up and ask what router to get, what speakers, whether phone and computer upgrades are worth it, and all that. There are multiple ways in which my know-how could help my mother. No dice. She could easily manage these things if she wanted to, but it suits her purposes better to be helpless and have to rely on me to make all the arrangements that depend on access to the internet. Which are a lot of arrangements, and growing more and more all the time. It would be convenient to me if she could use the internet, so she won't do it – see the pattern? In her defence, or partial defence, she also is one of those people with a mysterious force field that makes things break or stop working. Nobody in England has their fridge, boiler or water supply fail more often; nobody's microwave as frequently blows a fuse; nobody's double-glazing cracks more often or sink clogs as often or hearing aids malfunction or run out of battery more. It's as if her ambient, all-purpose difficulty leaks into the air around her and, simply, breaks things. (People, too.) Given that, it was perfectly likely that her oven was actually broken in some mysterious, you-would-have-thought impossible manner, requiring elaborate repair plans that would devolve to me.

'How's Tony,' she said. Aha, I thought. So the theme of the visit was now clear. Her attitude to Tony varied between none too subtle hints that he was a nogoodnik, a sponger, a man who managed to combine the otherwise uncombinable attributes of being a bore, a bureaucrat, a dead weight, with those of being a sponger, an opportunist, a freeloader, a failed musician; or alternatively that he was a rock and a gem, a paragon of stability, and I was lucky to have him, I didn't appreciate my good fortune, I had no idea what it was like or how precious and rare it was to have a truly good, truly reliable man in my life. The true great pain of loneliness, harshest and bitterest and most shameful and most protracted of life's pains, was something that could never be understood by one such as me, who had had the miraculous good fortune to find a trustworthy life partner.

So, yeah. Those were her two takes on Tony.

'He's fine,' I said. 'Busy.'

No reply. My mother moved across the room and looked out at the 'garden', the small square patch of moist stone outside her back window. The silence stretched for a while. The Tony stuff was always particularly charged because the great wound, the great tragedy, the defining event of my mother's life was her own disappointment in— well, I would say love, but it goes beyond that. Not just love but men, hope, life itself. It was the relationship that ended all future relationships for her, that blocked her and broke her and made her the person who she is. It happened at university and by her own account, and I believe her, she's never been the same person since. That failure is the thing that made her what she is. 'That man', as she would very occasionally refer to him – and never by name – had ruined her life. He stood in a proxy for all men. So any glimpse of me having anything that resembled a successful relationship was both a provocation and a crushing reminder of her own failure at life's central task.

'It must be wonderful to be busy. To be in the middle of life.'

And there it was – pressing hard on what she felt to be the centre of her tragedy, the centre of life's unfairness to her.

There was a thin film of green mould growing in the top corners of the counter-top recess where the oven sits. As soon as I saw it, I knew what that meant: she'd got through another cleaner. My mother is uncontrollably rude to cleaners, and the task of finding new ones defaults to me. This happens somewhere between two and three times a year, on average, and I live in fear of the day when the various agencies I use collectively decide that they're never again going to send someone to work for her. I've already noticed that the rates they charge are right at the top end. She hadn't told me about this new cleaner debacle, so it would be coming up soon, unless she chose not to remember so that it gave her something to call me up over and chase me about.

I turned on the oven. Nothing happened. I opened it. The solenoid seemed to have come loose, or something – there was a disconnect between the setting on the dial of the cooker and what was happening to the heating element. I fiddled with both the dial and the element but nothing made any difference. My mother's gadget-busting force field had worked its dark magic once again. I tried all the things I'd already tried twice for a third time, and then gave up. I sighed and straightened. My mother was still looking out the window into her non-garden. Therapists say that you can often intuit what a person is feeling by paying attention to what they make you feel. (They also tell you to use this trick with care, because it can drive you mad.) I had been in my mother's company for about twenty minutes, and I felt tired, sad, frustrated, hard done by, and bitter. I felt unappreciated and lonely. Life stretched out in front of me, joyless. Nothing good would ever happen to me. It wasn't just the champagne comedown. It was her. That was how she felt, so that was how she made me feel in turn.

'OK, Mum, I'll have to ring and get someone in,' I said, trying not to imagine how much work, how much time-juggling, that would involve, and that it would be likely to involve at least two visits – one for the engineer to come and assess the problem, another for him to come and fit the new part or new cooker or whatever it was. I would have to be there for both of these. From experience, it would be whatever was most complicated and expensive in terms of the time cost to me, and involve the highest and most intense level of recriminations.

'I told you so,' she said, even though she hadn't.

'What's next?'

'I can't get through to my doctor to make an appointment,' she said, and I felt the next hour sliding away from me.

★ ★ ★

Why do I put up with it? Why do I put up with her, you might ask? Some of you, the more materialistic and darker hearted (greetings, comrades!), will already have done the maths. Flat worth £1 million or thereabouts. Good! But proceeds must be shared with my sibling in Sydney. First £325,000 is free of tax, plus another £175,000 tax-free band for a principal residence, divide the residue in two, knock off 40 per cent tax for the government in view of the fact that someone as narcissistic and distrustful won't have done anything to mitigate the inheritance tax bill (correct assumption), and there's still £400,000 for me. People will put up with a lot for more than a third of a million pounds.

But this doesn't work for my mother. Remember, she's a narcissist. Everything is all about her. Even after she dies, as far as she is concerned, everything will continue to be all about her. Not that she really thinks she's going to die. She talks about it, a lot, in the key of 'when you get to my age, and you realise you don't have much time left, you start to look back on your life and . . .'

or 'sometimes when I think about how ill I feel all the time, how I can't see and can't hear, I wonder how much longer I want to go on, or even if I want to go on at all'. And plenty more in a similar vein. But I don't think that translates into any actual consciousness of her own mortality. At some level, she genuinely thinks she's going to live for ever. Whenever she talks about the death of an acquaintance, she always shows the narcissist's distinctive, defining lack of empathy – she makes it sound like a mistake, a piece of stupidity or deserved ill fortune, on the part of the person who's died. So when she's dead she's likely to have had a go at making everything continue to be about her, which might be by asking for her ashes to just be chucked in the bin because no one ever cared for her in life, or might be by endowing a foundation to recite a poem in her honour at the Albert Hall on her birthday every year, or might be by giving all the money away to a charity that looks after hedgehogs. Or all of those. The salient point – my brother and I would be unwise to expect a red halfpenny from her will.

So that's not why I put up with it, with her, with everything. The answer is: I don't. Or rather I'm planning not to. I have wrestled for years with the idea of cutting off from my mother, and the thing that has kept me back from doing it is the thought that I don't want to seem like a bad person. I don't know where it comes from, that tug, the power of that thought – it definitely isn't something I got from her.

But I decided to move past that. I've lived with her shadow over my life for three and a half decades, and that's long enough. I'm going to cut myself off from my mother; I'm going to get her out of my life. And before I do, I'm going to close my account: I'm going to show her that I have taken notice of everything she's said about how her life was ruined, how her happiness was cancelled, when she was not all that much younger than I am now.

That's why I wrote my script.

* * *

One good thing about having a twin who has chosen to live on the other side of the planet is that you know without ambiguity the answer to the question of whether or not they are there for you. They absolutely and unequivocally aren't. This gives you, the abandoned person who is carrying all the load, certain privileges. If you know your parent is toxic and you flee them, and leave a sibling behind in the process, there is going to be Stuff.

Compounding the Stuff: the fact that Tristan went to make his life in Australia is the reason our mother no longer talks to him. I can't follow the logic other than as a narcissistic thing. You left me and made me feel bad therefore you no longer exist – something like that.

I rang Tristan. I knew it was five or six in the morning in Sydney but I didn't give a shit. He made waking-up noises. I was relieved, I didn't want him to already be up doing something exercisey or self-improvey.

'Everything OK?' he eventually managed.

'Just been to see her.'

'Oh shit.'

Then I vented for about half an hour. By the end of it I didn't feel better, except insofar as I'd made him feel worse.

6

I've been doing this interviewing thing for a long time – for exactly *coughs loudly* years now, in fact – and I have felt a whole lot of different things when doing it. I'm not talking about the times I have been so hungover that I had to sneak to the loo to be sick (sorry, Alicia Keys), or desperately trying to hide the ladder I put in my tights while getting out of the taxi and hoping the celeb, whose name I won't reveal, wouldn't notice. (Oh all right then: Jean-Paul Gaultier, and he did, but he was so nice about it, it was almost as if he didn't.)

This isn't about those feelings. This is about another feeling: fear. I'm talking about the feeling you get when you're going to see someone who makes you scared that you're going to wet yourself. I'm not talking about physical fear: I'm not talking about the fear you get when someone is throwing a tantrum at you. (Professional secret: you actually love it when that happens. It makes fantastic copy.)

I'm talking about the feeling you get when someone is so sharp, so mentally and psychologically on it, you worry they're going to see straight through you. I'm talking about people who are just plain scary.

I'm talking about Phoebe Mull.

Phoebe is the author of this summer's most talked-about TV, a steamy, sexy, bitter, nasty, devastating piece full of self-confessedly autobiographical detail.

And that is part of the reason I'm scared. She really doesn't give a monkey's what anyone thinks of her. Phoebe sees through people, spares no feelings, takes no prisoners. She's so sharp she could cut herself. Except, on the evidence of the programme, she's much more likely to cut you. Especially if you're a boomer. *Cheating* is very strong on the mutual loathing of millennials and boomers.

But it turns out that this terrifying apparition of unsisterly husband-stealing and frightening candour isn't, in person, at all what you expect. For a start, she arranges to meet me at her maisonette in Acton. A-listers never want to do that. They go to any lengths to avoid it. They don't want you seeing their furniture and fittings, much less describing them. They don't want you telling people about their curtains or what kind of towel they have in the downstairs loo. Much less do they want you describing their housekeeper or nanny. (And yes, if they have kids they also have those – always.) But Phoebe doesn't seem to know that, or if she does, she doesn't care.

Or maybe she does know, and does care, but has decided that this is how she wants to play it. When you've seen her programme, you know she's capable of thinking like that. She's had the classic TV writer's career: ten years' preparation for overnight success. She worked in the writers' room on a BBC soap, then another writers' room on a Channel Four comedy-drama, then she picked up episode credits and a couple of co-writing credits. Now she has her name in lights on a show she has written all by herself. 'The programme I always wanted to write, the story I burnt to tell,' is how she puts it.

Second thing that isn't as you expect: she lets me meet her partner. Again, the A-listers don't do that. If you're interviewing Mariah Carey (good luck!), you don't get Tommy Mottola thrown in for free. If you're interviewing Beyoncé (because she's plugging something, because she doesn't already have enough money, apparently), you don't get a complimentary side order of Jay-Z. But if you go to interview Phoebe, the door is answered by a gorgeous, sleepy-looking barefoot man in his early thirties, who looks like a musician who's just got out of bed - which, it turns out, is exactly what he is. Tony is Phoebe's partner - has been for more than five years - and is the first clue that Phoebe's show isn't as strictly drawn from life as people are taking it to be. They aren't married - they don't believe in it, Phoebe tells me - but they have taken a new joint surname, Mull.

'Phoebe is just on a Zoom,' Tony says, charming and shy, as he leads me through to the kitchen slash dining room. He mumbles an offer of tea, coffee, water or something stronger, and then wafts away. I hear feet on the stairs - it's a duplex - and then a few minutes later, guitar noises start coming through the floor. It's floaty and folky and a bit poppy. It sounds a little how you expect it to sound, once you've seen him. I like it.

I get a good look around, exactly one of those good looks the A-listers never let you have. The taste is classic young professional bourgeois Bohemian contemporary. Nothing brown or old or inherited. Quite a lot of the stuff is new, like, fresh from the shop new. Ikea and Smeg. Coffee by Gaggia, not Nespresso. *Cheating* has 'the best pre-launch buzz I've ever seen,' says her suave super-agent Aloysius

Jones, and there is talk that an American version is on its way, 'by a big name we're not allowed to disclose yet'. It's no mystery where some of the money has gone. I take a quick peek into the fridge – I never said I was a good person! – and happen to see a bottle of vintage Bollinger. It retails for £115. There's a small pot of Exmoor caviar too. Yours for £125 the 50 grams.

I think I manage to get the fridge door closed before Phoebe comes in. A tall woman with red hair and a confident walk, a level gaze, a retro Miu Miu dress and the loveliest jade earrings you've ever seen. She looks you in the eye and takes your hand firmly. A hand shaker, not a hugger or an air kisser. The general air is slightly cool, cool in the sense of not warm, but she immediately starts making up for it.

'So so sorry! So rude of me! Especially as you were bang on time! Family drama – you know how it is.' And then she, off the record, explains some family details that do perfectly explain exactly why she had to take exactly that call at exactly that precise moment. And you find yourself saying that yes, yes indeed, you do know how it is, because you do, and right there you see her secret ingredients as a writer: empathy, relatability, and a touch of manipulation. (Because yes, actually, it was rude. And yet she's got you letting her off and seeing her side of the story.)

Orphan power, she calls it in conversation, though she isn't an orphan herself. She was raised, one half of a pair of twins, by a single mother, a subject about which she says next to nothing: she is an example of that modern kind of candour, a woman who is willing to talk at length about sex and money but won't say a word about more private subjects such as family or love. Relatedly, her relationship with handsome Tony is completely off-limits. I have to go behind her back and truffle around to find out more about him, that he is a primary school teacher nursing a long-time dream of making a go as a songwriter. Phoebe and he met 'on a dating app' – that selective candour again. I have a piece of advice for him: if he wants to appeal to the opposite sex, he won't do much worse as a dreamy primary school teacher than as an aspiring Chris Martin. But maybe that's just me.

So Phoebe will tell you her favourite sexual position and how much money she has in her bank account, but she won't tell you her mother's first name. A modern girl, sorry, woman. She will tell you how she snuck around and lied and two-timed her partner (the one before dreamboat Tony, obviously) but she won't say what she's working on now, and she won't admit to being pleased by the early attention to her show, because she pretends she hasn't read any of it. (Why do writers and artists, in fact every genre of luvvie, do that?)

And yet there is that core of toughness in her. The series is a modernised, updated story about a man-eater, a home-wrecker. Phoebe herself doesn't seem at all like that: she's too cool, even slightly aloof. Aloof like a posh person, which she isn't. It doesn't seem sexual. It's more like she's someone who's going to do what she wants and doesn't much care about you or what you want; who keeps her own counsel and is making her own judgements, all the time; someone capable of putting her own needs completely and ruthlessly first. That is so rare that it is bracing and even thrilling to encounter. How likeable it is, I'm less sure. But I do know she couldn't care less about that.

It interests me that her career, before her break into screenwriting, used to be in HR. I don't find it at all difficult to imagine her explaining to someone that the time had unfortunately come for them to be let go.

'You're not very nice, are you?' I say at one point in the interview. Professional secret, if an interview is going easily, too easily, you sometimes throw in a much sharper question, just to see how the other person reacts. It's not fair to the subject to ask only softball questions: it makes them sound boring. You learn quite a lot about a person in that initial split-second when the tone changes. Some people flare up, some work even harder at trying to be charming. Fight or flight.

Phoebe doesn't even blink. No loss of temper, and no renewed effort to make me like her. She even looks a tiny bit amused.

'No, not really,' she says. 'Niceness is overrated.'

Cheating comes out on Netflix on 31 July.

PART TWO

7
KATE

That day began with the first thing I had been looking forward to since Jack died. It was about three months later. The occasion was my biannual lunch with my favourite former prison visitee, at our mutually favourite restaurant. Wiltons in Jermyn Street is as pure Establishment as a mere restaurant, as opposed to a club, can get. Panelled wood; a strong aura of Parliament and public school and pinstripe; the opposite of the stripped-down modern aesthetic that Jack practised in his work – and that's why I love it. Also, it has the classic quality of a treat or gift, in that it is something you really enjoy but would never spend the money on for yourself. The greeter took my coat and showed me through into the dark warm dining room, where Conor was already waiting for me, as I knew he would be, sitting at a corner table, eyebrows slightly raised at something he was reading on his phone, well-cut blue suit but no tie, pocket square, Patek Philippe visible on his wrist. Pale. Thirtyish. A stranger making an assessment of man, room and context would think, he's something to do with money – hedge fund? He looked up as I approached and then got up to give me a perfectly calibrated wordless hug. It's a thing you notice in grief, the difference between people who know exactly what to do and the broad mass of the clueless and useless.

I don't want to make it sound as if I stay in touch with all my former clients. I'd say on average I keep in contact with about a third of them, mostly over email. Conor is one of only three or four whom I still see in person. An obnoxious observer would say that it's partly because Conor is among the most middle-class of my clients. The obnoxious observer would not be entirely wrong – though there are quite a few middle-class people in prison, mostly for white-collar crime as well as the occasional paedo. But yes, OK fine, Conor is middle-class, polite, well spoken. The same obnoxious observer might unkindly notice that he is good-looking, unusually so, by far the best-looking client I have ever had, high cheekbones and curly black hair – OK, fine, that too. He is also the richest former client of mine, again by far. The white-collar types you meet in jail were once rich, or more subtly were living as if they were rich, but by now they have all, more or less by definition, been cleaned out. Conor is the opposite of cleaned out. But none of this is the reason I feel a connection with him and look forward to seeing him.

The reason Conor is so important to me is because he is the only client who has ever told me, directly and forcefully, that I saved his life. That if it hadn't been for me, he would have died. He said that and I believed him, and that's why he is in a special category for me. This isn't false modesty about my other clients: I do know that I've helped people, most often by simple presence and consistency in their lives, accompanied by whatever kindness I can bring. Prisoners are usually men who haven't had much consistency or kindness and while they don't exactly bloom in its presence – nobody blooms in prison – they do often react to it with an unfolding or unfurling.

Conor was different, though. The first time I met him was in Wandsworth. HMP Wandsworth is a chaotic, frightening place. Conor hadn't been inside for long. He seemed sullen and surly and closed off and the first three visits were a disaster because he basically didn't speak. He was doing a five-year stretch for drug dealing and I must admit that I had him identified – stereotyped – as a classic professional drug dealer who was caught and whose time inside was just the cost of doing business. Career criminals who feel no remorse and are simply passing the time until they can get back to work aren't easy to relate to, at least not for me. I had Conor pegged as one of those. You have to feel a click for the work with a client to actually do any good. I was on the verge of telling the charity that they needed to assign Conor to somebody else.

But he seemed different on the day of my fourth visit. When I came into the meeting room – square, functional, high windows with reinforced glass, a room where you feel that nothing good has ever happened – he was lifting his head from his hands and there was such a look of defeat in his face. He looked beaten and broken and that in turn made me realise just how young he was – mid-twenties – and also that I had him wrong. He wasn't shutting me out on purpose, it was just that he was trying to cut off his feelings and disappear into himself to get through this. I could have told him that that wasn't going to work, not with a proper stretch inside. A few weeks, yes. But Conor was facing a few years. Even if he was lucky and careful and nothing went wrong and he did the easiest version of his time – parole after half his sentence, sent home with an ankle tag halfway to parole, so serving a week for every month of his sentence – he would be doing more than a year. Nobody can hide from themselves for that long in prison.

I don't remember what we talked about that day. But I do remember that there was a before and an after. Conor began by showing how he was feeling, then talking about what was happening, and then finally by saying what had happened to put him in prison. And it turned out he was more or less the opposite person from whom I had thought he was. He was a privately educated finance person from Dublin, close to his parents, who were the other people who visited him and whom I felt I got to know well through his description, but to this day have never met.

He was also, very unusually for a man in prison, innocent. Of course, everyone in prison is innocent, to hear them tell it. You're told that often – 'everyone in here is innocent' – by the warders and, it has to be said, occasionally by the lags themselves, once they get to know you, with a laugh. But of course hardly anyone is actually innocent, and when you meet one of the rare exceptions they are often distinguished by their anger, and the anger of everyone around them who knows their story. When the lawyers are furious, that is often a sign that a miscarriage has occurred. Conor was innocent – but there had been no miscarriage. He was not angry, but he did feel cheated and defeated; swindled. He had been charged with drug dealing, and the reality was that there had indeed been drugs at his flat, held in keeping for a friend; and yes he had known that the friend had dabbled in the drug business; and yes he had known that the suitcase under the bed in his spare room probably had MDMA or similar. And yes, even this probably wasn't the whole truth, and Conor, open as he was with me, was still holding back the full extent of what he knew. (The friend with no obvious external source of income who asks you to look after packages for him and occasionally chucks you gifts of inexplicable generosity? And you never wonder what's happening?) But the gist of his story both matched and explained the official version, in the case notes I had been given. Conor's friend had asked him to take care of a 'larger than usual' package. It turned out to be a suitcase. The next day, his flat in Borough was raided and searched. He was arrested, tried, convicted and sentenced as a drug dealer, and not as a banker who had been doing a friend a favour and had been naive. The police hadn't been able to find any payments into his bank accounts, and that convinced them that he was hiding assets. It seemed to me a clear sign that he hadn't been paid and had been merely doing his friend a very rash, very reckless favour – but that's not what the police and prosecutors chose to think.

'How on earth did they know to raid you exactly at that moment?' I asked him, when he finally told me the long version. 'Two days earlier and they wouldn't have found a bean. Two days later and they wouldn't have found a bean. What are the odds?'

He looked at me and his expression did not change and then I got it.

'Ah,' I said.

'There you are.'

'"The police are the criminals",' I said, quoting a maxim of Jack's. It used to annoy me when he said it, because he delivered the line with such confidence, on the basis, as far as I knew, of almost no experience dealing with either group. But of course that didn't mean he was wrong.

'Yeah – sort of. And there's a trade in favours. The dealers sometimes need a bit of help to see off the competition. The police sometimes need a few convictions to make the clear-up rate look pretty. But the cops and the dealers both know the supply of drugs is never going to go away because the demand for them is never going to go away. It's basic economics. Society doesn't want to face that truth, so there's a gap, a gap between the reality and the way everyone behaves. And when you get a gap like that, things happen.'

I thought about it for a moment. Conor seemed calm; by now, having met him once a week for months, I knew how wrong I had been about that initial impression. But there were still times when I had no idea what he was thinking or feeling, and this was one of them. He could have been philosophically resigned; he could have been in well-hidden despair; he could have been seething.

'So your friend, or so-called friend, stitched you up. Dobbed you in to the police. In fact, did worse than that, set you up and then dobbed you in.'

He gave a small semi-shrug, more an acknowledgement that he had heard what I was saying than full agreement.

★ ★ ★

'This is a stupid question but – how are you?' asked Conor in Wiltons.

It's a thing you get sick of being asked, after a bereavement. You get particularly sick of being asked it in a leaning-in, sincere, pressing way; the kind of 'how are you' that is begging you to emote, to share, to break down, to dissolve. I hate being solicited to grieve openly. If I'm going to fall to pieces I'd rather do it on my own time and in my own company, thank you very much. And yet, I also hated it when people would make no acknowledgement of any kind at all, behaving as if Jack's death was an embarrassing mishap and they were doing me a favour by not mentioning it. So I accept that I was difficult to please. No, more than that: I accept that I was a very difficult person to talk to without feeling that you were saying the wrong thing and making me completely furious. Not many people got it right, but Conor was one of them. I felt that he was allowing me enough space to answer the question lightly, or heavily, to deflect, to engage or even, if I wanted to, completely deliquesce.

'Much as you'd expect,' I said. 'Waves of pain, waves of grief, waves of numbness, the occasional small chunk of time here and there when I'm not thinking about it, which is a huge relief. The thing is that I don't find it particularly cathartic. Lots of tears, wailing, and at the end of it, nothing has changed. Jack's still dead.

I know that not everyone is wired that way, but that's how I am. So thank you very much for asking, and if I need to talk about it I will, but I think we'll both be happier talking about something else.'

So that's what we did. We ordered what we always ordered – game for him, grilled sole for me. I barely drink alcohol, so we stuck to mineral water. Everything was, in its staid, old-fashioned, reassuring style, perfect. It was steadying that this was the kind of place that made you feel as if everything would always be the same. We had the same kind of conversation that we always had. Conor made small talk about the art he'd been collecting, the latest episodes in his ongoing girlfriend difficulties, the tax-free killing he'd recently made selling wine he'd bought and held in bond, and how his new expensive old car didn't have to pay the congestion charge because it was officially considered a classic – a loophole he'd recently discovered, and of which he seemed inordinately fond. It became steadily more obvious that he was for some reason in an exceptionally good mood. Jack used to quote a line of Boswell's, about how at the end of a successful evening he was left 'hugging himself in his own mind'. Conor looked like that at lunch.

'Come on, out with it,' I said eventually, after the waiter had taken away the remains of our main courses. I was full – which made me realise that this was the first time I had eaten with genuine appetite since Jack's death. A credit partly to the cooking but more to the effect of Conor's company. 'You're up to something, you're dying to tell me about it, but you don't want to seem too jolly.'

'No fooling you, Kate,' he said. 'It's not something I'm proud of. But at the same time I'm incredibly proud of it, if you see what I mean. Morally, maybe a little dubious. In terms of character and conduct, well, let's just say it's not the first thing you'd tell your parole officer. But also, really very fucking funny and gratifying and all round brilliant.'

'Lucky I'm not and never have been your parole officer then,' I said. I knew Conor's parole had been spent long since, otherwise we wouldn't be meeting somewhere so ostentatiously spendy.

'I never really told you much about Ambrose,' he said. 'The guy who got me sent to prison. My ex-friend. Author of all my troubles. Finance guy who made some money, left the business, got into clubs and bars, and then got into drugs as a sideline or overspill from that, I think – I didn't want to know the details and he never offered to tell me.'

That was something we had talked about when Conor was my client: how he had drawn the line around what he could guess but didn't want to know. It was the reason why in the final analysis, though he was sort-of innocent, it was only sort-of. He was innocent of being a drug dealer but not of deliberately concealing the truth from himself. He had long since come to admit the reality of that, and it was one reason why he had ended up such a sane and balanced person – a paradoxically good advertisement for prison.

'Well, anyway, we've never spoken since . . . since what happened, but I've kept tabs on him. We have mutual acquaintances, most of whom don't know the truth about what went down, and I, not to put too fine a point on it, stalk him on social media – he doesn't know I'm doing it, but some of the accounts that follow him aren't, you know, actual human beings. They're me. And I'd been planning, well, how to put it . . . a bit of this and a bit of that. And one of the things I've been planning has come off. And that's the thing that has been, as you correctly noticed, putting me in such a good mood.'

'We're talking about the thing that is best served cold,' I said. Conor did something that is often said to happen, but which I don't think I've ever actually seen anyone do in real life: he rubbed his hands together in glee. The waiter came over with dessert menus, hovered briefly, and then we waved him away. Espresso for Conor and mint tea for me.

'Yes indeed. Revenge. I did what could be argued to be a bad thing. From a conventional perspective. But which is in fact a good thing, as far as I'm concerned. See if you can guess. It involves every English person's favourite thing, property prices.'

'I've no idea, Conor,' I said. 'My mind doesn't work that way. Let me guess, you put his house up for sale on a property website without telling him and booked in visits and he had lots of people coming and ringing the doorbell thinking they had arranged a viewing.'

He gave me a surprised look and said: 'Actually, you know, Kate, that's not bad. I might try that one some day. But no, it was a lot more brutal. I bought the house next door to him. Through a shell company so he'll never know who owns it. And I've rented it out on Airbnb, and I only rent it to people who I'm sure are going to use it for parties. And I happen to know, from his socials, that it's making his life a living hell and he can't bear it any more and he's thinking about selling up and moving himself, just to get away from the noise and the parties. So what I'm going to do is, I'm going to suspend the parties for a bit, lure him into a false sense of security, and then I'm going to restart them, say in six weeks or so. The best thing about it is – actually, that's not true, the best thing about it is the revenge – but the second-best thing about it is that the house I bought is going up in value by thousands every week and also earning me income through the rentals while doing so. It's basically a machine that's inflicting psychological torture on my enemy and printing money at the same time. How great is that?'

'Another thing you could do is, you could buy another house near him, across the road, say, and start parties there and alternate between the two,' I said.

Conor again looked surprised, impressed too. 'You have a talent for this,' he said. 'I hope I never cross you.'

'I hope so too, darling,' I said, sipping my mint tea.

You're probably wondering: how could Conor afford to buy a London townhouse, and contemplate buying another one, as if with loose change? Well, some of that was no doubt his quiet version of swagger. In Britain, if you want to boast about how much money you have, you do so by talking about property prices. But he did have a very great deal of money and it was the other reason his attitude to prison was so complicated, a kind of rueful or even half-amused fury: anger at the injustice, combined with awareness that it had turned out to be a bizarre kind of good luck. Not the kind of good luck that people congratulate themselves on when they survive an accident; the kind of good luck that was directly linked to the bad thing that had happened, and which wouldn't have had a chance to manifest if the bad thing hadn't brought it along.

The authorities couldn't find the money Conor had been paid, and suspected him of hiding it offshore. They knew that as a finance person he would know very well how to do that. That's why he got five years. They were half right: Conor wasn't hiding money. His friend didn't have much cash free. What he did have in its stead, and what he used to pay Conor, was cryptocurrency. By the time Conor was able to access his accounts after prison and parole, his stash of Bitcoin and Ethereum and 'various other bits and pieces' had gone up in value by a factor of a thousand. A sum worth in the region of £20,000 when he was arrested was, thanks to the combined good offices of the drug dealers who stitched him up, the Metropolitan Police, the Crown Prosecution Service and HM Prison Service, worth in the region of £20,000,000 by the time he was free of parole. Hence the ruefulness, the amusement, the consciousness of good luck.

'But wouldn't the same thing have happened anyway?' I asked him, when he first told me this story, which as chance would have it was in that very same restaurant. He almost choked on his mouthful of woodcock.

'Good Lord no,' he said. 'I never had the slightest intention of investing in crypto. I just took it in payment for a laugh. I was basically doing Ambrose a favour, not trying to make money. I don't – didn't – even believe in crypto and had no interest in how it works. The minute it would have gone up by ten per cent I'd have sold it and bought something real like, I don't know, a car or something. The idea that I'd hodl—'

I made a face.

'It means hold, in crypto speak – it comes from a mistyping – anyway, the idea that I'd hodl for four years and watch the value go up by three orders of magnitude is insane. I mean, it's not as if I chose to invest in the stuff. If I hadn't been in the clink I'd have dumped it right at the start, and we wouldn't be sitting here, and I wouldn't be wearing this' – he gestured at his suit – 'or this' – he waggled his watch hand in the air – 'and I wouldn't be having mock arguments with my fiancée about whether to have our honeymoon on Aruba or Bora Bora. Not that I was poor before. But I wasn't, you know, what's the word I'm looking for, oh yes, here it comes: rich.'

'It suits you,' I said. Conor looked pleased.

8
KATE

The good mood I was in from lunch carried me through the rest of the otherwise inconsequential afternoon and meant that when the time came to go to book group, I was feeling sufficiently strong. Perhaps that's the wrong word: I wasn't anticipating an ordeal, and I wasn't expecting any big scene. But this was going to be my first time in the company of more than one person since Jack died, and I knew that I would have to feel braced: not braced for action, not primed to react or step in or fight my corner, but just braced for a roomful of people directing sympathy at me. I thought the best thing would be to get there early, so I wasn't walking into a room of eager consoling faces: the first exchanges would be on my terms.

Daphne's house is in a small Georgian crescent in a part of south London that wasn't fancy when she moved there, but is now full of the aspirational bourgeoisie, driven south of the river by house prices. I'd taken a taxi into the centre of town to meet Conor, but it was quicker and simpler to take the Tube to Daphne's. It was my first time on the Underground since Jack had died and I was nervous, though if you had pressed me on what I was nervous about, I would have struggled to give a clear answer. Perhaps it was simply that the Tube was one of those things you have to practise, before you grow accustomed to the crowds and the crampedness. It's such a strange thing to do, and it's equally strange that we all get used to it: sitting in a row of strangers trying not to look across at another row of strangers, if we're lucky, or standing hanging from a strap, breathing into each other's faces. The psychological effort comes from the sheer press of other people's lives: the temptation of entering imaginatively into thinking about who they are, where they're from, what they want: is that an estate agent, or a solicitor's clerk, or an actor on their way back from an audition, or a waiter on his way to work who still thinks of himself as an actor, while also knowing that he isn't really, not any more, he's living the slow torture of giving up his dream; that girl in the jeans with the swollen lips and the just-fucked hair, has she been doing what it looks as if she's been doing? And everybody in the train carriage has a similar weight and presence, a similar sense of carrying their story with them: all these selves, all these souls, every one of them a half-locked box of mystery that you maybe, but only maybe, could unlock, with a little time and attention. Because the truth is that most of us, though we pretend we want to be mysterious, actually don't. I learned that from my clients in prison. People are desperate to tell their stories. They run towards the camera, the notebook, the recording smartphone, the therapist's couch. They want to unburden and unpack themselves. Too much so, I often think.

You can lose yourself in wondering, down in the Tube. Or the other thing you can do is keep your eyes and your thoughts to yourself, close your imagination off from other people's lives and mind your own mind. But that's almost as hard and maybe even more unnatural – we are naturally curious, inquisitive beings. We want to know about each other. It's hard work shutting that part of our brain down. Hard work closing out all these other beings. One of the reasons we get so angry about beggars and the homeless, the destitute human detritus of the city, is that it is so exhausting putting in the necessary effort of ignoring them. What we all in our hearts want for them is to just not be there. To go away. But because we all like to think of ourselves as good people, we know that we shouldn't want that. So they make us feel conflicted and bad about ourselves – bad about our own bad character – and that makes us secretly hate them.

At Tottenham Court Road I got on to a Northern line train, which at around six thirty in the evening I expected to be rammed, strap-hang only. Greatly to my surprise, there was a seat in the middle of the row. Across from me, a middle-aged Chinese man in a tracksuit was reading a Chinese newspaper, with evident displeasure – whatever it was he was being told, he disagreed with it. Next to him, two young Black women were passing their phones backwards and forwards, exchanging strong opinions about whatever they were looking at, but not through the medium of speech: they were frowning and nodding, briefly raising eyebrows, giving abrupt grimaces and occasionally a quick decisive nod. They might have been assessing fashion or candidates for a flatshare or prospective boyfriends. I had a sudden sweet sad memory of watching *Dunkirk* in the cinema with Jack and sitting behind a teenage girl who spent the entire two hours looking at photographs of trainers on Instagram. It began by being annoying but in the end, Jack and I agreed, was strangely impressive: comparing trainers was what she felt like doing, so comparing trainers was what she was going to do, irrespective of place or context. These two girls could have been entirely on their own, so lacking were they in any self-consciousness, or consciousness of anyone else at all. I envied that. Was I, were we, like that when we were young? It didn't seem likely and if I was, that's certainly not how I remember it. But then, one thing we never know is how we appear to other people. Maybe people found the twenty-year-old me absolutely terrifying.

By this point in the summer, the Northern line was unbearably hot. Almost everybody in the carriage, apart from the Chinese man disagreeing with his newspaper, was on their phone. It was increasingly the case that not using one in a public place made you an outlier. That was fine with me; Jack used his phone, used gadgets in general, enough for the both of us. I used to tease him sometimes that he and his phone could go out to restaurants on their own and leave me behind; that he could go on holiday with his phone and just send me some pictures and it would come close to being the same experience. I suppose, though, that I didn't really mind. In a long marriage, it's sometimes nice to have a break. Like several of my women friends, I've always quite liked it when the men are watching football, or F1, or whatever. It means they don't need entertaining or looking after. It's oddly freeing. That's how I felt about Jack and his phone. I didn't have to be on wife duty. Well, that was something I'd never have to do again. King Lear was right. Never never never never never. The truest and most painful line in all English literature. I must have been studying it roughly around the time Jack and I met at university. I was too young to know what it meant. I would now, and for the rest of my life, connect it with my late husband. I felt my eyes start to prickle and looked up at the lights to stop myself crying. A woman in late middle age bursting into tears in a Tube carriage – I felt shame at the thought of being a spectacle no one wanted to see. And with that shame came a jolt of anger and with the anger I felt the moment pass.

Anger at who or what? Hard to say. Anger at fate for taking Jack. Anger at Jack for dying. Anger at the people who might be looking at me and telling themselves a story about who I was and what had happened to me. And then further anger at the thought that the story they were telling themselves was probably more or less accurate. Sad oldish lady crying, bet it's because her cat died or somebody was mean to her. When I felt the threat of tears pass I looked down and caught the man across from me, suited, professional class, looking at me. He just had time to wipe the look of sympathy off his face. It didn't help. The sting of strangers' pity.

The train thinned out a little at Clapham North, then properly thinned out at Clapham Common, then a little more at Clapham South, then I got to my feet as it slowed into Balham. The man in the suit got up too, and I could tell he was being careful about not meeting my eye. I had, of all ridiculous things, a sensation of having accomplished something, by getting through this trip in the crowd without doing anything to embarrass myself. I thought: I can still pass as a Londoner. I don't have the giant flashing sign over my head saying: Widow! Pity her! Avoid her! It'll rub off on you! Or rather, I do have the sign, definitely, in bright blinking neon – but I'm the only person who can see it.

We came up the stairs, tapped out of the Underground, and began heading to our disparate destinations, some bouncy at the end of the workday, springy with the sense of heading for evening adventures, and others unmistakably trudging, tired and heavy with gloom about whatever might happen next. It was at least ten degrees cooler at street level than it had been in the Tube. It felt so long since I'd been in a group of people that it was as if my senses were both stripped and heightened; as if, had I concentrated and given it my full effort, I'd have been able to read people's minds. That woman in front of me carrying two heavy supermarket bags, not balanced but alternately slumping on one side then the other – she's going home to somebody who doesn't love her. That young man stepping into the roadway to overtake sluggards – he thinks he's going to have sex tonight. That girl scrolling through messages at the bus stop: she's terrified that she's no longer in with the cool gang: she's probably right.

I began to walk towards Daphne's house, turned two corners, and then abruptly I was the only person on the street. The claustrophobia left me and I had the other sensations you have as a woman walking down a city street alone, the fear and the shame at the fear, and the anger at the fear, and the ashamed anger of perceiving yourself as vulnerable. This was compounded by the other vulnerability I felt in remembering that this was the first time I was going out to meet people in company on my own, as a widow, companionless. No Jack with me. Never never never never never.

Daphne had changed the colour of her door so it took me a moment to recognise it. It had been a matronly dark blue. Now it was a deep, welcoming, vulval red. Well – fine, whatever. Daphne's house is lovely, as all the houses of everyone our age are, because we bought them when they were cheap and looked after them; none of us would be able to afford them if we were younger versions of ourselves, who do the same jobs we did. Some people my age joke about this – 'we can't afford our house!' – and others secretly think that the fact they bought their house several decades ago and it went up in value by millions means that they are geniuses. And some say one and think the other.

I went to ring the doorbell but Daphne had seen me coming and opened it before I could press the buzzer. She stepped towards me and took me in a hug and I felt a complicated mixture of acceptance – it was good to be touched, to feel the human warmth – and revulsion. It was the curse of pity again. I found that I couldn't return the hug, and after a few seconds she let me go. I could smell the pre-book-club dinner that she had made for herself, though I couldn't exactly identify it. Something warm and with plenty of alliums. Not the kind of food you would make if you were going to be meeting a lover. Onion soup?

'You're all right,' she said, a statement rather than a question.

'I got here early,' I said. 'You know. I haven't read it. I haven't even brought my copy. I'm just here for—'

She interrupted me before I had to say whatever sad thing I was going to say: I was there for the companionship, the practice at getting out of the house, a first trial attempt at being with other people.

'—I know.' She put a hand on my arm. 'Tea? Coffee? I know you don't normally, but something stronger?' I shook my head. I could tell that she wasn't quite ready for guests yet, so I told her to act as if I wasn't there while she did the rest of her prep. She got on with her pottering and tidying and laying out of snacks. I stood and looked at her books and pictures.

It was strange, but not unpleasant, to be in someone else's house again. There was no sign of Daphne's work life to be seen, though from the impeccable upper-middle-class taste of the decor, and at the same time absence of any signs of financial wealth, it might have been possible for a stranger to guess that she was exactly what she was, a senior civil servant. Work and friendships took the role in her life that children took for many people of her age and background. I noticed that there were more family pictures than the last time I had been there – not her own children and husband since she didn't have any, but photos of her parents and other antecedents. Daphne had always had a slight tendency to ancestor worship, and it was bleeding into her decor. Her mother, whom I'd never met in life, in pictures looked like an angry lesbian, and her father looked like a mouse. In the stories Daphne told about them, they were titans of charisma and daring. I had always thought that highly unlikely.

It's lucky that our friends hardly ever know what we're thinking.

There are four other people in the current version of our book group. They all arrived in character. People-pleaser Tabitha came at eight on the dot, bringing chilled wine, a huge basket of peonies and a can of fancy olives. Helen and Rachel arrived five minutes apart at 8.10 and 8.15, pretending that they hadn't already met for a natter in the pub beforehand. Helen brought chocolates and Rachel a box of expensive Turkish delight. Despite being closer to sixty than to fifty, the two of them still had the air of recovering mean girls, women who had been bitchy alpha females in their school days and weren't quite sure whether they were ashamed of their former selves, or slightly missed them. I have to admit that although both of them were still married to the same men they'd been with since we first knew each other, I did wonder if they were certifiably a hundred per cent heterosexual. The closeness between them was like that of former lovers who had remained friends. Daphne and I had speculated about it and I'd even once or twice come close to asking. Their air of being involved in a conspiracy of two was heightened by the fact that both of them did work that involved keeping other people's secrets: Helen was a therapist and Rachel created recipes for famous cookery writers, who then claimed them as their own. She was normally discreet about this but would occasionally report going to dinner at someone's house and being served one of her own recipes, inevitably credited to the famous chef to whom she'd sold it.

When you were with Rachel and Helen, you knew that they would debrief each other about you afterwards – that was part of the price of admission. You also knew that both of them were secret-keepers so whatever they said to each other about you would go no further. Once you accepted that, they were good fun and good friends too. I had been putting up with it for twenty years so why should I stop now? Jack had a theory that people tend not actually to like their friends, just to be thoroughly used to them. He also believed that people work too much at trying to keep relationships going, because the truth is that most relationships go on for too long. We cling too hard to our families, our lovers, our friends. We should be more willing to accept when things have finished. Now that Jack had suddenly died, I was in a strong position to assert that he was wrong about that.

Evelyn arrived last, as she always did, at half past the hour, in a nimbus of contradictory excuses and messy hair. She was wearing bright-green dungarees, a floral blue shirt and dangly red earrings, a combination that only she could make work. Although Daphne was my oldest friend in the group, the person with whom I went back furthest, and in some official sense my best friend, Evelyn was the woman in the room I liked best: an opposites-attract thing. I had met her when I was teaching at the Courtauld; she had come as part of a placement programme for working artists to exchange ideas with academics. She was a potter, attractive, disorganised, had a permanently complicated love life – an admirably complicated one, you might say, for somebody our age – and she was also, of all of us, the most successful in her own right. In fact she had already been famous when she joined the group two decades ago, after meeting Rachel at a lunch and complaining that nobody ever recommended her interesting books any more. I am enough of a snob to like that about her. Instead of bringing something for her hostess, she brought something for me, a small package that she told me to unwrap and turned out to be a deeply beautiful orange and green ceramic ashtray: completely useless, but in its way a perfect thing. For the second time that evening I felt my eyes fill with tears. Our hostess rescued me.

'Shall we?' Daphne said, standing and not so much gesturing as making it obvious what we were supposed to do next. I suppose in the civil service you learn how to give an order without making it sound like that's what you're doing. We got up from the kitchen table, collected glasses and bowls, and headed through to the cosy sitting room; it was overstuffed, to my taste, but then I had been married to an architect. I took my favourite of Daphne's chairs, in the bay window. I'd never noticed before that we all tended to sit in the same chairs in each other's houses – staying in character again, I supposed. A lot of adult life consists of staying in character, even when you no longer want to.

'I'm not going to pretend I've read it,' I said, 'so act as if I'm not here and I'll chip in if anything occurs to me.'

'Right,' said Daphne. 'Well!' And then she started talking about the book, or rather – subtle difference – what the book had made her think. I tuned out. I thought about how much comfort I got from being in this room with these women, and how grateful I was for it, and how lost and lonely I would be without the comfort of this company. It was an unexpected thought, since I very much see myself as someone who didn't need much help or support, apart from Jack.

I felt different now, though. This book group had been in my life during my marriage with Jack and it was still in it now that he was dead. I had learned already, in these early days of widowhood, that there were any number of things for which that would no longer be true – experiences, connections to the world, people, who were part of my marriage but were no longer part of my life. Some of these things were the simplest, most fundamental physical sensations: waking up in bed with someone next to you. Knowing that someone was in the next room. Coming home to a house and being able to tell that it was not empty. (That has always seemed underrated to me as a human capacity that verges on the mystical, the instant awareness of another being's presence or absence in any given space.) Living in and around another person's smells and sounds and thereness. All that was over for me, as were many other things too, and the hardest part to accept was that this was all normal, something that happened to people all round the world every day, something that was happening to someone somewhere right now, right in this very moment, some loss that would never be restored, after which nothing would ever be the same again. Never never never never never. But these people in this room were still here.

By now, the book group had gone off the book and were talking about something everybody was watching on television. Apparently, it was the current show that the whole world seems to be bingeing at the same time. I'd never heard of it. Daphne was talking but I tuned her out and looked over her head at the carefully 'curated' selection of pottery on the shelves behind her.

One of the reasons I find my prison visiting meaningful is that I understand the importance of having somebody who is *there*. Daphne was in my life when I met Jack; she was the first person I told about liking him. She was there through the various dramas when he and I got together. And in turn, she has told me, I made the world seem a bigger place for her.

I won't say that this was the last few seconds when I was happy, because I wasn't happy. I was deep in grief, lost, desolate, empty. But there was a completeness to that state: I knew what had happened: I knew what I felt. That feeling ended in that room in that moment, as I heard somebody say something I never imagined it possible to hear.

'And what about the thing where he keeps calling her "disco doll"? What's the line, "I want you disco doll", or something?'

'"I want your body, disco doll",' said Evelyn.

I felt the floor slide out from under me.

* * *

When something traumatic happens out of the blue, people often say that they don't remember the details, just that there was a catastrophic event, and time was split in two. There was life before the disaster, and life after it, but the disaster itself has disappeared. I envy those people because I wasn't so lucky. I can remember all the details of the rest of that evening. I can also remember the fog of dissociation that came over me, so that although I was present and conscious and aware of what was going on, I also felt that I was mentally somewhere else; that it was all unreal and couldn't possibly be happening.

The first thing I did was slowly and carefully get up and, as calmly as I could, walk to the bathroom. I locked the door behind me, moved the bathmat in front of the loo, knelt down, and threw up. Then I threw up again, and then once more.

Usually, when you are sick, you feel better. I didn't. What I now felt instead was dizzy and faint. At least, that's what I felt physically. Emotionally, I think I was in more pain and turmoil than I had been when Jack died. I was sure what those few words I had overheard meant, and yet I couldn't understand how they could possibly mean what they implied. It was impossible. And yet there was only one explanation. Which meant it was not just possible but certain.

I got back to my feet. I don't know how. I rinsed my mouth out and splashed my face. I looked terrible but at that point I looked terrible all the time anyway. In any case there was nobody to care but me, and I didn't. I went back into the sitting room. They were at the stage of the evening devoted to complaining about the government, intermixed with gossip about mutual acquaintances. Daphne glanced up but the others kept talking. I made an excuse about how I was exhausted and needed to go home. Daphne gave me a look, a sharp one, but offered to sort me out a taxi, which I accepted. I went home in a blur.

At home, I watched the first two episodes of the show they were talking about. It was on Netflix in the section 'For You', which was so hurtful it was almost funny. The programme told the story of an affair between an older married man and a younger woman writer. It was obviously supposed to be confessional and autobiographical. It was about the intergenerational tension between people my age and the young. The older married man was an architect. He lived in a house in our part of London. Not exactly our part of town, but not far away. He had a wife the same age as him. The actress playing the wife wasn't exactly the same as me – she was tall and fair instead of medium short and dark – but again, she wasn't far off. The 'me' character was a teacher. The girl having the affair looked like the TV writer in her photo, gobby and over-made-up, with dyed red hair. I was reading online while I half watched – I couldn't bear to concentrate any harder than that. It seemed that the show was driven by the author's anger at everything – at the complacent husband and wife, at their smug middle-class life, at herself for her complicity with everyone else's norms, at herself for not marching into the middle of everything and blowing the whole thing up. The writer claimed to be coming clean about something that had really happened. It was clear that everything was going to end in disaster for everyone involved.

At first, the killing point for me was the intimacy between the cheating couple. The show was all about sex – that was the centre of it, the whole point of the story. As a viewer, I would normally have thought there was nothing wrong with that. But time and again the older man and the younger woman used phrases and jokes and nicknames that only Jack and I used. I don't want to spell them out because they were things that were never supposed to be written down. I had thought these were our deepest secrets, the things we kept entirely for each other. Our private space. But it turned out that this was just Jack's way of carrying on, and he was as capable of doing it with another woman as he was with me. It wasn't just me for whom he would use these nicknames, make these jokes, ask for these particular things to be done. Some of them were the biggest secrets, the biggest intimacies, in our marriage. The way the programme told the story, it looked as if the affair had gone on for about two years. More or less the two years before he had died. Jack had lied to me and cheated on me all through the last of our time together.

One of the worst things that happen when people get divorced is that they have to rewrite all your memories of the good times you had, and change them into unhappy memories, or, at best, into the precursor to unhappy memories. You have to rewrite them in the knowledge of what was to happen later. You see good times as the build-up to bad times. You pick over happy memories looking for signs and clues that you missed. The places you used to go to in your head, to make you feel comfort, the memories you replay to ease your pain, or help you through a difficult patch, or just to make you feel good for a moment – they're all gone. They don't mean what you thought they meant.

I had thought Jack was a loving, devoted, faithful husband, one who was, in a secret way nobody else knew about, dependent. Dependent on me. I knew he needed me and that made me feel loved and safe. I now knew that he was a liar and a cheat and a player and the things I had thought were uniquely ours, the private language of our intimacy and our marriage, was for him just a set of signature moves, a game.

What's the worst possible thing you can imagine happening to you?

9

INT - JERRY AND CHARLOTTE'S KITCHEN - EVENING

An expensive kitchen and dining room, open-plan, with a big island and double-sized American fridge and fitted storage spaces. Your first thought on looking at the room is: fuck, I wonder how much they spent on that. Copper pots hang off hooks; knives on a knife rail. JERRY is standing at the kitchen island opening a bottle of champagne. There are three glasses in front of him. CHARLOTTE is sitting at the long wooden dining table.

                    JERRY
Awkward.

He holds a champagne flute out to her.

                  CHARLOTTE
Awkward? Don't be stupid. We aren't children. We know how this works.

Jerry gives a small laugh.

                    JERRY
Yes, we do.

He raises the glass to her and she does the same back. He takes a sip of the champagne.

                    JERRY (CONT'D)
When I say awkward, I was thinking of the first time. You remember.

                    CHARLOTTE
The first time we . . . tried it, or the first time you brought it up? Or the first time we met this one?

                    JERRY
When I brought it up and when we tried it.

                    CHARLOTTE
Of course I remember. You were so nervous when you came out with it. Just adorable. It was like you were a fourteen-year-old asking a girl out for the first time. I couldn't for the life of me think what you were going to say. It wasn't very Jerry at all.

                    JERRY
Very Jerry, Jesus, what does that mean?

                    CHARLOTTE
Oh, come off it, you know.

                    JERRY
        (less cool than he wants to be)
I did feel nervous. It's hard to talk about these things . . . or rather it was hard, it isn't any more. It's hard at

first. You don't know how the other person is going to react. Embarrassing . . . No, it's more than that, it goes deeper, it's about shame. The things you are ashamed to bring to light.

                    CHARLOTTE
Even in front of me.

                    JERRY
Or especially that.

They each take another sip of their drink.

                　JERRY (CONT'D)
Because obviously I had no idea how you were going to react.

                    CHARLOTTE
You thought I might recoil in horror. Or divorce you. Or demand we start couples' therapy.

He's trying to remember.

                    JERRY
Mainly, I think, I was worried that you might think I was ridiculous. Or might think I didn't want you any more, or not in the same way. That you might think the reason was that I didn't think you were enough. Not meeting my needs. God, it's awful how one can't talk about this stuff without sounding like some crappy therapy column. 'So you're feeling insecure

because your husband just suggested a threesome and it makes you wonder if he doesn't like you any more.'

                CHARLOTTE
  (smiling)
I never thought that.
  (beat)
And 'threesome' doesn't really describe it, I don't think. I'd say it was a little more specific.

                JERRY
  (now he's smiling too)
Specific. Good word.

                CHARLOTTE
A lot more specific.

                JERRY
Well, yes, as it turned out. We knew each other pretty well. All these years. But there were still things we didn't know. Things we didn't know about each other and found out.

                CHARLOTTE
And had fun finding out.

                JERRY
If fun is the word. I suppose it is. But it goes deeper too. Fun and also something more than fun.

CHARLOTTE
You're very serious tonight. The young people say 'it's just sex'.

JERRY
Ah, but we're old enough to know better.

CHARLOTTE
Learn by doing.

Jerry laughs.

JERRY
You're saucy tonight.

CHARLOTTE
Just as well, given what we've got planned.

JERRY
It meant so much to me. That you went along with it. And then I realised that it wasn't just going along with it, it was something that you wanted too.

CHARLOTTE
(almost whispering)
It's sexier if we don't talk about it.

JERRY
I know. But just this once.

CHARLOTTE
OK, just this once. I did turn out to like it. I still do. You know that. Maybe

it was something you saw in me. Or we saw in each other, without realising. It just took all that time to come out.

                    JERRY
Talking of coming.

Charlotte's turn to laugh.

                    JERRY (CONT'D)
Well it's true. I don't think I've ever seen you come so hard. I thought your eyes were going to roll out the back of your head.

                    CHARLOTTE
You're making me blush. And I'm too old to blush.

The doorbell rings. They look at each other, smiling, expectant.

                    JERRY
And here she is, right on cue. Shall we?

10
KATE

I've always been proud of my toughness. I loved the idea of my invulnerability, my obduracy, my thick skin, my will to survive, to push through, to ignore pain and overcome difficulty. And then I found that wasn't enough; or I wasn't tough enough, which amounts to the same thing.

I think that if Jack's death had been Jack's death and nothing else, I would have got through the bereavement, and all the processes of grief, without having to go to talk to someone. But the humiliation, the complicated humiliation of what happened with that horrible TV series was just too much. Grief is catastrophic. Grief is the roof falling in. But when the roof falls in, you can dig yourself out of the rubble. Or wait for someone else to come and dig you out. This was more than that. It was the added compound of shame and humiliation and the need for secrecy that took me to the edge. It was the loss of all the happy memories. I had a story about my life. It made sense. Even the loss made sense, as a terrible plot twist. After all, one of us was going to die one day. But all the time I had been living the life I thought I had with Jack, meanwhile he had been, not to put too fine a point on it, fucking this young whore on the side without my even beginning to suspect. And telling her everything – every single secret thing about our life.

Grieving, lost, lonely, ashamed, humiliated, isolated, betrayed, furious and – and this magnified and compounded everything else

– stupid. So, so stupid. I felt all of those things simultaneously and more intensely than I'd ever felt any one of them.

That's the point at which I realised I needed to go and talk to someone.

I wouldn't have dreamt of confiding what I was going through to Daphne. I wouldn't have even known where to begin. But she had seen something happen to me during the book group – she knew me too well – and came round the next day, and every single day after that too. Although she could be irritatingly practical, minded to fix things and to fix me, that didn't mean she was oblivious. It was about her fifth of these visits, a wet weekend afternoon after the book group. I was in a bad way. She started doing irritating things both with the bunch of flowers she'd brought and with the other vases of flowers in my house, which were in various stages of fragrant semi-decay. She was bustling around talking about this and that and generally minding my business when she suddenly stopped and turned to me and said:

'You're not all right, are you?'

Friendships ordinarily function inside set parameters. You are completely open and honest, but these free exchanges happen within electric guard-rails. This remark was Daphne jumping those rails. It might not sound dramatic, but it was so far outside the normal boundaries of our relationship that I was genuinely shocked. I tried to reply along conventional lines about how I was fine, but I found that I could not speak. I began to choke and cough and immediately I was wracked with gasping, heaving sobs; a form of weeping that was more like being sick. I had never done that before and have never done it since, but there in front of Daphne I was wholly undone. It was this grief that was not just grief but was also rage, humiliation, betrayal, and the need to keep it all secret.

I was astonished by myself. Daphne seemed to be less surprised. After a minute she came over – I remember the delicacy with which she put down the vase she was carrying before she did so – and hugged me. She was not a natural hugger and nor am I, and this was only the third or fourth time, in decades of friendship, that we had ever done that. She was stronger and held me tighter than I had expected. It took a moment for me to accept; then I cried harder, but more like ordinary crying, not the desperate half-choking wail of moments before. I don't know how long we stayed like that. It felt like a long time. I let her go, took some tissues from the box on the counter, went to the loo to tidy myself up. My mascara had run and I had a bad case of what Jack used to call 'panda eyes'. The memory made me feel better. I came out to the sitting room, where Daphne was back at her arrangements.

'I think you should go and talk to someone,' she said. Daphne being Daphne, of course she had a name in mind. And that was how I began therapy, which was how everything changed.

★ ★ ★

I disliked Carlos on sight. I never found out why he had a Hispanic name, since he presented as the most Anglo-English, Home Counties person imaginable. He had prints of Constable pictures and hunting scenes on the walls of his consulting room off Cavendish Square. He was a short fair unsmiling man, usually dressed in tweed or corduroy, who always had small places where he had not accurately shaved around the base and sides of his neck. So he would be mostly well turned out, but with random patches of bum fluff. This particular failure of middle-aged male grooming was a pet peeve of Jack's, and something he often pointed out as the difference between being well-turned-out and 'looking like a dressed-up yeti'. This annoying thing about Carlos reminded me of Jack, brought him into the room – and was therefore, oddly, helpful. That was the pattern for what it was like with Carlos. He was irritating, often got the wrong end of the stick, and never got the funny side of anything resembling a joke. Since many of my memories of Jack involved shared jokes and private language, that meant he never really got the point of Jack; which in turn forced me to think hard about what it was about Jack that I was trying to convey; which made Jack very present in the consulting room; which was, as it turned out, a good thing.

I lay on the couch, which was excruciatingly embarrassing the first time, for about five minutes, but I quickly got used to it and saw the point of avoiding eye contact. I realised afterwards, after talking to people who had been through grief counselling, that this was more like full-blown Freudian psychotherapy than something specifically for grief. I lay there and he waited for me to talk and I waited for him to talk and it was as awkward and weird as I had always imagined therapy to be. But when I started talking, I found, to my surprise, that I was replaying the story of how Jack and I had met and how we had got together and reliving a whole drama that I hadn't thought about in decades.

PART THREE

11
KATE

'Anal sex'.

That was the first thing I ever heard Jack say. I was in the bar of the posh college down the road from my less posh, more academic one. The bar was in the half-underground genre of student bars, with a barrel ceiling and trestle tables and walls thickly layered with an archaeology of old student posters and flyers advertising this, protesting that: *Cyrano* at the Playhouse, Support the NUM, Which Of You Cunts Stole This Bicycle – Reward For Information. Several of the posters had been defaced with a homemade ink stamp declaring 'Tory Crime!' The atmosphere was so saturated with old beer, it was like a drink in itself. Every second person was smoking rollies.

I have long since forgotten why, or with whom, I was there. It was probably to do with acting, with a play I was going to see or had just seen; my first two years at university, I did a lot of that, before realising most student drama was rubbish and I had no talent for it anyway. I was in a below average production of Brecht, a piss-poor modern dress all-female *Faustus*, a grisly pantomime and a definitively puerile, unfunny college review. I was probably in the bar in connection with one of those. Maybe I had even gone to the bar – though in the posh college they didn't call it the bar, they called it the buttery – to put up a flyer, or meet someone about an audition. Whatever the reason and whoever I'd been with, I no longer remember.

But I do remember Jack. He was sitting at the next trestle table over from me, not exactly holding court, but clearly the centre of attention in a noisy, laughing, not completely sober group of about eight fellow students, half boys and half girls.

'Anal sex,' Jack was saying, loudly, as a punchline. I grew to know him so well, every contour of his face and body, his smell and his walk, from the pattern of hair on the back of his hands to the rough skin on the soles of his feet that I would nag him to file down; I could have spotted him in a crowd a mile away, or picked him out of a police line-up with his back turned and wearing some other man's clothes. But I never forgot the shock I got seeing him for the first time, slightly flushed, sitting with his good posture and big shoulders and unthinkingly athletic figure. I have hundreds of pictures of him in every state of dress and undress, but I never took or saw a photo of him that matched the impact of that first look.

'That's going to be the name of your new airline?' said a girl across the table from him. 'Anal sex?'

'Think about it. What's the most successful new branding enterprise in the history of modern aviation? Easy – Virgin. From that beardy twat Branson. But it's brilliant too. You remember it. Everyone else is called, I don't know, Boring National Airline Company. British Airways or Swissair or Lufthansa or whatever. Who cares? They're all the same anyway. But then Branson comes along and bang, there's an airline called Virgin. And people go, ooh! Virgin! Shocking!'

'I know I'm shocked,' one of the group said, taking a swig of his pint. 'I for one am shocked. Shocked to my core. So shocked!'

'Right. We're not shocked. Obviously. Apart from Linda' – this being a tease-flirt directed at one of the company, who giggled. We were all so young that somebody in that company probably was a virgin, of course, and that fact hung faintly in the beery air.

'But we're sophisticated and cool and worldly. We're not shocked. Still, we remember the name. We remember the idea. Virgin. An airline that sounds a bit different. And before long the people who are shocked now won't be shocked any more, because having an airline called something like Virgin will seem perfectly routine. And then, in order to be a little shocking, to get that jolt you get from the new, the not yet normal, not yet boring, you have to go a bit further, you have to move to where the customers are not now, but where they'll be in a few years. Right? So: welcome to my new airline: Anal Sex.'

There was some laughter, some muttering, some 'come off it'. The tables were so close that I had full eavesdropper's access to this group, who I thought, from their confidence and their body language and their volume, were a year or two older than me – third years where I was in my first. I was, I hoped not quite openly, eavesdropping. One of the men, looking at Jack, took a long slow swig of his beer without smiling and without looking up, and I could see that the two men didn't like each other. I could also see that he was itching to take Jack on conversationally but didn't feel strong enough to do it. He was frightened of Jack, just a little. I rather liked that.

'Initially, people will go: gasp! They will keel over, they will swoon, they will faint with horror, they will write letters to their MP, address petitions to the Queen and Mrs Thatcher, they will vow boycotts, threaten to emigrate, tear up their passports, their library cards, their books of Green Shield stamps. Or at least, some of them will. But there are others who will say: do you know something, I like the sound of this Anal Sex. There are some who will say, let's try Anal Sex. A group who will wonder, Anal Sex, how bad can it be? Once we were shocked by Virgin, but then it turned out to be a perfectly good airline with better service and cheaper prices, so now we are shocked by Anal Sex, but perhaps that will turn out to be a perfectly good airline with better service and cheaper prices still.'

Now it was Jack's turn to take a sip of his drink. His friends – his audience, his claque, his clique – did not interrupt.

'I haven't got to the good part yet.'

The semi-antagonist, the potential enemy, said, with his mouth half hidden behind his pint glass:

'Oh please Jack, do get to the good part.'

'It's what we call the different parts of the plane, the different classes. First class, obviously, is Front. Or The Front – I haven't decided yet. Economy class, equally obviously, is Back. Or The Back. And now we get to the best part. Guess what we'll be calling business class? Go on.'

There was some mumbling but nobody said anything coherent.

'OK, ready? This is the genius part. Wait for it: Business. Isn't that genius?'

'Genius,' said Linda.

'And then we roll out the brand, just like the beardy twat himself. Anal Sex records. Anal Sex hairdressing salons. Anal Sex chocolate.'

Laughter, pretend applause. Normal conversation resumed in side chats and mutterings. The set piece was over. The man-who-I-didn't-yet-know-was-Jack had clearly finished his riff. One of the other boys started saying intelligent but contextually off-tone things about branding. One of the girls and one of the boys extracted themselves from the trestle seating and headed back to the bar for another round. Jack, with the attention now off him, went quiet, and looked down at his drink for a moment, and it was that, more than his looks and ease and confidence, that had the clinching effect on me: he looked shy and private and a little damaged, as if there was a side to him that he knew he couldn't let out in company, a side to him that he had to hide and protect and let nobody else see. That was what did it for me. Love at first sight is said to be a fiction or a social construct, and maybe it is, but what I do know is that in that moment, as I looked at him, I had an overpowering idea. Or perhaps it was a feeling rather than an idea. I looked at this man and I felt: mine. Simple as that: mine. It wasn't that I wanted him – though I did, obviously – it was that I knew he already belonged to me. He was mine.

And then a girl came into the bar. I was looking sidelong at the man I didn't yet know was Jack and his table of friends, so I had a full view of the length of the crowded, noisy, warm mass of drinkers. I saw the girl scan the room, performing the act of 'where are my friends' – and I did feel it was a performance, even then, even in that first moment. Then she switched to 'oh there they are! silly me!' and came towards our end of the bar. She was pretty, skinny, blondish, tallish, dressed in a suede skirt and a long belted jacket and a maroon sweater – a careful, self-conscious, very put-together version of Bohemian chic. You could have put her on a poster for a movie in black and white. She walked slowly down the room, slaloming a little between the trestles, and came up behind the group I'd been watching. She rested a hand on the shoulder of the man I liked and he turned to face her and she slowly, slowly leaned down and kissed him on the mouth, not a social kiss, a lover's kiss, and a proprietorial one at that. The kiss went on for a little bit too long. I could tell the rest of the group were embarrassed. Then she came up for air and one of the men said brightly, 'Hello, Sarah!'

★ ★ ★

'Stalking', as it's now called, didn't really exist in the eighties. Don't ask me why not. Jack would probably have had a theory about it, or at the very least a riff. Perhaps the boundaries between people are more porous today, since we have full access to all the information known to humanity, everywhere, all the time; we blur into the world around us and our stories leak out too, like a trail of cuttlefish ink, and we can't resist the temptation to follow the trail, to sniff around after each other's traces like dogs on a scent.

It wasn't like that then. There were limits to what you could find out about someone without their knowledge or consent.

So what I did wasn't stalking. At the time, I thought of it as a form of detective work. Bear in mind I had no idea who Jack was at that point, no idea of who his friends were, which college he went to, what he was studying. My hunch was that some or most of them were at the posh college, the one with the buttery and the reputation for being both grand (socially) and left wing (politically) and unusually full of itself, even by Oxbridge standards. They took up space in that room as if some or most of them belonged there. I was at a three-hundred-years newer, swottier, more distant college. My likely hunting ground was the posh college, though I didn't know that for sure, and didn't want to hang around the place like a ghost while I waited to bump into the man who was going to be mine.

I did have a flash of panic, of the thought: but what if I never see him again? What if he's mine but I lose him? What if he's mine but is already lost? But I was able to calm down as I sat with the idea. From the cool kids' conversation I began to glean that some of the group were actors or actor-adjacent, and I knew that would make things easier: student theatre is a finite world. The mystery man was comfortable here, which probably meant he was a regular or semi-regular. If all else failed I could just hang around this bar until we met again. I lingered over my drink for as long as I could, eavesdropping and gathering data, but it got harder when the person I was waiting for finally arrived. Soon after, the group I was looking at glanced at watches, finished drinks, and left. I remember that it was early evening so they were going to a play or dinner or a party or perhaps all three, in that order. We finished our drinks too and went to do whatever it was we were going to do, but then I had my first idea, my first flash of inspiration. I stopped just as we were crossing the quadrangle and said:

'Oops – shit – just realised I dropped something.'

I doubled back and as I was going in, took the pocket diary I used in those days out of my handbag. It was a long thin volume in red leather. I held it up and went over to the counter, where the barman, an ex-policeman (as quite a few college barmen were in those days), was pulling pints of bitter.

'I'm so sorry,' I said, flustered and flaky in the way that older men often like, 'I was sitting over there' – vague wave – 'and as we were going I saw that a girl at the next table had dropped this, but I just chased after her to give it back and I don't know who she is, can you help?'

He gave a backwards jerk of his head to acknowledge that he had heard me and was thinking about it.

'She was wearing a suede jacket. Blonde girl. At the table with about six other people.'

The former copper turned and went to the other end of the bar. A young man was leaning against the top, with the air of someone who was very used indeed to doing exactly that; he had a proper beer gut, not a common sight on a nineteen-year-old undergraduate in the mid-1980s.

'Oi Clive,' said the barman, 'who was that blonde girl at the corner table – you know her?'

Clive took the opportunity to suppress a belch as he thought this over. When his cheeks were puffed out, slumped over at the bar with his stomach out, he looked as fully frog-like as it is possible for a person to be.

'Sarah Hadling, second year, does English, hangs out with those,' said Clive, waving his arms in a narrow circle towards the table where the group had been sitting. That told me two things: the girlfriend went to this college and so, university life being what it was, it was likely that her boyfriend did too; and this group were regulars at the buttery. And in that moment I realised that the best route to my future man was through his girlfriend. His current girlfriend.

★ ★ ★

Age changes your perspective on many things, and right at the top of the list is the change to how you perceive the passage of time. While this was happening, I thought I was being slow and careful and meticulous – excruciatingly slow. I was measuring my actions, being deliberate and cautious to a fault. I was the tortoise not the hare. Looking back, what I see now is the acceleration and compression of young life, especially student life. We were all in such a hurry; we had no idea at all how young we were, how ignorant we were, how much time we had. Lifelong friendships would be made in days, irrevocable harm done to relationships in minutes; you would start an eight-week term as one kind of person and end it a completely different type, with new interests, new friends, new politics, new clothes, new everything. The fact is that it took me a week to be known to Sarah, two weeks to be her friend, and four weeks to become her best friend.

I began by going through the names of everyone I could think of to try and find someone who went to the posh college. The difficult part was that because it was posh and I was not, in the nature of things I would know hardly anyone who went there – but there was a merciful single exception: a friend of Daphne's called Vera Wilson.

Back in those days there was a useful, brutally dismissive term for everyone who was not posh, southern, and studying an arts subject. They were known as 'northern chemists'. Daphne, despite being middle-class and southern, was a natural-born northern chemist, and so was her friend Vera. Daphne and I had met on our shared staircase and had become friends. She in turn had a friend at the posh college, Vera. They had met, of course, at a lecture. I met Vera a couple of times in Daphne's room. She was permanently dressed for heavy rain; she had lank dark hair, glasses, and moderate to non-existent social skills. We had few interests in common, but we knew each other well enough for me to drop in on her in her room unannounced without it seeming unduly weird or desperate. I chose to go around the evening after I had seen the man who would turn out to be Jack. I went in the early evening after hall, suspecting that One, she would have been to eat in college and Two, she would have gone back to her room on her own and would be working. I was half right: she had indeed had her dinner in halls, but she wasn't alone. Vera had set up a card table and she and three other people were sitting around it playing bridge by – least expected thing of all – candlelight. One of them was Daphne. That was the first moment when I realised that this person might be someone different from who I thought she was.

'You stood there blinking in the doorway as if you'd seen an apparition,' she said to me, years later.

'You sat there with your bridge friends staring at me as if I was the ghost of Christmas past,' I said back. At the time I was mainly annoyed: I had been planning to drag Vera out of her lair, pour a drink or two into her, and at a minimum get an invitation that would start bringing me into the orbit of the posh college and give me a chance to meet Sarah Hadling. At a maximum they might already be friends, or in adjacent rooms, or who knew what. But instead of arriving in Vera's room like a welcome breeze from the wider world and sweeping her off her feet with a glimpse of glamour and fun and sexy Oxford, I was standing there dancing attendance while the bridge players shuffled and dealt.

We made a plan to meet for coffee. She had no lectures, and in those days I didn't bother with lectures anyway. (People didn't, on the whole, with the exception of unfortunates in the northern chemist subjects. The world was in many respects a more forgiving place. The winners' enclosure was small, but once you were inside it, you were there for life. That's what we felt.) The process of arranging to meet Sarah could hardly have been easier. The tricky part was coming up with an excuse for why I was curious, but I got there via a general enquiry about the kind of person who went to the posh college, then a follow-up about some types I had overheard in the buttery, then zooming in on my specific target. I needn't have been so careful. Vera was like Daphne: she had a general willingness to get involved, an all-purpose interest in other people's business, and assumed no ill intent on my part other than a perfectly normal (to her) nosiness. She knew exactly who Sarah was. As a happy side effect of the posh college only recently having taken female undergraduates, it had a women's group, and both of them were regular attendees. Vera, again like Daphne, was the kind of person who becomes secretary of any club or society or group on the second meeting, and chair in short order thereafter. She was more or less running the women's group already and knew all the other women in college, and had both set the strategy – campaign for one issue at a time – and picked the issue – tampon machines in the girls' loos. To match the condom machines in the boys'. A simpler time. Sarah was part of the campaign. My own college already had tampon machines. This, I told her, was relevant information for her campaign: 'come and have a look at our loos and you'll see'. And that's how I first got to meet Sarah, in the course of a walking tour looking at tampon machines.

So what was she like? Short answer: first impressions were deceptive. But first impressions lasted for a while and it took some time to get beyond them, because front was important to Sarah. Destructively so. She liked to look put-together, composed, cool calm collected. She liked it to be thought that she was the person she dressed as: arty, London or Paris or anyway Big City, and not any of the various off-the-shelf tribal identities that were around in those days: Sloane, post-punk, Greenham woman, northern chemist, *Brideshead* wanker. You might say that her category was Uncategorisable Arty London. (I once overheard her describe herself as 'an ironist'.) She was pretty and she knew she was pretty, but her look was designed to signal that she didn't spend all day thinking about the fact.

After that first time looking at tampon machines and taking notes (or rather, Vera taking notes, detailed notes), we arranged to meet for a drink. I think we both knew that we were more each other's kind of person than either of us was Vera's. It turned out that yes, Sarah was an actor. I waited for her to mention her boyfriend because I thought she would smell the level of interest and intent on me if I asked first. I had to wait quite a long time and it wasn't until the end of that first drink that she asked if I was 'seeing someone' and when I said no and returned the query she said 'well, yes, actually,' while shyly raising her glass to her mouth with a small smirk. We were in my college this time, in the bar that nobody ever thought to call a buttery, though to be honest it was much more to my taste as a room, a bright metal and glass space that was nice as a café by day; the kind of room that in a later era people would camp out in with their laptops.

'Who is he and what's he like and what does he do and is it serious and whatever other questions people ask,' I said, taking a drink in my turn, deliberately asking too many questions so that I wouldn't seem too interested in any specific one of them.

'His name is Jack Hittlestone,' she told me, and that is how I learned the name of the man I lived with for the next four decades. 'He's at the same college as me. Doing a degree in history but he's already decided he's going to train as an architect. We met in freshers' week and, well, we sort of clicked and we've been going out since halfway through the first term.' That meant, for a little over a year. 'Hard to say what he's like, really – I sort of know him too well' – another small smirk – 'to be able to say. Funny and clever. Good-looking. Anyway, I like him.'

'Posh, if he's here. Lefty posh. No offence.'

'Yes, clever, lefty parents, sent him to the local comp, lots of culture and stuff in the family. A bit like you,' she said, more dangerously than she realised. 'People like him. Not rich though. Not like some of the properly rich pretend lefties you get around here. It's one of the things we have in common. It's his birthday coming up and I want to get him this architecture book he's been talking about for ages, but he can't afford it, and nor can I but I'm going to anyway, so I'll go around in rags for the rest of the year but it'll be worth it.'

'What's the book?'

She told me. I thought about what she was saying and thought about her and thought about how to get from where I was to where I wanted to be.

'Let's get it for him then. No need to go around in rags, I promise.

They wouldn't suit you anyway.'

'I can't really afford it, is the truth. It's one of those oversize lavish architecture books. Like an old family Bible.'

'What are you doing tomorrow morning? Got any lectures or anything?'

She made the 'I don't go to lectures much' face.

'No real plans.'

'Then it's settled – we're going shoplifting.'

I was pleased to see that she was a little shocked but trying to look cool about it. I went on:

'Done much? Shoplifting?'

'Define "much",' she said. Remember that this was Oxford university, in which one of the basic rules of life is reversed. I can't remember who told me the rule, but I still remember how it worked. In normal life you smile at people to make them like you and say clever things to make them think you're intelligent. At Oxford you smiled at people to make them think you were intelligent and said clever things to make them like you.

'No, actually, not much,' she went on. I took that to mean none at all.

'So these are the basics. It's once and done. You don't reconnoitre and then do it the second time – they'll remember you if you went there to case the joint and then the book goes missing the next time they see you.

'You either do it the first time you go to a place or you take the time to become a regular and keep going back even after you've taken the thing. Are you a regular?'

'Blackwell's in general, yes. In the architecture books section, no.'

'So it's Plan A. No problem. Do you want to be the snatcher, or do you want to stage the diversion?'

'Er—'

'Let me put it this way: do you want to be the sneaky one, or the theatrical one, the centre of attention?'

'I don't know what I'd be doing to stage a diversion, so I'd better be the sneaky one. Also, I think I know roughly where the book is and what it looks like.'

'OK. You go in slow and have a good look from the other side of the room, as far away as possible, but don't make it obvious. You don't want to be casing the place at the last moment. Think about it like you've forgotten the keys to your house, and you're having to use a trick you know to get the door open. Do you look shifty, from side to side, like you're worried about what people might think you're up to, like you're worried about being caught? Like hell – you look as if you own the place, because you do. That's crucial. So the way you check if there are staff watching or something is in advance of the snatch. You don't look around during, you look around before. Then you're just a normal browser. Got it?'

She nodded, frowning, with the air of a person regretting her life choices.

'But where do I put it?' she said. I reached across the table and took her arm.

'Leave that to your Auntie Kate,' I said. 'I have a bag. I'll bring it tomorrow. You just drop it in. And there's one last thing: when you go into Blackwell's, you look around to see if there's a security guard, and if you see one, you go up to him and ask him where you can find the architecture section.'

'That's mad.'

'Right. Because which shoplifter would draw attention to themselves by going up to the security guard. Which is why it works. They strike you off their mental list – they don't see you as a potential shoplifter any more. Trust me.'

She didn't look like she trusted me.

★ ★ ★

'I gather I have you to thank for my birthday present,' said Jack. This was four weeks after I had seen him for the first time, and about a week after we had first officially met. We were at a party at a chaotic student house in the north of the city. Whoever was in charge of the music was in love with Wham's then recent single 'Wake Me Up Before You Go-Go' and was playing it at roughly four-track intervals. I wasn't complaining – it's my favourite George Michael song.

'I don't know what you're talking about,' I said.

'Sarah says it's the most impressive thing she's ever seen,' he said, maintaining eye contact.

And the truth was, it had been pretty impressive. I'm not tall, but when I was in my early teens I nonetheless had a growth spurt, and during it, for about eighteen months, I was prone to fainting. It didn't happen often – six or seven times – but it happened often enough for me to know how it worked, what it felt like, and, most crucially, what it looked like to everyone around me. The first time I fainted was the most dramatic. That was partly because it happened in full public view, at a bus stop, and also because, since it was the first time, it was the only time that I had no idea what was going on. The first time you faint you think, what the hell is this, and the intensely unpleasant experience is compounded by a form of existential panic, by the thought that you are going to die – that you are being swept away by something over which you have no control. All the other times, there is at least a moment when you have the chance to realise, oh no, I'm about to faint. It's still horrible, but it is a fraction less horrible than the first time, when you have no idea what's happening to you. Then you wake up and are – or at least I was, on that first occasion – looking up at half a dozen aghast, ashen faces. It's not that you don't know where you are, it's that you don't even know who or why you are, and why is the sky straight ahead, and why are there all the terrified strangers up there too? Have I died? I remember thinking that as I came round and began to realise that I had fainted – thanks in part to a kindly middle-aged woman who was bending down over me and saying 'you fainted' over and over again.

There were no upsides to that experience. Except that I did learn one thing: how dramatic and attention-grabbing a proper full-scale faint could be. And making a little bit of noise just before keeling over does nothing to diminish the effect. When my brief growth spurt ended and I stopped fainting for real, I took up pretend fainting – mainly for shoplifting, though also occasionally for getting out of social situations and work deadlines. Not too often, obviously: maybe ten times in all.

The first pass at the planned shoplift did not work because it was a clear and unseasonably warm early winter's day, and there was no credible reason for wearing shoplift-friendly clothes – big coat, big bag, and the shoplifter's friend, the umbrella. Not that we needed those coverings, necessarily, but one of the things I had learned was the necessity of being flexible and prepared – the bag might split, or the book be the wrong shape, or a bookshop staffer might start looking at one of us funny before we had had a chance to cache it properly. Anything was possible. So we needed the baggy clothes as backup, and if you need them, you have to go on a day when everyone else is wearing them too. The closest I had ever been to getting caught was in Debenhams, when I and a school friend went to pinch some make-up. We went in with umbrellas on a radiant June afternoon when every other girl within a five-mile radius was wearing the skimpiest clothes she could find. My friend did the distraction, I did the lift and drop into the upturned umbrella, but a security guard, who I later realised had been suspicious as soon as he set eyes on us, chased me. I only got away because going around the corner of a stairwell I was able to tip out the contents of the umbrella into a bin while out of sight. By the time he caught me and searched me, I was clean. I never went back to that branch of Debenhams.

When our first attempt was aborted, Sarah and I went to the covered market for coffee and to regroup. Two days later, one day before Jack's birthday, it was chucking it down and the entire city of Oxford was dressed for monsoon. We met in the pub before going to the bookshop and I was surprised that I could smell alcohol on Sarah's breath. She was more nervous than I had realised and without working out exactly why, I knew this was going to be good for me, not necessarily with the shoplifting but later, with whatever happened next. Perhaps it was just that I thought needing a drink meant she was weak. I bought her another one – vodka. I stuck to water. I didn't want anyone who might attend to me after my faint to notice that I had been drinking.

We talked it through one more time. We left the pub and she went into the bookshop. I waited five minutes and followed. I wandered around the shelves for another five minutes, then, as per the timing we had agreed, drifted through to architecture. Sarah was standing in a corner flicking through a book. There were two other people in the architecture section and by the exit there was a staffer at a till that served all the different mini-departments in that part of the shop. I went and stood by a table in the middle of the room. I picked the table where a duffel-coated man in early middle age was flicking through a pictorial history that – no judgement, but I did notice – seemed to consist mainly of full-page photographs of naked female sculptures. He looked up and we made eye contact and I briefly smiled, just to make sure he had fully noticed me. I fiddled about with books for a moment or two, picking them up and putting them down, and I saw that Sarah was in position, because she had made our agreed signal of switching her bag from her right shoulder to her left.

I gave a sharp intake of breath, designed to be heard. My new friend looked up.

'Ooh,' I said, more or less. It didn't sound quite as stupid as that in real life. 'I—'

I swayed a little and put an arm out towards the table for support.

'Excuse me, miss, are you all right?' he said. He had quite a loud voice, which was going to be useful.

'I . . . I . . . I think,' I said. I fell forwards on to the table of books and rolled off sideways on to the carpeted floor, taking a fair few architectural picture books with me, and making a truly epic amount of noise and drama in the process. An absolute classic, one of my very best. I kept my eyes closed and counted up from one to ten and then down from ten to one, and opened my eyes. Three faces were peering down at me: the man in the duffel coat, the staffer from the till, and – for a moment I wondered if I had truly fainted, or bumped my head, or was hallucinating – a much older man wearing, of all things, a monocle. I made incoherent noises for a few seconds and then, with assistance, sat up.

'Please take your time. You have had an episode of syncope,' said the man with the monocle. That was Oxford for 'you fainted'.

I knew better than to come round too quickly but also knew to seem confused and embarrassed. I asked for a glass of water and the man from the till went and got one. I drank it and they helped me to my feet and I brushed myself down. I could see that Sarah had gone and was keenly hoping she had managed to grab the book first – not least because this was a trick that would only work once.

'Do you need help getting somewhere?' said duffel coat. He couldn't stop himself looking expectant. Fainting woman = damsel in distress = opportunity to try it on. Honestly, men.

'No,' I said in a small voice, 'thank you, I'm not going far, but thank you.'

He and the bookseller were not so easily deterred, however. Both of them insisted on walking me to the door of the shop and seeing me on to Broad Street outside. I had to work quite hard to brush them off – no no I'm fine, no no I am, no no I insist – and eventually I managed to turn and leave, making an effort not to break into a jog as I did so. About ten yards down the pavement, I felt somebody grip my arm. It was the bookseller. Duffel coat had gone. The bookseller's face was pinched and angry and his grip on my arm was hard.

'Do you think I'm stupid?' he said.

'I – sorry – what?'

'Do you think I'm stupid?'

By now I knew, or had guessed, what was coming.

'I don't understand the question. Of course I don't think you're stupid.'

'Well fuck you and don't ever come back. Or your friend.'

'I have no idea what you're talking about.'

He gave my arm one final hard squeeze and let me go.

I have to admit I hadn't seen that coming. Sarah was waiting for me in the same fuggy pub we had been in before. She had a vodka in her hand and had one waiting for me. She had the book in front of her, still in its protective plastic wrapper. I smacked my drink down in one. I took off my coat and my sweater and rolled up my sleeve to show Sarah the bruise on my upper arm. I told her the story of how I came by it. She was impressed.

'I wonder why he let you go?' she said.

'Who cares? There's nothing they can prove. They have no evidence that we know each other or that I was faking.'

We drank to that.

Did I stop shoplifting? Of course not. I couldn't afford pretty things and there was no other way of getting them. But I never did it in Blackwell's again.

'Did Sarah tell you about the drama?' I said to Jack at that Jericho house party.

'Absolutely. She said you were like Clint Eastwood. I hope it goes without saying that because I'm a man, that's the ultimate compliment.'

'I'll take it as such. I'm so sorry she couldn't be here,' I said.

'Essay crisis,' he said, looking away for a moment. I could tell that he liked me; possibly a little more than was convenient, or than he was willing to admit. We were standing close – had to, because of the noise. But maybe not only because of the noise. It was a typical student party, packed and sweaty, with drunk students arguing about politics next to a table full of bottles and people in the next room snogging, dancing, and trying to get off with each other. Cocaine wasn't a big thing in those days, and even if it had been nobody there would have been able to afford it, so the only drug available was marijuana; you could tell who had been smoking because they were sitting on the sofa on a spectrum from catatonic introspection to stoned quasi-philosophical mumbling. The party-giver had turned off the overhead lights – classy! – and the room was lit instead by side lamps, which had been covered with red pillowcases. It worked pretty well to make the otherwise infernal scene look warm and welcoming. 'Wake Me Up Before You Go-Go' came on again for what felt like the hundredth time.

I don't think I am the kind of person who wants what other people have. I'm not by nature envious. I don't try to nick other people's friends, or copy their opinions, or their ideas. I don't even ask people for recipes. When I see something I want, though, I will take it. And that was what I felt about Jack. I have never taken a man off any other woman apart from Sarah, and if the same sequence of events were to be repeated, with the same characters and the same consequences, I would do the same things that I did then.

What is attraction? I don't know and the truth is I don't think it matters. The best way to think about it is exactly as the name suggests: things being pulled together under their own mass. Like gravity. I felt it and I knew now in that moment that Jack felt it too.

'Essay crisis,' I said back to Jack. He turned to look at me and we held each other's gaze. At first it was a look that we were holding for too long, and then it turned into something else, and I knew. I can't describe what I felt. It wasn't sexual; it went beyond that.

'That book,' I said. 'I had a look at it. A record of all the things in this city that haven't been built. All the brilliant ideas that were dreamt up and thought through and should have been made, but weren't, because the money fell through or the patron died or the place where they were going to build it changed hands, or whatever. All that possibility. All those things that didn't happen. It's sad to think about, isn't it? The things that could have happened but didn't. The things that should have happened.'

12
KATE

It was six weeks after I'd first seen Jack, four after I'd gone shoplifting with Sarah, that it finally happened. As I said, it seems quick looking back; when I was twenty, it felt like it was happening in geological time.

Because we were living more or less in each other's pockets, we'd seen each other multiple times that week. Friday and Saturday were especially busy. On Friday we went to see a performance of *Three Sisters* that had Sarah already furious, because she'd wanted to play Masha and the part had gone to a college frenemy of hers. From my own drama activities, I knew the director. I knew that Sarah had never been within a country mile of getting a part – 'she's totally wrong for it, I'd be better off casting the college porter' was his verdict – but that I kept to myself. At least, I kept it to myself until later, when I was together with Jack.

To make Sarah's daylong sulk turn into a nightlong sulk, Masha was brilliant, frail and compelling. Afterwards, steaming in the winter cold, with Sarah additionally steaming with envy and resentment, we went for a 'death kebab' from the 'death kebab' van. That was the only late-night option in mid-eighties Oxford, and it only made people ill some of the time.

I noticed Jack slathering his kebab with twice as much hot sauce, then twice as much yoghurt, as either Sarah or I did. I liked that about him: liked his appetite. We turned and headed back the way we came. Down the High Street and then out down the Cowley

Road, towards the pocket of town where we lived in our three separate sets of crappy student digs. The walk was about twenty minutes to Sarah's house, the closest of the three, and she didn't speak once in that whole time. She just strode and sulked and seethed.

We dislike the people we have wronged, just as we feel warmly towards the people to whom we have shown kindness. When I think about Sarah, I have to correct not just for subsequent impressions of her, for the person she eventually proved to be, but to allow also for the fact that I did what I wanted, and got what I wanted, at her expense. It's nothing but human nature to feel a permanent residue of ill will towards our victims. Even allowing for that – making due compensation for the double perspectival shifts of who she turned out to be and what I did to her – I have to say that Sarah was a nightmare. A subtle and under-appreciated kind of nightmare, one of the worst and most toxic: the born victim. Being a victim was so much and so completely what she wanted that it would have been uncharitable to deny her that status.

I have sometimes wondered if she had regrets later not just about what happened in general – I know the answer to that – but about that specific evening. And even more so, that specific walk. If she'd spent that twenty minutes laughing and joking, and talking about how terrible she thought the production was, and how bad Masha was, and how Chekhov couldn't write women, maybe mixed in with a bit of giggling and flirting with Jack and then maybe taking him aside for a second and whispering to him; and if we'd all gone by a different route, to my place first, the long way around, and if she'd taken him back to hers, and they'd spent the night together: if all of those things had been what happened, instead of what did happen, maybe everything afterwards would have turned out different: she and Jack would never have broken up and my certainty about us being destined to be together would have been proved a delusion.

I wonder if later she thought about that, and blamed herself. Not for everything else, not for the overall failure of the relationship, not for her personality and her way of behaving and all the other things that drove her boyfriend into my arms, but just those twenty minutes. I wonder if she regretted those twenty minutes.

Or maybe she regrets a different thing: the fact that she never saw me as a threat. If you know your partner is attractive and know there's a member of the other sex who also finds him attractive, and you're hanging out together all the time, maybe you'd have a tendency to think that two plus two equals four, given all the times in the history of the world when two plus two have equalled four. I think it's just that she was young and clueless. When you're twenty-odd you don't really know anything about life and about people, but you have a tendency to think you do. I think if she'd been ten or five or maybe even three years older, she'd never have made the mistake of not seeing me coming. But the fact was that she didn't.

There's a tendency for the dramatic person to underestimate, dismiss or even just fail to see the non-dramatic one coming up on the inside rail. I've heard it said that the moral of every single novel by Anita Brookner is that in real life, when it's tortoise versus the hare, the hare wins every time. Every single time without exception or qualification. In real life, though, that's not true. Sorry, Dr Brookner. Tortoises win all the time.

In any case, what happened instead – instead of Sarah seeing that her entire future was on the edge of a razor – was that she silently marched to her house, silently fished out her keys, silently opened the door, silently went in, and noisily slammed it behind her. Jack and I were left there on the street. As soon as the door slammed behind her, we looked at each other. I waited for him to go first.

'Wow,' he said. I laughed.

'Double wow,' I said. He laughed.

It was five minutes' walk to my flat, down a back street on the other side of Cowley Road. If I had to describe how I behaved, I'd say it was the opposite of how Sarah had just been behaving. I was upbeat, jokey and responsive to jokes. Who said that people don't want to be charmed, they want to be charming? Good advice.

Jack told me later that up until now he hadn't been sure about whether I wanted him. If he had told me that at the time, I would have been aghast. I felt like I couldn't have been more obvious. But apparently, I slow-played it and underplayed it and did a perfect job of acting cool. On that walk, he said, he was sure. And as soon as he was certain how I felt, he became certain how he felt too. That was the moment when he realised, as suddenly and completely as I had that first time I saw him. We didn't really have a choice. It was us against the world and always would be.

We got to the peeling, rickety front door of my shared house. I'd been waiting until we got there to say something. Even at the last moment I wasn't sure I would, until I knew what the feeling was like, on that walk. At the door, I stopped and stood in front of Jack, stood close, and looked him full in the face. He was about six inches taller than me, so I was looking up at him. I said,

'They're both away. Tonight. If you want to come in.'

It was obvious what I was implying. For a moment, Jack just looked at me. He told me afterwards that he couldn't speak.

He swallowed and nodded. And said in a voice that I can still feel, from the tips of my toes to the roots of my hair:

'Yes, please.'

★ ★ ★

I'm not twenty, and I know more now than I did then. So I'm not especially proud of what happened next. It would be hypocritical to apologise for anything I did on the journey, because all I cared about was the destination. That said, there was something harsher than it had to be about what happened next.

After that night, during which neither of us got any sleep, and which neither of us ever forgot, we went to the local greasy spoon and each ate multiple thousand calories of fried food. I'd been there many times, but never with a man. Both of my housemates were girls. The Greek waiter proprietor and his waitress daughter gave me some side-eye as they took our order and served us. There wasn't a single solitary atom of me that cared. I was so happy that if I'd lifted my arms above my head and willed it, I could have flown straight up into the stratosphere. Jack with his slight morning stubble was the most beautiful thing, not just the most beautiful man, I'd ever seen. I had known he was going to be mine and now he was and everything was perfect.

One slight problem.

'How are you going to tell her?' I said to Jack.

By what even now still seems like an excruciating coincidence, all three of us were booked in for a formal dinner at the posh college that same Saturday night. Formal dinners were something that happened once or twice a term, in honour of a founder or benefactor. The bad news was that you had to dress up in a gown and it went on for a while; the good news was that the food and wine were excellent, and, crucially, cheap. This formal dinner had felt like a good idea at the time when we all agreed to it, a way of getting a fancy slap-up meal at less than cost price, at a point where none of us had two five p coins to rub together. The evening was intended to be part of my campaign to present myself as the good-time potential girlfriend, preferable to Sarah's 'unpredictable moody taking things for granted second year of relationship' incumbent girlfriend. Now, it seemed like a less good idea.

Jack shuffled things around on his plate for a few moments. Then he realised that he was extremely hungry, and ate several mouthfuls. He finished chewing – I don't think I ever saw Jack talk with his mouth full – and went back to looking thoughtful.

'I don't know. But as directly as possible, I suppose. That has to be best.'

'Yes,' I said, 'rip off the plaster in one go.'

'Kinder that way.'

'Yes.'

I felt like the sun had gone behind a cloud. I was still as happy as I could ever remember being – but there was no point denying that there was, if not an obstacle, then at least a big thing that needed to be done, before the rest of our life could begin.

Looking back, it is remarkable how many things are utterly banal and ordinary in the big scheme of things, and yet how completely consuming to the people in the middle of the story. Perhaps it's especially true about youth: when we're young, we're all consumed by drama, all the time. There's barely a day free of it, and most of it is about relationships, and what fraction of it can we remember a month later, a year later? And as for a decade – there's no need to say 'forget about it': you already will have. It's almost as if there's an inverse relationship between how strongly we feel about something when we're young and how much it will seem to matter ten years later. From that perspective, of a full decade, all those feelings and dramas, and loves and hates, and crushes and aversions, and who's in and who's out, and what he said to him and what she said he said, and what she said that he said that she said I said about her – all that, all of it, it's steam on a bathroom mirror.

While it was happening, I thought this triangular drama with Jack and Sarah and me was the single most consequential thing in the history of the universe. In particular, that day, when Jack and I had got together and Sarah didn't yet know, felt as if the entire future of the universe was poised on a fulcrum, as if we were living in one of those science fiction movies about alternative timelines, where everything in existence is decided on the split-second choice of a single instant.

Did part of me think that Jack actually wouldn't go through with it, would go to tell Sarah, and she would do one of her numbers on him, and he would change his mind and back out? The answer is yes. I never told Jack I was thinking this. I never admitted it. But the truth is I was worried. Sarah in her dramatic mode could be a force. The older version of me has seen this happen: a man (or woman) says to a woman (or man), I'm leaving you, and the other person says: oh no you're not. And then everyone involved is completely miserable, for ever. I wanted to be sure that Jack was strong enough to hold Sarah off. But I wasn't, not completely.

It was early afternoon when we headed back from the café, queasy with fried food and anxiety about whatever was going to happen next. We said goodbye on my doorstep. All three of us were supposed to be meeting at the posh dinner a few hours later. I agreed to rendezvous with Jack fifteen minutes before, in the buttery. By then it would all be over and our new life, my real life, would have begun. At least, that was the plan.

I've always liked the saying, if you want to make God laugh, make a plan.

I put on jeans and my second-sexiest top and my least sexy sweater and my shoplifter's coat and put my gown – which everyone needed for the formal dinner, but wouldn't wear in the street because it looked ridiculous – in a plastic bag. The idea was to swap the sweater for the gown after I got to the posh college. We all wore less make-up in those days so I think I kept to lipstick and nothing else. I tried to think about small things instead of the huge change that was about to happen. I remember walking down Cowley Road towards the middle of town thinking: all these people going about their business just have no idea about the immensity of what's going on, how my life was at a turning point, about to be completely different, completely marvellous. How I'd got everything I wanted.

The loo was outside so I changed before going in. I checked myself out in the mirror. I was shining from happiness and anxiety and sex. I went into the beery student fug of the buttery and there, sitting at the same table where I had first seen them, were Jack and Sarah. It is the closest I have ever been in my life to having a sight make me immediately ill. They were sitting with their heads near to each other and they looked the absolute picture of co-conspirators. Then Jack realised I was there and leaned back slightly and looked at me with his eyes briefly flashing wider and I've never experienced a moment of silent communication to rival it. His look was saying: 'I wanted to tell her but I couldn't; the plan is still the plan; I'm so sorry.' I looked back at him and tried to make the look say: 'I understand, and the plan is still the plan.' Sarah looked up and saw me and the silent desperate exchange of panic and reassurance was over, and we were into what was supposed to be the evening of three friends together for a boozy semi-free dinner.

We ended up doing the break-up in the worst way possible, and that is the thing that I regret – not the outcome, just how we did it. I have replayed that night to myself many times, wondering what I, what we, should or could have done differently. The simple answer is that we should have told Sarah right there and then that she and Jack had broken up and that Jack and I were now together. It would have been impossibly awkward and would, of course, have caused a catastrophic scene. It would have been harsh, but it wouldn't have been cruel.

The fact is when I was imagining doing it in one simple swift, brutal, manoeuvre, I'm leaving out the effect of Sarah: the force field of drama she generated. It was always going to be super-awkward and difficult and stormy. We just chose to do it later. A mistake, but an understandable one.

All the way through the evening I was running scenarios in my head about how we'd tell her; about what would happen when we did, and what could happen if we didn't. I was possessed with a complete certainty that I mustn't leave Jack and Sarah alone together at the end of the evening. She would get her hooks into him and it would all be over, and the fact that he hadn't been able to tell her already was a bad sign. I knew that we had to get it done that very night. That thought was consuming me while at the same time I was sitting there in the grandeur of the panelled, candlelit hall, messing around with but not managing to eat my food, telling myself I mustn't get drunk but being so nervous I felt as if I had no choice except to empty my wine glass as soon as it was refilled.

Sarah had had a mood change from the previous night and was bubbly, verging on slightly manic. Perhaps she sensed something. I kept catching Jack's eye. He looked sweaty and uncomfortable, and as if he was going through something very similar to what I was going through, about a third of him present, the other two thirds lost in writing various dramatic scenarios for what was going to happen next.

It happened at the end of the evening, the thing that I still regret. We didn't plan it. We didn't discuss it. In truth, I don't think either of us actually thought about it. We just came out of the hall, queasy and two-thirds drunk. We stood there for a moment. Jack reached out his hand and at the same moment I reached out mine. We looked at each other. And then we looked to Sarah. I don't remember which of us it was who spoke; maybe it was both of us. But whoever it was said,

'Good night.' And we walked off together and left her.

★ ★ ★

I didn't expect her to break.

I knew that there was a gap between how she liked to present herself – styled as a cool, low-affect, the 'at home in Paris' type of London girl – and the real person, who was more up-down and volatile and unconfident than she seemed. But really, for whom is that not true? She was more emotional than she liked to appear and could be, to use the word we used at the time, hysterical. But that manifested itself in things such as more dramatic than usual essay crises or getting in a flutter when she had mislaid something, or was late, or had locked herself out. Jack once told me a story about coming home to his shared house and finding her sitting on the doorstep in bucketing rain – she had thought he had promised to be in, there had been a misunderstanding. She hadn't gone and sat in a café, she hadn't left a note and walked back to her own flat, she hadn't gone to the library or her college and done some work; she had just sat there and got soaked and marinated herself in the drama.

I knew about that. I didn't know anything like the scale of it: the depth of her need, the size of the inner hole she was hiding. To put it bluntly, I had no idea just what a bitch and nightmare she could be.

We had twenty-four hours of calm at the start. On that first Sunday after the formal dinner, Jack and I holed up at my house

– we thought that Sarah would be less likely to come there and cause a scene – and spent most of the time in bed. I remember on the morning of the second day saying, 'maybe it'll be fine', and Jack saying in reply, 'yes, maybe it will'. She might go quietly; accept what had happened; be angry and sad for a while, and then move on.

It began the next morning, on the Monday. Jack had to go back to his shared house to pick up some papers he needed, on his way to a tutorial. I wasn't with him so don't know exactly what was said, but I do know that Sarah was waiting for him, again doing her party piece of sitting curled up on the doorstep like an abandoned kitten. She had obviously been there all night. Jack didn't go into the details, but he was still pale and shaky when I saw him that same evening.

The next day it was my turn. Sarah came to a seminar I was attending at the English Faculty. This regular meeting was a course on Romantic poetry, led by the current Cool Lecturer, who was one of the only people at the university with knowledge of and interest in the latest French theories. Death of the author, primacy of the text, semiotics and aporia and all that – today, I think I would have been better off studying hieroglyphics or numismatics or just about anything else, but at the time I loved it. Roughly twelve of us used to go, to a small seminar room at the Faculty building in St Cross Road. The session was about to start when Sarah slipped into the room. She was wearing a buttoned-up black overcoat, one I'd never seen on her before, and her face was not pale but actually, genuinely white. Her eyes were glittering with fatigue and rage. I felt a jolt of adrenaline and my first instinct was to jump up and run away, to leave the seminar room as quickly as I could. But I realised: if I do that, I'll never stop running. She'll be always waiting around the next corner and I'll keep dreading this exact moment. Better to face the crisis here and how. She walked around the table and sat directly across from me. I counted to ten and looked over at her. She was staring at me and was someone I had never seen before – somebody on the edge of madness. I hadn't thought my heart could be beating any faster, but it turned out that was wrong.

The lecturer came in, tousled his curly dark hair, reached down towards the undone top two buttons of his shirt, visibly thought about doing one up before deciding not to, and began talking about Keats. I was sweating, panicking, waiting for Sarah to do whatever it was she had decided to do. He stopped talking, there were a couple of desultory interjections from students, he started talking again. More Keats. Sarah put her hand up. That's not how it works in that setting – it's not primary school. The lecturer looked confused, but he stopped, re-tousled his hair, and said:

'You have a question?'

'Does Keats have anything to say about whores?' asked Sarah. I felt the room sway and had another banging jolt of adrenaline.

'Excuse me?'

'Does Keats have anything to say about whores? You know, whores. Prostitutes. Or snakes? Does he say anything about snakes? Not the animal, the kind of people who are like snakes. The kind of people who lie and cheat and pretend to be someone they're not. Who fuck other people's boyfriends and steal them and shoplift and lie and are whores. So that's what I mean – does Keats have anything to say about people like' – she pointed at me; she had been staring directly at me all during this – 'her?'

This exchange was by a margin the worst thing that had ever happened to me. It was so awful for me that I only later thought about how uncomfortable the experience must have been for everyone else. With the benefit of full hindsight, I am deeply impressed by how the handsome lecturer reacted to Sarah's psychotic break.

'Keats wasn't very invested in ideas about ownership and possession. In fact, the Romantics as a whole show very little concern with the contemporary capitalist imaginary of property. If we make the comparison with Pope, going backwards, or Browning, going forwards, we find that . . .'

By this point I had gathered together my coat, books and bag, and was walking to the door. I had to go past Sarah as I left, but I didn't look at her. According to other students in the seminar, I seemed calm and composed and in no hurry. I'm proud of myself if that's true.

★ ★ ★

It went on for two weeks. Because we'd been spending so much time together, she knew what seminars and lectures we went to, and when and where our tutorials were. She knew when we had promised friends that we'd go and see their productions. This was the end of term, so in the drama circles in which we'd sort of met, it was an important period, with end of term performances all happening in the last two weeks. She knew the details of all that. She used that knowledge to torture us, and to be fair she also used it to torture herself.

There was never an explosion or confrontation as dramatic as the one during the Keats seminar. There didn't really need to be. A person who has gone beyond embarrassment or shame is capable of inflicting an immeasurable amount of embarrassment and shame on everyone else. It was the most stressed I'd ever been.

Part of the torture was that her appearances were intermittent. The next couple of times when she could have turned up to torment me, she didn't, because she switched to stalking Jack instead. She didn't always speak. She didn't need to. Her appearance was enough. It never really changed from that seminar: white face, black coat, staring eyes. When she did speak, it was never a public rant, but it was just to corner one of us – when I say corner, I mean actually physically take up space so that we couldn't get out of a room or couldn't get through a gap between desks or out the door of a coffee shop or up a staircase. She would say, you destroyed me, you've ruined my life, I'm going to kill myself and it'll be your fault, I'm pregnant and I'm going to have Jack's baby and I'll be alone for ever, because of you. Should I jump off a bridge or in front of a train? Are you trying to force me to have an abortion? Are you trying to drive me mad? What did I do wrong? Please, please, please take me back, please, please, please let him go and come back to me, please please please, whatever it was I did to annoy you please forgive me, I promise I'll never do it again if you only tell me what it was, I'll tell everyone, I'll destroy you like you destroyed me, you've killed me, when I kill myself, it's just following through on something you've already done.

Those are some of the things she said.

I stopped sleeping. Jack stopped sleeping. One morning I was looking at myself in the mirror, with saddlebags under my eyes and weird new worry lines on my face and forehead. I thought, we're going to have to leave the university. We can't come back next term. We're going to have to take a year off, or something, because we just can't keep this up. I was pretending to do my work. I was turning up to academic events when I was supposed to, because otherwise, it would feel too much like a defeat, it would feel as if she'd won. But not an atom of anything connected to my studies, or indeed anything else, was staying in my brain. The thought of this stretching on open-endedly was just too horrible to think about.

Jack and I had even begun to discuss it. We would take a year off and not tell her where we were living. We'd get bog-standard jobs and earn some money to go travelling. It actually sounds quite nice in retrospect; at the time, it was a wild and panicky idea, a fugue.

And then one Monday, two weeks after the weekend when everything changed, it all stopped. We didn't realise at first that it was over. Jack and I went through our respective days, both of which we had been dreading, because they were full of things Sarah knew about and which we had learned she was likely to come to, in order to torment us. But she didn't: in the evening, when we compared notes, we realised that it was the first day we'd had free of her since it all began. The next day was the same. And then we heard that Sarah had dropped out and left the university. She had gone home. Neither Jack nor I ever saw her or spoke to her again.

13

INT - KITCHEN - NIGHT

A suburban terrace house, done up in the current white-walled London style. A family home. There are children's artworks on the wall and lists stuck to the fridge with magnets. The house has been knocked through so we can see into the sitting room. The kitchen is empty but we can hear voices from the hallway. TOM, the host, is opening the door to JERRY and CHARLOTTE.

> TOM (V.O.)
> Come in, come in. How lovely.

> JERRY (V.O.)
> I hope we're not late. Or indeed early, which is just as bad.

> TOM (V.O.)
> No, no, perfect, perfect.

> JERRY (V.O.)
> Charlotte tends to be early because she wants to be liked, whereas I tend to be late because I want to be needed.

                    CHARLOTTE (V.O.)
          Oh do shut up, darling.

                    TOM (V.O.)
          Perfect, perfect. Let me take your coats.
          Tara is just putting the kids to bed.

They come through into the kitchen. Jerry is openly
looking around at the house - he has never been
here before. Tom takes a bottle out of the fridge
and holds it up to offer them a glass.

                    CHARLOTTE
          Oh yes please.

                    TOM
          English. Nearly as good as Champagne
          though, with global warming.

                    JERRY
          Better!

Tom pours three glasses, gives them one each, holds
up his and takes a sip.

                    TOM
          Cheers! Would you excuse me for a moment,
          I'm just going to go up and help Tara
          sort out the twins. We'll be down in two
          ticks.

He leaves, and we hear his feet go up the stairs.
Charlotte moves to Jack and lightly punches him on
the arm.

CHARLOTTE
'Better.' God, you're awful.

JERRY
They're sweet.

He crosses to the kitchen island, next to the stove, and looks at the cookbooks on display. He picks one up and holds it up for Charlotte's inspection. It's by Ottolenghi. They share a look.

CHARLOTTE
Promise me you won't. 'More damage than the Luftwaffe.' Not tonight.

JERRY
On my life, of course not.

A baby monitor, in the corner of the kitchen, crackles into life.

TARA (V.O.)
Finally.

TOM (V.O.)
I was as quick as I could be.

TARA (V.O.)
I've nearly got them down. Carry Zachary for a minute while I get Seb settled.

Faint baby noises over the monitor.

                    TOM (V.O.)
            (sounding like an entirely different
            person from the one in the hall)
But did it really have to be tonight?
I'm so fucking tired, I can hardly see
straight. I've had the shittest day at
work and these two are going to wake us
up every thirty minutes all night long
and I feel like my head is going to
split open. And you chose to spring a
spontaneous dinner party. Genius idea.

                    TARA (V.O.)
'Spontaneous' – how dare you! I must have
reminded you ten times in the last ten
days. And how dare you act like you're the
martyred one. You swan around all day in
the office telling people what to do and
being the big boss while I'm stuck here
on my own all day being run ragged. I'm
running on nothing but adrenaline and ten
minutes' sleep a night and you act like
you're the tired one who is doing the
hard stuff. How about we swap? How about
I get to go to the office and have my ego
stroked and you spend all day every day
trapped with one-year-old twins?

                    TOM (V.O.)
Well, if it's so fucking hard and such
a big fucking drama being at home, why
invite your friends for dinner on top of
it all? You know I don't even like them,
they don't like me, it's completely your
idea that they're here.

Charlotte and Jack, who were looking amused at the start of all this, are increasingly embarrassed.

                    TARA (V.O.)
Yes, fine, keep me isolated all day then
don't let me see anyone I like, great
idea. Why don't we have your fantasy
football morons round again instead and
let me shop and cook and clean up for
ten drunk bankers again, that was such a
lovely treat for me, you really do know
how to make a memory.

                    TOM (V.O.)
Oh, do fuck off.

                    TARA (V.O.)
No, you fuck off.

                    TOM (V.O.)
I've fucking had enough. How long is
this going to go on? Two hours, three
hours? And then, an hour to get to sleep
and then we'll be waking every thirty
minutes after that and then I've got
a nightmare day at work again tomorrow
and all for the pleasure and privilege
of sitting around with people who can
barely keep their faces straight for the
contempt they feel for me. Their smirking
faces as they deign to hang out with the
philistine. Thank you so fucking much.

                    TARA (V.O.)
I sometimes feel the whole reason you
wanted us to have children is that you
wanted to destroy my life and my career
and keep me locked up. You want to have a
life, you love your life. You just don't
want me to have one.

Charlotte and Jack look at each other.

                    CHARLOTTE
Oops.

                    JERRY
We could turn the monitor off.
    (beat)
No, actually, wait, we can't, they're
going to need it.

                    CHARLOTTE
They're going to realise any second now.

                    JERRY
God, how embarrassing. But also, quite
funny.

                    CHARLOTTE
Stop it, Jerry. I mean he's right, we do
feel contempt for him. Come on.

                    JERRY
You're thinking what I'm thinking. I can
tell.
    (beat)

                    CHARLOTTE
          OK.

They put their glasses down and, as quietly as
they can, walk out into the hall. We hear the
front door close.

                    TARA (V.O.)
          Oh shit!

                    TOM
          What? Fuck!

Two sets of footsteps come down the stairs. Tom and
Tara come into the kitchen, looking wary. They look
at each other. At first, they're aghast. Then they
start laughing.

                    TARA
          Looks like you're going to get your quiet
          night in.

14
KATE

I was looking at the crack in the ceiling above my therapist's couch. It was a wavy crack with a faint edge of blue to it; it looked like a map of a river. Sometimes the river seemed to change course from one session to another – at least, that's what I thought, though I also knew that wasn't possible. It looks like the Thames, I told myself. No, the Danube. No, the Mississippi. No, it's just a crack in the ceiling, and I'm lying on my back looking up at it and wishing this were over. You lie on your back and look up at the ceiling when you're talking to a therapist and when you're lying awake in bed and when you're being fucked. That thought popped into my mind more than once during therapy. I didn't share it with Carlos.

Grief is hardest in the middle stretches. At the beginning you're so busy – busy with practical details, with things to arrange, administration to do, forms to fill out, emails to send, accounts to close and rename. People ask you how you're feeling every time they see you. Not middle-class life's routine 'how are you?', but the real question. That's because being recently bereaved is an official acknowledged role. But it doesn't take long before that fades away. You can no longer start every conversation talking about your loss. People get bored, they start to flinch away: you can see it in their faces. It quickly goes from, 'poor Kate, I really feel for her' to 'oh God, here we go again'.

Once the drama and intensity passes, that's when the real difficulty begins. The grief and loss kick in hardest. You fall down the hole in the middle of every day. Never, never, never, never, never. This is difficult for everyone; the hardest part of grief. The trouble for me was that this was also the time it appeared that every single person on the planet was watching that TV series.

We all know the phenomenon of contemporary culture whereby there's one particular book, one movie, one TV show that everyone's consuming at the same time. It becomes the only thing people want to talk about. My horrible misfortune was that *Cheating* became that show. Everywhere I went, it was the same conversation. What do you make of *Cheating*? Have you seen *Cheating*? Have you seen the latest episode? Do you think *Cheating* is as good as everyone says? Do you think *Cheating* is better than *Succession*, *White Lotus*, *Coronation Street*, *Dallas*, *Godfather II*, *Sopranos*, the Old Testament, Tolstoy? What do you make of the actor who plays the husband? What do you make of the girlfriend? Is she supposed to be as horrible as she seems? Do you think you're supposed to hate the wife or is that just my bad character? Do you think you're supposed to like the husband, because I can't stand him? Is there a single person in it you don't hate or is that part of the point? Are the boomers worse than the millennials or is it the other way round? Who's more oblivious and spoilt? What's she going to do when she finds out? She won't find out, will she – there's got to be a season two? I think the husband and wife are going to get together and kill the girlfriend. I think the husband and girlfriend are going to get together and kill the wife. I think the two women are going to get together. Don't tell me about this week's episode. I haven't seen it yet. Do you want to come over to watch *Cheating*? I think I need to stop watching *Cheating*, it's giving me ideas.

It was torture. Having Jack's infidelity and deceit and the intimately upsetting details of his betrayal rubbed in my face every time

I left the house was difficult in and of itself. It didn't help that Netflix had taken out bus and Tube ads. It was like being followed by a stranger shouting abuse. The pain was made so much worse because I couldn't talk about it. Even with my closest confidants – not the same thing exactly as closest friends, with Daphne and Conor being the two main candidates – I found that I just couldn't go there. That was partly because it was so painful. But it was also because of shame and embarrassment. My relationship with Jack was the single thing I was proudest of in my life. It was also a point of difference between me and most of my girlfriends – I had had a decades-long successful marriage, and none of them had had any relationship even vaguely resembling that. So I felt better than them, partly because of Jack. That is hard to admit, but it's true. If my life with Jack had a lie at the core of it, that meant my life story wasn't what I thought it had been. Which in turn meant that I wasn't who I thought I was. And so in dealing with other people, I couldn't be quite the same person that I had been before. I hadn't just lost Jack, or the part of myself I had lost with Jack; I had lost my own life story.

Carlos the therapist was the only person I could talk to about what had happened. 'Part of what a therapist is for, is so that you can bore them,' Daphne had said, briskly. 'Nobody wants to say the same thing to their friends, over and over. Nobody sensible. Nobody who actually has real friends. With a therapist, you can repeat yourself until you're blue in the face.' Philip Roth said that the only time people tell the truth is when they are complaining or when they are talking to their therapist. In my case, they were the same. The bizarre thing was that it was easier to confide in Carlos because I didn't especially like him; if I had felt more empathy from him, it would have been harder. He didn't pity me. Or if he did, he didn't show it. (Which might mean he was a better therapist than

I thought at the time.) Another point in his favour is that I didn't interest him; I didn't pique his curiosity; he wasn't titillated by my account of Jack's betrayal; or, again, if he was, he kept it to himself. Because of that, I was more likely to confide in him. I've never liked or trusted people who seem curious about my personal affairs.

There was one conversation in particular that kept coming around.

'It is the shame, that's the thing I feel most acutely. The humiliation. Replaying things in my head over and over. The things only Jack and I shared. And then it turns out he was sharing them with this other woman too. Jokes and nicknames. Silly little things. And now several million people have seen them acted out and she knows it was me and Jack and she is probably telling everyone she knows.'

'The shame you speak of – some of it is sexual,' said Carlos.

'Of course it's sexual. It's sexual betrayal. Humiliation and shame are deeply part of that. I would have thought you would know that,' I said. I was spiky with Carlos. He never showed any sign of noticing or caring.

'And perhaps some of the shame attaches to the things you and your late husband did,' he said. 'Not every aspect of your intimate life together was entirely within contemporary bourgeois norms.'

He kept coming back to this. I suppose there is no way around the fact that Jack had certain proclivities and I either had them too or was willing to indulge his and came to enjoy doing so. In a long marriage, the things one partner does for the other can begin in a willingness to please the other person and blend into a desire to satisfy oneself. Jack liked to watch, in one specific form: he liked to watch me have sex with other women. Not often. To a comic, perhaps even slightly ludicrous extent, this was something we saved for special occasions. 'Christmas Eve and Ho Chi Minh's birthday' was Jack's joke on the subject. We used an escort agency and we had certain favourite girls who we saw more than once. I felt no shame at all about it, though I did feel it was deeply private, the absolute definition of something that was nobody else's business. I'm not gay, or no more so than anyone else, and I had never felt attracted to women in any other context. This was something I liked to do for Jack, and came to like doing for myself too. It had felt normal – not something I would be delighted to hear broadcast to all my friends, but normal for Jack and me, our little secret. And then it was acted out on the television screens of the nation, episodes dropping weekly, and everyone had something to say. I had never said a word about it to anyone, and now I couldn't say anything about it without talking about Jack's betrayal; and it was being repacked as entertainment. And Carlos just couldn't shut up about it.

'I do wish you'd shut up about it,' I said.

'This is a subject you can't bear to discuss. That is a working definition of a thing about which a person feels shame,' he said. And then we'd go over it all again.

Daphne's prediction had been right: in therapy I kept saying the same thing, kept telling the same story, over and over. Jack and how we got together, Jack and his death, Jack and the television show. Love, loss, betrayal. What happened in Oxford, what happened at home, what happened at the book group. Over and over. Sometimes, while I was talking, I would find myself wondering what Carlos did when he wasn't there in the room listening to clients – what his other life was like. Apart from the impossible conservatism of the Constable and hunting prints, which surely – surely? – couldn't be his, the consulting rooms gave nothing away about his interests, wife or lack thereof, family or lack thereof. He never got any better at shaving. His hair, which had seemed fair when I first met him, now seemed colourless. His buttoned-up ultra-English demeanour hinted at a form of disguise or escape:

nobody with that first name could be as stolidly, solidly Anglo as he presented. But there were no clues. He let nothing slip. I suppose I keep coming around to the thought that although I never warmed to him, he actually was pretty good at his job.

In the evenings after my sessions I would go around to Daphne's house. The therapy was like exercise, or at least how exercise is for me: I didn't enjoy it but I felt better afterwards. It left me needing human contact with an actual human, not a shrink. Daphne knew where I'd been and knew well enough not to ask what I'd been through. She made tea and gave me biscuits and pottered about her kitchen giving a running commentary on whichever of her many projects was currently occupying her. Her experiences at the prison visit charity (she'd been the person who introduced me, and for a while had been on the board). Her work as chair of the organisation for civil servants who used to work in her old department. Her work on the board of an arts outreach organisation. Her successful plot to depose and replace the controller of her street's WhatsApp group. I pretended to listen and she pretended not to notice that that was what I was doing.

I tried hard not to become obsessed with Phoebe Mull, the writer of the TV show, but I still read everything written about her in print. In interviews and press she consistently seemed cocky and obnoxious, and evasive with it; it was noticeable that while she was free with her opinions, she was much less so with personal information. She made it clear that the show was at least partly based on something that had happened to her – an affair that she had had. That could only mean with Jack, though she gave no hints about the person's identity. You couldn't find where she had grown up, where she had been educated, what her original surname had been; she wasn't married but had a 'partner' and they had taken a new surname, one of those idiotic modern pseudo-feminist gestures that younger people seem to find meaningful. I know that there are many new tricks to stalking, new developments since the days I was getting together with Jack and did my best to find out everything I could about him and Sarah. I was well aware that the internet is the best thing that has ever happened for stalkers. But I didn't want to start because I knew that if I did, I would find it impossible to stop. I thought about asking Conor, the most digitally competent person I knew, to do a deep dive on her and her background, but he was much too sharp not to realise that there was something weird going on in that request.

Perhaps most of all, I couldn't stop myself obsessing over the question of how she and Jack had met. They were in completely different worlds, a TV writer in her early thirties and an architect a quarter of a century older; I don't think we knew – we certainly didn't socialise with – anyone at all in her line of work. That's the marital 'we', which Jack didn't like and never used. 'We think *Citizen Kane* is overrated, we could never be friends with anyone who voted Leave, we don't like chianti – do people think that when you get married you turn into Siamese fucking twins?' It's as if being a couple means you take an oath permanently abrogating any claim to independent thought. It's the mental equivalent of holding hands while walking down the street and forcing people into the gutter by not allowing enough space on the pavement. As if your status as a couple would be called into question if you ever in any context used the first person singular.

But it turned out that the marital 'we' was even weaker, meant even less, than I had thought. There had been nothing resembling a 'we'. Jack had been having at least one affair; and did anyone who had affairs ever have only one? Was it likely he had spilled all the intimate details of our life together to one woman and one woman only? For instance, there was the story of Mitchell and Leah, new friends who we had met through a client of Jack's architecture practice. We had them over to supper and went back there and had a completely disastrous evening, featuring a huge marital argument on their part, which left us with no choice (we felt) except to take French leave and go home before they realised we had overheard the whole thing on the baby monitor. That was a very embarrassing story all round, and one we never talked about except to each other, not because it wasn't a good story, but precisely because it was such a good story it wouldn't fail to get around, both to the arguing couple and to Jack's clients – and then he would be the gossiping architect whom people shouldn't trust. We often discussed it with each other, but never with anyone else. At least, that's what I had thought – but no, it turned out that Jack had been telling his girlfriend about it. Telling at least one of his girlfriends about it. And about everything else in our lives too.

'I can't bear the thought of the conversation. Not just the fact of Jack telling her but the detail of it. I keep imagining it. Where were they? In some coffee shop somewhere? In a bar? Did he take her somewhere fancy, somewhere he didn't used to go with me? Did they, I don't know, go to the Ritz or the Connaught or something? Or maybe they used to go to one of the places I used to go to with Jack. The wine bar where they have the Beaujolais he liked. So maybe I've been there with Jack since the times he went there with her and the staff have been hiding the fact . . . no, I can't stand to think about that, and anyway it just can't be true, Jack would never play games like that.'

'I'm interested in that phrase, "games like that",' said Carlos, reliably missing the point, and as usual trying to bring the conversation back to sex. 'Of course, there were other sorts of games that he, that you also, did like to play, weren't there? And you have a degree of shame attached to these games.'

'It's really irritating, boring, and unhelpful, how you bring everything back to sex, do you know that?' I said. 'There are other forms of intimacy besides sex and other forms of betrayal and violation other than sexual ones.'

'And yet it is the sexual betrayal and violation, to borrow your charged terms, that you feel most intensely.'

'Because they most embody the main issue, which is that things I thought were intimate and private between Jack and me turn out actually to have been a kind of gossip he shared with his' – I groped for a neutral, uncharged word, knowing that Carlos would pick me up on anything else, before giving up – 'whore.' And of course in this instance, he was right, because the most upsetting of all the possibilities of how Jack had talked about his and my secrets was precisely in the most intimate setting: in bed. In bed with his mistress, his girlfriend, his whore, he had talked about the things that he had done in bed with me. There was no way around the scale of shame and betrayal embodied in that.

'So it is this violation of intimacy and trust that is the real wound,' said Carlos. 'Not the fact that he was having sex with this . . . woman. According at least to the story told by this television series.'

'Of course it was the sex too, don't be thick. Of course it was the sexual betrayal. But yes, the violation of my trust. Treating me like a fool. Disrespecting me and talking about me to this – this creature.'

I looked up at the ceiling and the ceiling looked back down at me. The Thames, the Rhine, the Rhône, the Danube, the Amazon, the Nile. It wasn't any of those. It was just a crack in a therapist's ceiling. It had heard many painful, shameful confessions before mine.

'This betrayal, this set of revelations or apparent revelations, does damage to your memories of your late husband. You have lost him but you also have lost the meaning of what happened between you. You thought it was one thing but now you have to see it was something else.'

I experienced a flood of feeling, a physical sensation of something pouring through me and past me, before I could name what the emotion was. Grief or anger or both. This was the only time, in all my sessions with Carlos, where I felt overcome by a reaction to what he said. I don't know if it was real insight or if it was by blundering around and throwing things out at semi-random that he accidentally hit on something perceptive. My eyes stung and I did not want to speak because it would come out as a gasp. I had never cried at my therapist's and did not want to begin now. I did not want Carlos to see me cry. I knew that I was unravelled – that was no secret. But for him to see me unravelled was something else.

I did not want him to see me. I did not want him to see me . . . there was an idea in that which snagged my attention, made the current of my feelings whirl and eddy before they accelerated away again. To see me was different from hearing me. Sight and sound were different.

That was it – that was the thought. The scenes from the TV with Jack and me, the incidents that he must have described to her, were word perfect. He had a very good memory (and was a good mimic too) and he had told her stories and she had remembered them with cruel completeness. Our sex lives, our in-jokes, our intimacy were all there on screen. And had torn my heart straight through my chest, and held it, still beating, in front of my eyes. But things in the TV show did not look the way they had looked in real life. Nor did people. On screen, Jack's dialogue was right but his presence, his physicality, his bearing and demeanour, were wrong. The actor was too skinny, too cold, he was about distance and watching where Jack was all about intimacy and warmth. The actor was a generic well-looked-after good-looking man in his middle fifties, whereas Jack was much more specific than that. He was not interchangeable. The show's version of me was a brittle, actressy caricature of me – a description of me put together by someone who had taken an instant dislike. Minor characters too bore no relation to their real appearance. Even the escort who featured in the show's most embarrassing scene was completely wrong: blonde and petite and fidgety where in real life she had been tall, brown-haired, and imposingly calm.

As for the house, our house, that was also wrong. Some of the downstairs was right – the kitchen was modern and open, the sitting room a rough first draft of Jack's version, they had correctly guessed the kind of sofa – but the rest of the house was off. Our bedroom didn't look at all like the TV couple's. It was much warmer and more feminine, more glamorous and sexy and even a little camp. The TV series had gone with a standard idea of an architect's house, all shiny surfaces and glass and metal. And then Jack's love of technology, the gadgety side of his houses, the automation and digital assistance, wasn't present at all. It was hard to think she knew him, while at the same time it was clear they had had an affair and been completely intimate. Jack had no secrets from her, and yet she knew nothing about him. The words that came out of 'our' mouths were uncomfortably accurate but the look of the show was askew. It was the other way around from most TV and movies, where they spend all their effort on the look.

'It's not just me who sees something else,' I said to Carlos. I was still looking at the riverine crack above my head. 'She, the person I won't name, sees something else too. She's looking at our lives and getting everything wrong. It's as if she has an ear but no eyes. It's like she's blind or something. Maybe she is blind, and they just left it out of the profiles out of, I don't know, political correctness, or whatever that's being called this week.'

I felt Carlos shift around a little on his throne of judgement. He was progressive and prided himself on the fact. I could tell. But he had never said anything about it. That was the kind of insight that was missing from *Cheating* – the things you knew about people, that they hadn't just come out and told you. There was a kind of insight missing from Carlos too. He could see some things but not others. Maybe all shrinks were like that, only good at seeing the things they were good at seeing. Perceptive and blind at the same time. As if they could only hear some things and see a certain limited perception of reality.

That was the moment when I realised what had happened. I didn't know how it had been done, not exactly; but I knew what had been done. I think I may have gasped. Carlos let the silence hang for a while, and my mind ran through a hundred, a thousand, different scenarios. The headline news was: I was sure I knew what she had done. Not why or how, but what.

'You are thinking something,' said Carlos, an unfamiliar tone in his voice. I don't think I often surprised him but he sounded, in that moment, a little bit surprised.

'Yes, I am,' I said, and I sat up. 'Thank you. We're done here, as far as I'm concerned. You'll invoice me for the full month, I suspect.'

I got up and headed for the door and turned to face Carlos as I opened it. Very gratifyingly – the only gratifying thing, on a personal level, that happened during my therapy – his mouth was hanging half open with shock.

'Seriously, Carlos,' I said (calling him by his first name for what I think was the only time), 'thank you. I couldn't have done it without you.'

I left it to him to try and work out what it was I had realised.

PART FOUR

15
PHOEBE

It was an autumn day at Soho Farmhouse.
'You did tell me that this place was Butlin's for cunts,' said my brother. 'I have to admit that I thought you were joking. I didn't realise it was the bare factual truth.'

I shrugged and drank some tap-water. When I'm paying, it's nothing but tap. I said:

'Welcome to Hell.'

The covered courtyard area at Soho Farmhouse is either one of the best or worst places on earth for people-watching. Best if you're looking for people to laugh at or hate. Worst if your mood is low and you don't want it lowered any further. I was sitting with my jet-lagged brother. We had evolved a tradition – maybe 'tradition' is too strong, 'thing' would do – that when Tristan came to visit he would spend the first couple of nights in a hotel. Then he would come and stay in the spare room. Ostensibly, this was to do with jet lag and the fact that our body clocks, moods and lives would be so out of sync that it would take time to catch on to each other's tempo and remind ourselves of who we were. 'Synchronising our periods' is what Tristan called this. The real reason was that for the first few days on getting back to the UK, my twin would be completely, definitively insufferable. Every second sentence would be an unfavourable comparison of England with Australia, or a drive-by insult about some aspect of my life, flat, friends.

Why did I put up with that? Well – if that was the person he was all the time, we would no longer be in each other's lives. What was really going on was that Tristan was acting out his guilt about having done a runner from our mother and left me to do all the shitwork. I understood this but understanding it didn't make the reality any less annoying. What usually happened was that after a few days he would calm down and get past whatever psychic soap opera he was going through and start acting like a human being. An admittedly bitchy and often difficult human being, true. But bearable, as opposed to not.

So that was why we were at Butlin's for cunts. I'd brought Tristan here to decompress, get over jet lag, and do some catching up on neutral territory. By the way, on the two times I've gone to visit him in Sydney I haven't needed to spend the first few days in a hotel. Just saying.

The weather was marginal, a mid-September afternoon just warm enough to sit out but giving maximum opportunity for fussing and layering up. Not that the clientele need much excuse for making a fuss. Two middle-aged women at the next table were wearing tennis gear and had clearly just had a group lesson or activity of some sort. They were getting to know each other by putting on and taking off branded clothes – Loro Piana sweats, Moncler gilet, all that rich-people wank – and talking about their troubles. Both of them had properties in London and the Cotswolds. One of them had five extra properties, which she let out on Airbnb. The workload! The other was running a renovation project so big it needed not one but two structural surveyors. It was hard. People didn't understand!

A family was squabbling over the allocation of their free use Soho Farmhouse Pashley bicycles. They were one of those English families of two blond parents plus three blond kids that make it look and feel as if the Nazis won the Second World War. When I looked a while longer, I could make out that the children were squabbling and the mother was refereeing. The father, who had a serious, internal expression on his face, was not taking part. He looked like a man who was compiling a list of every single thing he would rather be doing instead of what he was actually doing.

At a table close to us, a small child in a pink boiler suit and blue bucket hat was being ignored by her gay dads, both of whom were superglued to their iPhones. I could see the screen of one of them: he was looking at antique sewing machines on Pinterest. The kid had picked up a coffee spoon and was shaping up to make a bid for attention by doing something dramatic with it.

Behind me I could hear someone say that Monday was the quietest night, and that was when you would often spot Guy Ritchie.

Tristan had that look on his face. I knew he was eavesdropping. He was pretending to be scanning the courtyard benignly, taking in the sights, nothing special on his mind, certainly not a whirring dynamo of pure evil. If you have a twin who you haven't seen for eighteen months, one of the things that strikes you hard is how much they have changed, and the other thing is how little. I could see the fatigue in him. Twenty-four hours after a twenty-four-hour flight from Sydney, the skin around his eyes was drawn and he was pale under his tan. He was looking a touch older, but better preserved than ever. He has always been the king of taking care of himself. But he was also and always Tristan and I could tell what he was thinking.

Our waitress arrived, smiling, carrying a tray with Tristan's drink. She put it on the table and said,

'Our house picante. At the moment it's a t and t. Enjoy!'

Tristan smiled his sweetest smile, which – I was well qualified to know – was also his bitchiest.

'Thank you!' As she walked away he said,

'The three ts – tequila, tonic, and tweakments.'

'She's making the best of herself.'

'It's called labradoring – making a dog into a better-presented dog.'

'You're the biggest bitch I know.'

'Thanks, darling sister. I feel the same way about you.'

Tristan took a sip of his drink and made a face with his mouth pursed and a slight twisting grimace. I could see another face underneath his face. For that second, it was as if our mother was right there with us. Eighteen months apart felt like nowhere near enough. It didn't help that I knew what he was going to say.

'Too sweet?' I said.

'Too sweet,' said Tristan, surprise fucking surprise, since it's what he's said over every single cocktail that's ever been served to him for his entire fucking life.

I love my brother and since he's never around, most of the time I miss him. But when we're together we can wind each other up like nobody else on the planet. Or rather, like nobody else on the planet except our mother. The wind-ups take multiple forms, one of which is jokey banter with a slight edge that can escalate into a proper fight at any moment. Like this one. I haven't seen him for eighteen months, and he's saying bitchy things that have to me a just detectable (and meant to be detectable) edge that says: this place isn't as nice as you think it is; being able to come here/be a member here/afford to pay for it isn't as impressive as you want me to think; your life isn't as great as you imagine; you do know that you're a bit ridiculous, don't you?

Underlying all this was something else. The most validating incident in my working life had just happened. I had had a full-on, unambiguous, certifiable hit. I was, in my world anyway, and maybe a little bit beyond that world, slightly famous. And Tristan had said exactly zero words about that and made exactly zero acknowledgement or recognition of it. Not just since he'd arrived back in the UK, but at any point previously. He knew that I knew. Was he going to give me the validation? Was he fuck.

They say that the children of narcissists have narcissistic tendencies. ('They' in this context means shrinks. I've never been to see one but I've read some books. I will not be taking further questions at this time.) This maxim is completely irrelevant in relation to me, obviously, but I can see its application for Tristan. I can see it in his game playing and withholding and inability to give praise and refusal to accept pleasure and I suppose most of all in the fact that this moment, which should be at least to some extent entirely about me, isn't. But, you know, whatever.

Just as I was thinking this, he did an unfortunately timed thing. He began to talk about himself.

'I'm going to go and see her,' he said, maximising the drama by not looking at me when he said it, as if he was Norma sodding Desmond.

I said, 'You could always not.'

He didn't answer. He took another sip, made another grimace.

'No. Since I'm over here, I'm going to go see her. If she doesn't want to talk to me, fine. At least I'm sweeping my side of the street.'

'Imagine if you did that for real, though. Swept the side of the street across the road from her and left her side alone. You'd literally never hear the end of it. She'd fall over and get her leg in a cast and go round on crutches and say it was those leaves, nobody bothered to sweep them, not on my side of the street, but don't worry, I'll be dead soon.'

Tristan didn't smile. I could tell something was coming and I let him tell it his way.

'So the thing is, I have some news. I wanted to give it to her in person. But before that I wanted to give it to you too.'

He looked, very uncharacteristically for him, a little embarrassed. It was odd to see, because Tristan doesn't believe in embarrassment, any more than I do. It's an English trait, to be impressed by embarrassment; to perceive it as a significant reaction, in yourself and in others. What really is it, though? It's the fact that you have shown you want something. You can't feel embarrassed unless you're exposed to people's attention. You want, I don't know, to talk to the important person at a party, or get off with someone, cut to the front of a queue, get a pay rise, get an upgrade, get what you're owed, what you need, what you want. This is how life works: you decide what you want, then you go and get it, and accept the consequences. Where does being embarrassed fit into that? You miss out on so, so much by being prone to embarrassment. Fuck that, say I. And yet here my unembarrassable twin was, being embarrassed. It could only mean—

'I've been seeing someone,' he eventually said.

I tried not to laugh but made a snorting noise despite myself.

'Darling, you're the biggest serial monogamist in gaydom. Since you were fourteen, you've not been seeing someone for a grand total of about two weeks.'

Under normal circumstances Tristan would have risen to that, but he didn't, he just fiddled with his drink.

'Not like this. This is more serious.'

The way I remember it, several of the others had been plenty serious, but whatever, this was his life and he could narrate it however he wanted. Within reason.

'He's called Gary. I know you're going to make some joke about Gay Gary, but please don't. Anyway, the thing is' – and now he was looking straight at me – 'he's the love of my life and we're going to get married.'

I can't explain why this caught me so off guard. Tristan was the right age and as I'd just said, monogamy was his thing. But I was blindsided. It took me a couple of seconds, which was no doubt a couple of seconds too long, to say,

'Wow! That's great! I'm so happy for you!' I reached over the table and gave him a hug. He squeezed me back and when we separated he had stopped looking embarrassed and now seemed relieved.

'Thank you. I didn't know how you'd take it.'

'Honestly, it's so great!'

'Thank you again. He's . . . well, anyway, when you meet him you'll see. He's an interiors designer. His big thing is heritage. I know, didn't know there was any in Australia, jokes about convicts, blah blah. But he loves fixing and doing up old houses. And in fact, that's what we're going to do. He has a project to renovate some colonial houses in Hobart, so we're moving to Hobart. In Tasmania. That's the other thing I wanted you to know.'

I felt, of all excruciating things, my eyes begin to go shiny. Luckily, just as this was happening, the kid with the gay dads finally decided on the dramatic action it had been contemplating for a while, and threw the spoon it had been holding, with maximum force, at the water glass that dad number one had just set down. Direct hit. The glass went straight off the table, and decanted its contents onto the dad. The spoon ricocheted sideways and upwards, and hit him in the face. The kid burst into tears, the targeted dad was furious, the other dad was pretending to be angry while trying not to laugh. He started mopping up the mess with a napkin in his right hand, though I noticed he didn't actually put down his phone. Anyway, it got everyone's attention, including Tristan's, which was a relief.

I hate it when I have strong feelings that I don't understand. Yes, Tasmania was the other side of the world. But Tristan already lived on the other side of the world. Yes, Tristan had a new partner and it was serious. But – no offence, Tristan – it was far from the first time he'd had a partner and it was always serious at the start, even if it later turned out not to be.

So it couldn't be the surface realities of the situation that were upsetting me. Which meant that it had to be the underlying idea of what was happening. My twin brother moving further away. My twin brother choosing a partner for life. My brother settling down, permanently, as far away as he possibly could, short of volunteering to go to Mars. It wasn't about me, I knew that. And yet I defy anyone not to feel, if your twin was making that choice, that it wasn't a teeny, tiny bit about you.

Or maybe it's just that the children of narcissists have narcissistic tendencies.

What it did mean, though, was that any notion I had been holding on to, deep in the back of my mind, that Tristan was there with me in the work of dealing with our mother, was a fantasy. The idea that in a crisis, I could call on him; that he would be there for me when I needed; that at the end of the day, he would never stop being my twin, and as a result there were claims I would be able to make. All of that. These weren't thoughts I had ever dwelt on at any length – what with the whole 'running away to live in Australia' thing. But they were there nonetheless, a kind of backup, like the slightly boring bloke who's massively into you and who you know you'll always have to fall back on if all the men you actually fancy go off with other women. And then the boring backup goes off and gets married or something, and now you no longer have a Plan B. Tristan moving to Tasmania was like that. There was no way to avoid facing the fact that 'he'll always be there for me' was bullshit. It probably always had been.

I couldn't blame him. Actually, hang on a minute – that belongs on my list of sentences that are always lies. Along with 'it doesn't matter' and 'nobody will mind' and 'it's the thought that counts' and 'someone is coming to help you'. Of course I could and did blame him. But would I have done the same thing myself, if I could? Absolutely. As Tristan burbled on about his 'amazing' new life, I found my mind drifting back a month or so, to the big reveal I gave my mother, after it was clear *Cheating* was a hit.

★ ★ ★

I planned the whole thing with care. It was intended to be a huge moment for both of us. As part of that, I took my mother out to lunch. I had thought there might be a scene and I knew that she was less likely to blow up if we were in public – because love of drama and love of making a public scene are two very different things. She had the former but not the latter. I was trying to practise a form of familial-emotional jujitsu: her desire to preserve appearances was going to be used against her.

My mother has a specific modus operandi with restaurants. She likes the idea of them, or at least she says that she does, but always criticises the reality. They, like everything else in life, let her down. If this can be attributed to oversight, neglect, or ill will on the part of the person who chose the restaurant (and is paying for it), so much the better. Some of her dislikes are:

restaurant too loud
restaurant too quiet
restaurant too fussy (decor)
restaurant too fussy (staff)
restaurant too fussy (food)
restaurant too casual (decor)
restaurant too casual (staff)

restaurant too casual (food)
restaurant too expensive, even when she's not paying
restaurant too cheap, ditto ('I can't bear to think about what they're doing to those chickens')
table hidden away
table in full sight of everyone
waiter constantly interrupts (fair enough, I share that one)
waiter never to be seen
waiter treating her as if she's a hundred years old
waiter over-familiar
waiter over-formal
'we've been sat here for hours and they haven't taken our order, I've never been treated so badly in my life'
'I can't stand being rushed, it's not supposed to be McDonald's, I've never been treated so badly in my life'
restaurant attached to a hotel
being ignored because she's old
being hovered over because the waiter is attracted to me ('the man is drooling, it's disgusting')
bill brought too slowly
bill brought too quickly ('they're desperate to get rid of us')
toilet too far away
toilet too close ('might as well just sit us down in the cubicles')
toilet needlessly fancy
toilet 'disgusting'
management/owner trying too hard
management/owner not making any effort
full of boring old people
full of boring young people
nobody else in here like me, uncomfortable
everyone in here just the same as me, boring

    no hot water in toilet hand basin
    water in toilet hand basin so hot scalding risk involved
    toilet has no paper towels only air dryer
    toilet has no air dryer only paper towels
    toilet has real towels but who do you think ends up paying for them?

These are only the greatest hits. There's no pleasing her, but the mysterious power of a person like my mother is that just because there's no pleasing her doesn't mean you ever stop trying. Behind the anti-aircraft barrage of complaints and objections, a theme could be detected, which is that she liked expensive comfortable solidly bourgeois places. She didn't complain any less, just with less energy. Also, I'd learned to always take her to somewhere new, not somewhere I knew and liked – meaning that there was someone or something else to blame for the recommendation, rather than my own preferences.

I asked Aloysius, who keeps up with these things, and settled on Métier, a fancy new place in Chelsea within a short taxi ride of my mother. The mind games around taking her to lunch inevitably begin with the question of whether she'll be picked up at home and taken to the restaurant (which according to her implies that she's decrepit) or be allowed to get to the restaurant under her own steam (which according to her implies neglect). I took the risk of the second option, on the basis that if we went there together I might arrive so irritated that I couldn't get through what I was planning to say to her.

I got there a few minutes early. The room looked just right – tall ceiling, columns, some soft furnishings to damp down the noise but not enough to make it feel too much like a nineteenth-century Parisian knocking shop. The girl at the reception had nice manners and the waiter who brought the menu was good-looking but forgettable in a 'one of the professional dancers off *Strictly*' kind of way. He left two menus and came back with tap water for me. I could have done with a drink but my mother would have given me a look, so I held off. Aloysius had done OK with his recommendation, and I would tell him so.

From my seat on the banquette, I could see the entrance, and watched my mother come in through the curtained area by the front door and stand for a moment. There was one of those glimpses of someone out of context that makes you see them differently. She looked older and frailer than when I'd seen her last. She was thin, the not-OK kind of thin. In repose her expression was, as it had been her whole life, anxious, with an irritable edge; a person on permanent guard for disappointment or rebuff. Her clothes fought that: she was wearing her best Jil Sander, and if there was a single crease anywhere on her, I'd be surprised. As always with my mother, there was a histrionic touch to this. Part of her was hoping that someone would be watching her and thinking, I wonder who's that amazing woman?

She seemed to be waiting to be greeted and it took her a moment to realise that it was up to her to approach the front desk. She and the girl exchanged a few words and then she looked across the room to me and I thought: showtime. I smiled and waved. My mother didn't.

All this would have been depressing and difficult if it were a normal day and a normal lunch. But this was the time I had set myself up to tell her what I had done and also that I no longer owed her anything. I didn't quite know what that meant: it might be too dramatic to say I was never going to talk to her again. I was, though, determined to make it clear that everything would be different from now on: that I had done a big thing that rewrote the balance of accounts between us; that I was finished with being permanently on call, permanently in the wrong, permanently having to make things better for her and permanently made to feel that I was failing to do so.

She came over and sat down and made a twisting movement with her neck, a kind of tic she had when she was feeling stressed.

'Hello Mum!' I said, brightly.

She looked at me and nodded and twisted her neck again as she checked out the room.

'Phoebe,' she eventually said.

'Would you like a drink?' I was pretty sure that the answer would be yes, and that was a good thing, because a drink would give me a boost and would also make her, after an hour or so, start to be sleepy, which would be helpful in bringing lunch to an end.

'Please.'

I waggled my fingers at the waiter and he came towards the table carrying two printed menus on card and instead of taking my order for a drink he said something that made me curse my fate, fashions in London restaurants, and Aloysius, in that order:

'Can I explain about our thirteen-course small-plate tasting menu concept?'

★ ★ ★

With hindsight – now those are two words you never want to have to say at the start of a sentence – I should probably at this point have abandoned the whole idea of a slate-clearing, life-altering, side-of-street-sweeping mega-talk. I could have refiled the meeting with my mother under the category of 'total disaster from the very inception' and let lunch take its course. That would have left open the possibility of revisiting the talk at a later time. Instead, what I did was try and stick to the plan, only to have it comprehensively derailed by my mother's narcissistic love of creating difficulties. The specific category of narcissistic obstacle here was a game or subroutine called 'you can't make me happy, and if you try, I will punish you'.

I can't prove it, but I suspect that if I had a high-definition camera trained on her at the moment the waiter said his piece about the tasting menu, it would have caught her in a micro expression of pure joy. Why? At the thought of all the misery she was going to be able to inflict by complaining about her lunch. That's the thing about a certain type of narcissist: they feed off other people's pain, even the (you'd have thought) small and unsatisfying dose of pain you get by ensuring that someone's attempt to be nice to you goes horribly wrong.

This was done with the minimum amount of verbal communication, but lots of body language. Complaining body language. Radish carpaccio with lemon verbena dots (!?) – grimace. Hamachi crudo with bitter yuzu foam and chive garnish – subtly different grimace. ('How was that, Mum?' Shrug.) Cod cheek dashi with beetroot sorbet – touched with spoon, didn't actually eat. And so on. I grew more and more irritated, and as I did, felt less and less inclination to tell my mother what I had done on her behalf. This wasn't so much because I knew she would ruin the moment, and make it clear that the thing I had thought was significant meant nothing to her. That was OK: I expected that and was braced for it. I'm not stupid: I didn't think I was going to magically change her entire personality. No, the thing that made me abort my plan wasn't how she would react, but the fact that it would reveal just how much I had been thinking about her, how much I cared about her and her life story. I had exerted myself hard and at length to do this thing for her. And now I was going to tell her about it.

That was the satisfaction I found myself determined not to give her. She wouldn't show me any pleasure, I knew that. But she would know what it meant. She would see what I had done and realise, even though she would never admit it, how important she was to me and how much I cared about her. And I suddenly realised I didn't want her to know that I cared. Mum, you act like I don't give a shit. Fine. I'll live up to it. I'll act like I don't give a shit. This is what that looks like.

Look what you made me do.

* * *

Do I love my mother? I genuinely don't know the answer to that question. Perhaps the fact that I have to ask it means that I don't. On the other hand it often feels as if I hate her, and I might not hate her if the other thing wasn't present at the same time.

I do love my brother, though. Maybe it's easier because he lives so far away and I see him so seldom. Or maybe it's because he's the only person I can really talk to about her. So although he annoys me and can press my buttons with the accuracy and destructive effect of a cruise missile and is exactly zero practical use in dealing with my life's greatest burden – in fact, has moved to the other side of the planet to avoid helping – I do still love him and miss him and have all the warm glowy normal human feelings that I sometimes think I lack. And also he makes me laugh.

I told Tristan the story of the lunch. He made all the right noises. Then he changed the subject and started talking about his own plans. I went with it.

'Getting married and moving to Tasmania to fix up old houses. Sounds pretty gay.'

'Yes, it is pretty gay. That's kind of the point.'

'You'll be a big help with Mum. Thanks a lot.'

He had the grace to look, not sheepish – Tristan has never looked sheepish, and in fact I find it hard to imagine what that would look like – but rueful.

'I know, sorry. Feel bad about that.'

'Mind you, it's not as if you're any help at all as it is.'

'So at least you won't miss out on anything.'

He saw me start to flare up and could tell that he'd gone too far.

'Sorry – I do get it, I do. I don't know how you manage. I would do more if I could, I promise. But—'

The strange thing was, is, I believed him. He hadn't gone to Australia ten years ago planning to emigrate, but a holiday turned into something else and he was offered work (I've never been clear on how he sorted out the visa side of things, but anyway he did) and then he was living there. That was enough for my mother to break off all contact. She didn't answer letters or emails and she let phone calls go to voicemail without returning them. When he went to see her on his first visit back to London, she refused to answer the door. By moving to Sydney, Tristan was doing lots of different things to do with his life, his ambitions, his gayness, whatever. But as far as she was concerned, what he was exclusively doing was yelling 'I'm trying to get away from you because I can't stand you'. She knew that as clearly as if it were written in letters five metres high on a plane banner overflying her house.

'It's fine,' I said. 'Well – it's not fine, obviously. But it's fine. While also not being fine. You know what I mean.'

'I do,' he said. 'I really do. I wish it was different.'

'Just, you don't wish it enough to not live in Tasmania,' I said, feeling that I was comfortably within my rights to make this dig.

'Yes, just not enough for that.'

I put my hand on his arm and we looked at each other. In the end, finally, there was nobody else who fully understood about her, and that was why the thing that kept us apart, my mother, was also the main thing we had in common. This hand on the arm meant all of that and also that I forgave him. The shit.

'When she dies I'll come and live in Hobart in your fancy gay house. I'll be your crazy sister up in the attic and everyone will pity you. They'll be walking up and down the street in their little gay Australian shorts feeling sorry for you. They'll point at your place and talk about poor sad Tristan and his horrible life.'

'It's not really a shorts climate, Tasmania. It's much the same as England, weather-wise.'

'Don't change the subject.'

'I wouldn't dream of it. And by the way – how is Tony?'

Tristan held my eye. I could see the tiniest flicker of his secret evil smile. Tristan had known Tony before I did. They were at college together. In fact, it was Tristan who introduced us at some party with a preamble along the lines of 'he's exactly your type, good-looking but a bit boring'. This was, I was well aware, what my twin thought about my partner – that part of the reason I liked him was that I was the interesting one, who brought the drama and fun, and he was the 'contrast gainer'. Which was unfair, not least because Tony is a very gifted musician and although he works as a teacher, that's as much his main interest in life as my writing is in mine. There's also the fact that I love Tony, my chosen life partner. But having said that, Tony's instrument is the guitar, and his music is folkish in timbre, and to Tristan, both those things are inherently a bit ridiculous. (Did I say Tristan is nice? No, I didn't. There's a reason: he isn't.)

'He's very well, thanks.'

'Keeping up with the music?'

'Very much so.'

'No big break yet? But keeping at it?'

Tristan, holding my gaze, took a sip of his drink.

'Yes. And fuck you.'

'Well, good. But the fact is, we probably only have room for one star in this family.'

Which was about the nicest thing my twin had ever said to me. He was letting me know that he knew all about my hit show. I was so surprised, I didn't know what to say. He was still looking at me and we both knew what he was saying.

I wish that moment had gone on for ever. I wish it was still going on now. Instead, what happened was that my phone rang. I picked it out of my bag and saw that it was Tony.

16
PHOEBE

Tristan – though obviously I would never tell him this – was right. I've never had a boyfriend who coped better with real world stuff than I do, sorting out the plane/train/theatre tickets, paying for the TV licence, fixing issues with the council, checking credit card statements, anything. I like to be better at it than my bloke and I like to complain about it and have someone be grateful to me for sorting everything out.

Given that, it makes sense that I would end up with Tony, sweet and gentle and hot and useless. I'm the one who brings the talent, the energy, the difficulty, the drama and the appetite for getting things done. He's the decorative flaky one. That doesn't mean I don't get irritated when he has one of his episodes, which is why, when he called me that day, my first reaction was to snap at him.

'For fuck's sake, Tony – pizza? I get to spend a couple of days with my brother for the first time in forever, and you're calling me up about pizza?'

'Not pizza, pizzas. Plural. Like, twenty of them. Family size. Ordered to the flat. In your name. The guys are standing right on our doorstep wanting to be paid. Three delivery men. So I'm just wondering, did you order all these pizzas?'

'No of course I didn't order twenty fucking pizzas at home while I'm here in Oxfordshire, what the fucking fuck.'

'Well, they're here. Literally on our doorstep right now. Ordered in your name to our address.'

You know how sighing is always a sign that you're in the right, put upon, aggrieved but forgiving? I sighed.

'It's probably one of your pupils dicking you about. Just make it go away, all right? And don't pay for the pizzas. I'm going to put the phone down now, since there's nothing I can do about it from here and it's just an idiot prank by one of your retard students.'

'I guess. Maybe. I don't think the pizza delivery guys are going to be very happy about not being paid,' said Tony, at which I cut off the call.

Tristan was looking around the courtyard, pretending to have not been listening, but not pretending especially hard.

'Everything fine on the home front?' he said. I said:

'Oh do fuck off.' He laughed. I put the thing about pizzas out of my mind.

When I got home, Tony claimed to have stood his ground and not paid the delivery guys. I didn't believe him, but I also didn't give it any further thought.

★ ★ ★

'Momentum is a thing in this industry,' said Aloysius, two weeks later. For once we were meeting in his office, not in a restaurant, maybe to make the point that even as work talks go, this was going to be extra-worky.

My agents' offices are in Soho. The layout had the classic creative industry topography: individual offices and meeting rooms around the edges for the bosses, with a central well staffed by an assistant class of ambitious, resentful peons. Aloysius's office was an old-school chaos of books and papers mixed in with a new-school aesthetic of glass and metal and two computer monitors. He was dressed down, in black jeans and a dark-grey T-shirt that leaned hard into his 'exhausted dad' vibe. Al was drinking Red Bull from a glass, which wasn't something I'd ever seen anyone do. Behind me, at the door, his new assistant did a quick knock-and-open. He shook his head at her and she vamoosed.

I'd been here before, but never really noticed how businesslike this room was. What looked like mess was scripts by clients. What looked like random books on the shelves and the sort-of coffee table were books by clients. What looked like random posters were posters for shows by clients. It was all pretend casual.

'You are greenlightable,' he went on. I knew what that meant: because I had had something made and it was considered a hit, nobody would lose their job if they commissioned the next thing from me. It's impossible to exaggerate the extent to which most people in TV's concern, most of the time, is covering their backs. The upside of a successful risk is as nothing compared to the downside of an unsuccessful one. I knew that this was how it worked: starting out, it was impossible to get anything made, but once you had something made and people liked it, you went through a phase when you could scribble a shopping list on a piece of loo paper and someone would commission a returning series based on it. Which is why the first couple of things you see by a new writer are often better than anything else you ever see with their name on it. The good stuff earned them permission to make all the shit. Is this ideal? No. Is it how the industry works? Yes.

'You know showbiz,' said Aloysius. 'Never forget the lesson of Mugatu in *Zoolander*: Hansel's so hot right now. Except in this case it's not Hansel, it's you. And you have to make the most of it. So that's the question: what's next?'

Everything he was saying was positive. And yet there was something about his body language, or his emotional body language, that wasn't as upbeat as the official message. I don't find Aloysius difficult to read, and it was coming through clearly that there were difficulties going unsaid. I waited for it to come out, whatever it was.

'In an ideal world, of course,' he said carefully, 'we might already have a project on the go.'

I don't think his intention was to irritate me, since Aloysius isn't – isn't paid to be – a wind-up artist. Nonetheless, irritate me was what he did. I found it impossible not to hear in what he was saying an accusation that I was being lazy or slack or sluggish. That I already ought to have got going on another project. And perhaps inside the annoyance I was also feeling just a teeny, tiny bit – and I would have rather undergone a cavity search than admit it – that there was some justice in the idea that I had been dithering. I didn't have a project on the go for the principal reason that nothing was as close to my heart as *Cheating* had been. That show came straight from the spleen, or bile duct, or wherever it is that poison and bitterness draw their energising power. Surrogate revenge, an act of severing, my gift to my mother or my clearing of accounts with her. Whatever was next wouldn't, couldn't, have the same energy behind it. So yes, I was defensive.

'I'm not a machine,' I said. 'I'm not a one-woman industry. I'm not Shonda bloody Rhimes. It's just me and a MacBook. The entire reason people liked *Cheating* is that it was a highly personal project. That takes time, I can't just knock another one out like I'm, I don't know, making a tray of fucking oven chips.'

He held up his hands, as if to say: obviously not.

'I hear you, I hear you. Don't shoot the messenger. All I'm saying is, for the moment, you're you. You're a name, you're this week's name. Make the most of it. Because soon this week's name is last week's name, and last week's name just doesn't have the same vibe. Because last week was last week. Do you see what I'm saying? It's about the energy. The momentum.'

Part of me was spoiling for a fight, and another part could see there was truth in what Aloysius was telling me. It was the subject of a thousand knock knock jokes. 'Knock knock.' 'Who's there?' 'Mark Hamill.' 'Mark Hamill who?' 'That's showbusiness!'

'I can't just will it into being. I'm not that kind of writer,' I said.

'No, absolutely, of course not. It's easy to exaggerate this stuff, and to make it sound like you've only got ten minutes to make the most of it. And anyway, the main determinant of how something does, apart from luck, is how good it is. Lucky and good, that's all you need. And that slight sliding thing with the reputation of a piece, the initial word being, you know, supernova – well, if you get that rocket-boost, there's really only one thing that can happen next, one place for that to go, so it's nothing to worry about, in fact it's perfectly normal.'

I had a queasy sense that the conversation was going somewhere I didn't want it to go. Ever since the first draft of the pilot, I'd had nothing but praise for *Cheating*. In fact, some of the very first love came from this person right here, sitting opposite me right here in this very same office. I had caught and ridden a fair wind, and had grown used to that. This talk about sliding – it's not what I was expecting to hear and definitely not what I was wanting.

'I have no idea what you're talking about,' I said.

'The online stuff,' said Aloysius. He had never had to break bad news to me, and without thinking about it, I had assumed that would be something he was bad at doing. It was easy to picture him as shifty and uncomfortable around saying things that people didn't want to hear. But in fact he was fine at it. He was still and steady. Unflustered. I suppose agents get a lot of practice at telling creatives that they aren't going to get the outcome they want.

I shrugged and – probably – pouted.

'Still no idea.'

'You know, the IMDb thing. Rotten Tomatoes. The web, Reddit, forums. Twitter. The general stupidity contest that passes for online open quote culture close quote.'

'Aloysius, darling, if you don't start saying exactly what you mean, I'm going to get annoyed.'

He looked levelly at me for a moment. I don't think I had ever seen him do that before.

'OK. I was assuming you knew and were avoiding the subject. So there's no easy way of putting this, but what's been happening is, according to the sites where people can vote on what they've seen, audiences, in general, are going off your show. All the average scores are down and the sentiment tracker across posts and social media, which as you know is a Thing in this business, has got more negative over time. Much more negative.'

I felt sick – for a split-second I thought I might actually be sick. And then I thought: is this who I now am, am I really now this greedy and desperate for acclaim and praise? What the fuck? I thought my whole shtick was not caring what people thought. But I suppose it's like what they say about the first time you fly business class, and then the back of the plane is ruined for you, for ever: you don't miss what you never had. Everyone telling you how great you are. It turns out that's quite nice and you don't like it when it goes away.

I didn't try to play it cool.

'Fuck,' I said. 'Nobody told me.'

'I assumed you kept an eye on it,' he said. 'Most people do, though obviously everybody pretends not to. It's a bit of a curse, actually. Once upon a time there was no way of knowing what the plebs thought, except through the box office numbers. Now – unfortunately, it's a cacophony. And not in a good way. Not a jolly cacophony of excited, happy voices. More like tormented souls screaming in deserved hell-fire. For all eternity. That kind of cacophony.'

'And posting the resulting scores on aggregator sites.'

'And the matching opinions on discussion boards and social media. Yes. And these things take on a sort of momentum of their own, so someone points out something they claim not to like—'

'In plain English, they say that there's something they hate.'

'Well, yes, something that they say they hate, and then other people say they hate it too, and then other other people come up with aspects of it that they hate, and then they argue about what they hate more, and then more people come in with other stuff they hate, and on it goes. And your profile is higher than it was, and there's more press about you, so there's more stuff to pick up on and re-spin, not always in a positive way.'

I let it sit there for a while.

'Thanks a lot for that, Aloysius, good talk. I really feel great about everything now that you've told me I'm losing momentum and overdue on my next project and everyone loathes my show.' And me too, it sounds like, though I didn't say that part.

Because of course this is in your mind, when you've had something go well. Several ideas lurk in the background: everything that has gone well was a fluke and has nothing to do with you; that although people say they liked it, actually they hated it, and are just waiting for a chance to tell you so; that you have peaked, and nothing you do or make will ever be any good; that luck is finite, and you have just used up your full allocation for this year, or this decade, or this lifetime. It doesn't take much to make these thoughts barge to the front of your mind – not my mind, anyway. I don't wish other people all that well, most of the time, and I don't find it hard to imagine that general lack of well-wishing projected back at me. It is easy for me to hate and correspondingly easy to feel hated.

Now it was Aloysius's turn to let things sit for a moment.

'Hansel's still so hot right now, is what I'm saying, and what I want you to hear. Just, everyone is ready for the next thing. The *mot juste* would be, receptive. People are receptive. That's all. It's meant to be an encouraging message, not a warning one. Yes?'

His eyes moved to the doorway, where his assistant had materialised again with an expectant 'it's time for that upcoming thing' look on her pretty face. I was being, if not exactly dismissed, then manoeuvred out.

'OK, fine, I get it,' I said. 'Obviously I have some stuff on the go, obviously I don't love talking about it until it's ready to talk about, and obviously when it is, you'll be the first to know.' And with that the meeting was over.

Back out on the street in Soho, I had a feeling I don't remember ever having after seeing Aloysius: glad that it was over. That had been the closest thing to a bollocking I'd ever had from him, and I can't say I'd enjoyed the experience much. It didn't help that the city was going about its business and the cloak of invisibility that envelops you in London had fully settled on me. Two delivery vans were blocking the pavement on either side of my agents' offices. From one of them, a man was lowering a filing cabinet onto an upright carrying trolley. From the other, another man was doing the same with three huge bottles of water. He was wearing a T-shirt that said 'Rent-a-Cooler'.

Heat is relative. One person can't be hot without someone else being cold. It's also a spectrum, which goes like this: volcanic, smoking, hot, warm, tepid, who? I'd just been told that I wasn't quite where I thought I was, or where I wanted to be, on that spectrum. My moment was turning into something that was no longer my moment. It happens, though knowing that isn't necessarily much help when it's happening to you.

My mobile started vibrating. My first thought was that it might be Tristan giving me the news on how his encounter with our mother, scheduled for today, had gone. Instead, I saw that it was Tony and, before I had time to arrange my thoughts, had a lightning flash of irritation, along the lines of: now what does he want? (I did say – I was very clear about the fact – that I'm not a nice person.) I thought about ducking the call but I also know, from experience, that if you start ducking calls from your partner, you're declaring that the relationship is a dead man walking.

'Not a good time,' I said.

'Did you order a dishwasher, a washing machine, and a fridge freezer?' said Tony, sounding as if he was on the edge of hysteria.

'Obviously no,' I said.

'Well, they've just been delivered to the house. And the receipt says they've already been paid for, by you.'

★ ★ ★

It was strange to be going to the police station with Tony. I had never been in one as a – if you see what I mean – customer. Out of university, trying to get into TV writing, I did an internship on a cop show, so in one sense I know a bit about what the police are supposed to be like. 'What do you make of that, guv?' 'No idea, son.' That kind of thing. But I had never had any real interaction with the Met. Why would I? I'm middle-class. I couldn't even have told you where our local police station was until I arranged this meeting.

We turned up on time and sat in the reception area waiting for the appointment with Detective Sergeant Clarke, the name I had finally been given after four frustrating phone calls trying, first, to get to talk to an actual human being, and then to a human being capable of understanding what I was saying, and finally a human being who could put me through to another human being who could genuinely do something. The cop shop walls were decorated with posters advertising jobs with the Met, tempting people to apply to be Special Constables, and advising vigilance against terrorism. The anti-terrorist posters were pretty funny, because they had been done in a carefully unrealistic style to hint, but not to spell out, that the perpetrators – who were acting suspiciously around surveillance cameras, and suchlike – were likely to be Islamists. It's vital to be constantly alert for funny-looking people behaving in a suspicious manner. Just don't ask us what we mean by funny-looking.

Tony, sitting on the squeaky plastic chair next to mine, was radiating discomfort. He didn't want to be there. He had had a tentative go at telling me to ignore things until they went away, but I was so immediately angry that he backed down at once. I knew he thought I was being hysterical. (Not that he would ever use that word to a woman, least of all to me.) The things that I knew he was thinking – it's probably nothing, it'll sort itself out, it's just stupid kids, it's not worth making a fuss about – had never been spoken. Which of course made them come through all the louder, which in turn made me steadily more angry.

We had been waiting for the best part of half an hour when DS Clarke came in. Clarke wasn't at all what I was expecting, not least because she was a she. I had pictured a grizzled veteran of the beat, a no-nonsense old-school Cockney thief-taker. Instead, she was a composed, slightly brisk, tired woman in her thirties, wearing a trouser suit and a lanyard and carrying a thick file of papers, which evidently had nothing to do with us. Her dark hair was no-bullshit short and she had the air of someone taking time out from some more important duties to attend to a small problem. She would give it her full attention because she was a professional, but she wasn't here to charm or make friends. She came straight across to us.

'DS Clarke. You're Ms and Mr Mull. My apologies for the delay. Please follow me.'

We were buzzed through into the working part of the police station and then led into a featureless glass box of an office. If it had been up to me, dressing the set, I would have gone for a whiteboard with pictures of suspects tacked to it, coloured lines making a mind-map of murder, maybe a pyramid of photos of gangsters with some of them crossed out like in a movie about taking down the Mafia. You know, something cool. Instead, it was as empty as any room I've ever been in: frosted glass on the outside, blinds on the inside, a white table, a dozen plastic chairs. Clarke sat down at the head of the table and plonked the papers she had been carrying in front of her. She opened a notebook and took out a biro and looked at us in turn.

'So how can I help?' she said. I found it difficult not to translate this as: greetings, middle-class person with typical made-up middle-class problems who has come to make a middle-class fuss and waste a hard-working public servant's precious time.

'Well, it's like this,' I said, and began telling my story. As I recounted the things that had happened, it occurred to me that this was weirdly like pitching a script. I explained who we were and what the back story was and then ran through the list: pizzas; systematic campaign of bad reviews and negative chatter online; a couple of grand's worth of white goods being ordered on my card and sent to the house. Clarke looked steadily at me while I was talking and her expression did not change at any point. When I finished, she let the silence hang for a while. Tony was shifting in his seat but did not speak.

'I think it's best to take these one at a time. The pizza incident. Has anything like that happened before?' To Tony: 'You're a schoolteacher, is that correct?'

Tony nodded.

'Has anyone who works at your school been the subject of a prank like this before?'

'I would hardly call it a prank,' I said. 'That's like you've already decided what it is. This is a targeted campaign of harassment.'

'I understand your perspective,' said Clarke. 'But I'm wondering what might be the answer to my question?'

Tony shuffled some more. This setting and this conversation weren't showing him at his best. It was one of those moments when I found myself wishing he was a different kind of man – more assertive, more decisive, more (sorry) masterful. I could already tell that this was like going to the doctor when you know what medicine you want, and you have to be emphatic about your symptoms, because otherwise they will minimise your concerns and treat it 'conservatively', in other words do fuck-all. Give this woman the merest sniff of a chance to say that it was nothing really, and we would be out the door in seconds. I wanted Tony to go in as hard as he could. To make the unwanted pizza delivery sound like an assassination attempt. Instead, what he said was:

'They're teenagers. They do stuff. Write things on the boards, nicknames, whatever. End of term things. Yes, you could call them pranks. But to a teacher's house? No. It's over the line. Why would any of them even know where I live, for a start?'

Time for me to step up.

'We aren't fussers, we aren't hysterical people, we don't run complaining when somebody sets off a car alarm or there's a disturbance in the street or the neighbours are having a party or whatever,' I said, remembering as I did so that in fact I had once called the council about a neighbour's party, but that was only because it happened on consecutive weekends and went on all night and any reasonable person would have done the same. 'We're not imagining this. Don't you understand? This is not normal.'

Clarke didn't say anything. She wrote something in her notebook. She looked up at us, waiting for more. What a bitch. I didn't want to speak next and Tony seemed to have run out of steam so the silence built.

'Have you ever ordered from this particular delivery place before?' she asked.

'No,' I said, just as Tony said 'yes'. I glared, he looked sheepish. 'Once or twice.'

'So your details would be on their system,' said Clarke.

'Well, yes, but I don't see why that means—'

'I didn't say it meant anything.'

She made another note.

'You talk about a campaign of negative commentary. That's nothing like anything that has ever happened to you before?'

'Absolutely not.'

'But you did have some bad coverage before. Bad reviews, bad press, people not liking your work. Or you. I know – I've looked.'

From the way she said that, I realised that I wasn't imagining dislike and hostility on her part. For whatever reason, she had taken against us, or against me, or against the whole idea of this case.

'Of course I've had negative things said about my work, everyone has. I'm sure you as a police officer are used to criticism and negative feedback. I mean, let's face it, everyone in London hates the Met.' Yeah, have that, bitch. 'But this is, in my opinion, not the same thing. The show came out, everyone loved it, and then someone commissions a load of bots and sock accounts to spam every review site on the planet with one- and zero-star reviews, most of it specifically mentioning me. It's coordinated, anyone can see that.' Emphasis on *anyone*, meaning *even you*.

Clarke had a look on her face that in someone else might have been the beginning of a smile.

'I understand that it feels like that. People all saying the same thing, and it's something you don't want to hear. Almost like an intervention in AA. Unwelcome news.'

I felt myself becoming properly angry.

'It isn't at all like that. It's bot accounts with hundreds of followers saying misogynistic rubbish about me and my work.'

'Nobody says it's easy being in the public eye,' she said sweetly. The subtext was loud and not difficult to read: nobody says it, but we're all thinking it. 'Was there anything else that you wanted to bring to our attention?'

I told the story of the white goods. Tony nodded along with me as I spoke. I could tell that I had lost Clarke, or had never had a chance of getting her to listen, which made me put more and more energy into what I was saying, with less and less effect. I chased harder, she backed off further.

Talking to bureaucrats and minor office holders and people with small but significant amounts of power – people who in that precise moment have power over a supplicant – there's often a feeling that you are looking for a form of words, an incantation, a magic spell, that will unlock the humanity or common sense or basic decency or hidden empathy or really just anything at all inside the power holder, so that they'll start thinking what it must be like to be in your place, and start actually listening to you. That's the precursor, the indispensable precursor, to them being willing to help – even if what the help amounts to is just DOING THEIR FUCKING JOB. And that was the dance I was now engaged in with Clarke, putting more and more energy and attempted charm and vim and gusto and drama into trying to get her to DO HER FUCKING JOB.

'Unwanted delivery,' she eventually said, making a note on her pad.

'Theft – they used my card details.'

'Attempted fraud, yes. Would I be right in thinking that you suffered no financial loss and got a full refund from the card company?'

'That's not really the point, though, is it? The point is that it's part of this coordinated series of attacks.'

That ghost-faint smile again.

'I understand that it feels, seems coordinated, I truly do, Ms Mull.'

She made another note on her pad and then folded her hands on the table in front of her.

'For a case of harassment, or stalking, or anything along those lines, we need two things, however uncomfortable and unsettling the experience has been for the' – tiny micro pause, just to indicate she didn't believe what she was saying – 'victim. The first is evidence that this is what is genuinely happening. The second is some evidence that there is a perpetrator. In your case, Ms Mull, assuming as I think you do that you are the intended target of this supposed pattern of behaviour, there just isn't enough evidence that the thing you're talking about actually exists. A prank that might well have been targeted at Mr Mull. A series of negative comments about your television show from anonymous accounts – well, it's obviously unpleasant to be on the receiving end of people saying they don't like your work. But it would be a stretch to find in that anything that is illegal. In this country anyway. And finally a delivery of unwanted goods, which might be one of a number of things, the most likely of which in my view is a return goods scam.

You are perhaps not familiar with that. A person's identity details are compromised and goods are ordered to their home address. The target arranges for the goods to be returned. Then a criminal associate comes and pretends to be a legitimate agent of the vendor, and collects the goods for return – and that, there, is the moment of theft. So the stuff isn't stolen when it's sent to you, but when it's collected from you. That makes it a crime, but not the same kind of crime as the one you are talking to us about.

'All that is to the first point, whether there is a pattern here. The second thing we need for there to be a crime of harassment is some idea, some clue, as to who the offender might be, if he or she exists. And there I have to say we have nothing at all. Nor do you, I think I'm correct in saying. I'm sorry to disappoint, Ms Mull,' – looking not at all like someone who was in the tiniest bit sorry, and instead like someone who was enjoying this way too much – 'but there is nothing for the police to go on here.'

I was too angry to reply. But then something unexpected happened; something that doesn't often happen, and which I hadn't at all bargained for. Tony surprised me: he spoke.

'There's another thing,' he said. And turning to me: 'I haven't told you about this. It's awkward.'

Clarke looked almost as put out as I felt. 'OK, go on,' she said.

'It's not just stuff about Phoebe,' he said. 'There's been stuff about me too. It was brought to my attention by . . . a colleague. She was incredibly embarrassed about it and said she hadn't known what to do but was thinking about what she would want if it were her and had talked it over with her husband and had decided that she would want to know if it was happening to her, and so she should assume the same for me, so . . .'

Tony stopped for a moment. It wasn't clear he was going to go on. I hadn't thought it possible for someone to look embarrassed, angry, ashamed, uncomfortable, and desperate to unburden themselves, all at the same time. I snuck a glance at Clarke and she, for the first time since the meeting had begun, looked as if she was listening.

'It's anonymous stuff, of course . . . these kinds of things always are . . . they know better than to put a real name to it, for all the obvious reasons . . . and it happens to teachers a lot more than you might think . . . not least because it's so easy, it has no consequences, not for the people doing it anyway . . . they can just say anything they like, say it as a joke, like spraying graffiti, and then walk away, but again it's like graffiti, it stays there and won't go away, it hangs around, it's so destructive, people can't sleep, they can't think about anything else, lives are ruined, just casually destroyed, for no reason, because for every sensible person who knows what it's really like and what really happens there are five more who think there's no smoke without fire, God I think that's the worst expression in the English language, I really do, of course there's smoke without fire, with the internet it's all smoke no fire most of the time . . . it's just so unfair, so horrible and so unfair, because there's literally nothing you can do . . .'

I caught Clarke's eye for a moment and I for the first time could tell she was thinking the same thing that I was thinking. I said:

'Sweetheart, I'm sorry, but I have no idea what you're talking about.'

'It's these message boards where people say things about their school, their teachers, whatever . . . they say anything, they make up all kinds of stuff . . . just complete fantasy, the wildest and worst allegations you can think of . . . and then you never know who's seen it, let alone who wrote it, which of your colleagues or the parents of the kids or even the other kids, say next year's students, they're looking at this stuff, this filth, and they're thinking, maybe it's all true, maybe Mr Mull really is like that, maybe he does, you know, maybe he's one of those . . . It's the worst thing you can say about someone today, in this culture, literally the very worst, most damaging thing.'

'Tony,' I said, a feeling of horror settling in my chest, and at the same time incredulity and outrage, and at the same time part of me wanting to laugh aloud: 'are you saying somebody is accusing you of being a paedo?'

He was looking down at the table, shaking his head. For thirty seconds or so he didn't speak.

'Yes. On the boards and forums where people talk about their schools and mark their teachers.'

I thought: oh shit. Because Tony wasn't wrong. There were so, so many people out there whose whole world view could be summed up as 'there's no smoke without fire'. Any random lie, any shitty little untruth, as long as it gave them permission to judge or look down or despise or spit vitriol – they were there for it. People are so full of hate. They just want permission to express it. And when it comes to giving you permission to hate, there's nobody like a paedo.

'Have you made any sort of formal complaint about this?' said Clarke, sounding a lot more sympathetic than she had when I'd been talking about what had happened to me. Tony shook his head.

'The websites that do this, almost by definition they couldn't care less. Rating teachers. Spreading lies. They're in the business of making trouble and stirring things up. Why would they care?'

'Why didn't you say anything?' I said to Tony. He shrugged.

'You had enough going on. Plus, everything else seemed to be directed at you. The reviews, deliveries, that stuff. That was about you. This is about me. So, I don't know, maybe it seemed . . . not the same.'

I didn't find it hard to read the subtext on that one: everything to do with me was a top priority emergency, anything to do with Tony was just, you know, stuff happening. If this was meant as a bitchy zinger, it could not have been more effective. But because it was Tony, I knew it wasn't meant as a bitchy zinger, just as a truthful observation about how he felt. Which made it much, much more hurtful than any deliberate zinger could ever be. I felt full of rage at whoever the fucking idiots were who were behind this.

'Shit, Tony, I'm so sorry.'

Clarke was looking down at her pad and thinking and for a moment seemed, of all things, a little uncomfortable.

'I'm sorry, I have to ask this. Have there ever been any incidents at school that could lead to allegations of this type? Anything that could have been misconstrued?'

It was now Tony's turn to look baffled and furious. He even spluttered.

'What? God, no. I mean – no, just no.'

'Not even people complaining just to make trouble? I'm sorry, I'm sure you understand that I have to ask.'

'No.'

She made another note. Then she sat and thought for a moment.

'The . . . allegations, or slurs, whatever you call them, do they at any point make any allusion, any reference, to any of these other things that we've been talking about?'

'No.'

'Do they refer to Ms Mull at any point?'

'No.'

'Is there any sign of coordination or connection between this and the other incidents that Ms Mull and you are experiencing as harassment?'

'No.'

'Hang on a minute,' I said. 'Surely it's obvious, even to a sceptic, that this had to be part of a pattern. It's not happening in a vacuum. This is the fourth thing, after the sets of deliveries and the online campaign against me. It's a second online campaign. You have to be able to see that!'

Neither Tony nor I was calm. Clarke, on the other hand, was.

'I can see that this is a highly distressing situation,' she said to Tony. 'And these things that have been written about you are almost certainly above the threshold for libel. But that, as I'm sure you know, is a civil rather than a criminal matter. If they were to continue, and there's some evidence that it is a single perpetrator, then we'd possibly have a harassment case. But on the basis of what you're saying, we're not there yet.'

'I can't fail to notice that you have nothing to say about what's happened to me,' I said.

'This has obviously been a distressing period,' she said to me, sounding as if she didn't believe a word of it, 'but there is no evidence of a pattern of behaviour, just one incident that was probably a prank, another that was likely a delivery and collection fraud, and some people saying they didn't like your television show, which might be upsetting for you but is not illegal.'

And that was that. Two minutes later we were back on the street outside the police station. I couldn't remember a time before when I had ever been spluttering with indignation.

'I mean – fuck. What a bitch. And you! Idiots calling you a paedo and you didn't tell me about it. Not a word?'

He was looking down. I felt a wave of sadness. I know that I take up a lot of the available oxygen, and that I'm not always easy, or fair. I like to think that there are times when I more than make up for that. I could tell that this had the potential to be one of those times; one of the moments when I could reach out to him, comfort him, make everything all right. But I couldn't find it in myself to do that. I was stewing, steaming, boiling in my own feelings. I did nothing except stand there and let him feel sad.

17
PHOEBE

I have a morning routine when I'm working. Tony is up at seven. He's one of those weirdos who snap awake instantly as soon as his alarm comes on. I have trained him well. He organises his stuff before bed, which means he's up and washed and breakfasted and out the door to his school with no fuss. He makes next to no noise and I sleep heavily, so there are mornings when I hear some of this and mornings when I don't and instead I wake up to find that the other half of the duvet is unoccupied. I don't have a set time to get up, I just wake and either let myself drift back to sleep – if I feel like I haven't slept enough – or decide to face the day. The bathroom takes ten minutes if I have nothing particular on and I'm not meeting anyone that morning, or anything up to half an hour if I have to get primped and floofed. And then there's a strict rule: coffee, pint mug of water, and straight to my desk. Nothing to eat, no emails, no checking my phone, no opening the post if the post has come, which these days it usually hasn't. I am a shark. I am pure direction. I am velocity. I am all work and nothing but work.

All this is the theory. The practice: like everyone else, I check my phone before getting out of bed, carry it with me to the loo, faff about a bit more with it in the kitchen, and then arrive at my desk already partly annoyed, partly distracted, subtly demoralised, a little bit tired. Still, at least I'm not on social media any more – just imagine how much worse that would be. Since my meeting with Aloysius I'd had moments of being tempted to go back on there, just to find out for myself, just to see the worst. My awareness that that would be an unbelievably stupid thing to do was, for now, winning out.

But the semi-bollocking from Aloysius was still fresh enough in my mind to keep me straight. I put my phone into airplane mode. Discipline! Concentration! Focus! The next project!

It was about a week after we had been to see DS Clarke and been knocked back by her. I had heard back from Tristan about his attempt to re-establish contact with our mother. It had been a predictable, predicted, predetermined disaster. He turned up on her front step, and she closed the door in his face. I had a lengthy version of what happened from him, and no mention of it at all from her. Tristan told it as a funny story, but it wasn't hard to feel the pain behind it. I suppose if you were being charitable to my mother, or were a counsellor, you might say that the pain he was made to feel was an externalisation of the pain she felt about his moving so far away – in which case I would in turn say, on Tristan's behalf, fuck you. So there had been drama, but there were no more strange events – misdeliveries, trolling, whatever – and I was just beginning to hope that whatever it had been, it was now finished. I had run out of excuses for not getting on with work, but was also finding it impossible to get on with work. I was at my desk in the snug-like nook off the first-floor landing when the doorbell rang in the middle of the morning, with me having achieved exactly nothing that day apart from look at the same list of starting points that I had been staring at for months:

Sitcom: parents are vampires but they're trying to bring their child up human

Pub landlady who keeps murdering her husbands and getting away with it, cop is on to what she's doing, then falls in love with her

Main character falls off her bike, bump on the head, thinks she's on reality TV, friends and family go along with it

I sat at my desk and pretended to think about those ideas, while at the same time my eyes were flicking over to the other side of the screen, where a second Word document was open. Not a list of work schemes but a scheme of life accounting. It did not make for cheerful reading:

Career not in toilet exactly, but a bit stalled, and feeling more stalled than I would ever admit to anyone. Semi-fail.

Brilliant plan to clear the account with my mother and break up from her turns out to not be a brilliant plan. Fail.

Something horrible going on with stalking and/or harassment and/or bullying. To do with people hating me. Too weird to categorise but if I had to, open verdict tending towards fail.

Attempt to fix that by going to the authorities = a frustrating, infuriating disaster. Fail.

I didn't have an item on the list about Tony because although this was my workspace – Tony kept his laptop on the kitchen table, which was fair enough, since he used it for a couple of hours at a time maximum, whereas I was on mine all day every day – he sometimes came within sight of the screen, and I didn't want to write anything about him that he might read. If I had, it would probably have been along the lines of: Tony is Tony. There were a couple of different ways in which he might take that.

All in all, it was a relief when the doorbell rang. This would most likely be one of two things: either a delivery, preferably of something we'd actually ordered, or a charity mugger going house to house. So it was a surprise when I opened the door and saw a smartly dressed middle-aged woman in an expensive-looking dark-blue coat. For a second, I wondered if I knew her. I am bad with faces. Recognition, except of people I see daily, always takes a few seconds longer than it should. I don't interact with my neighbours much – that's one of the things I like most about London, the reciprocal right to not know your neighbours – so my first assumption was that it was somebody local. Have you seen my cat, do you have any spare parking vouchers, have you heard what the council is planning to do about bin collection. Something gripping like that.

'Hello?' I said.

'Phoebe Mull,' she said. It wasn't a question, but I nodded. 'I'm Kate Hittlestone. I wonder if we could have a little talk.'

She didn't wait for permission. She walked straight past me into the house. If I had had even five seconds to think about it and get my head together I would have blocked her, closed the door on her, or something. Instead, I froze. I shut the door, leaned my head against it for a moment, and then followed her through the hallway into the kitchen. She stood in the middle of the room, looking around. That look people have when they're checking out your stuff and judging you – judging you hard? That was the look on her face. I gestured at the kitchen table and she sat down. Playing for time, I went to the sink and poured myself a glass of water. I stood with my back against the sink.

Neither of us spoke. This gave me time to do a little judging of my own. The woman who had stolen my mother's boyfriend and ruined her life. The woman who my mother's boyfriend had preferred. The woman who had left my mother betrayed, humiliated, broken. By extension, the woman who had scarred my life by turning my mother into the person she was – damaged, histrionic, narcissistic, vampiric. Bitch, vampire, squid. That couple who had loomed so large, and who I'd been so keen to revenge myself on: this was the female half? She wasn't exactly mousy, but she was much more prim and buttoned-up and correct than I'd expected.

I had pictured someone voluptuous and sexy, Bohemian, someone with the dramatic chops to out-act my actress mother. But this was somebody from the Women's Institute or local bridge club, someone you might interact with when you drop off unwanted clothing at the charity shop. I had seen her only once in the flesh, for a few minutes one evening a couple of years ago. Much better than her appearance, I knew the sound of her voice, and had constructed a picture of her from that. I knew some of the things she got up to, and that contributed to the picture as well. The person in my head – it was worth being her nemesis. She was somebody on who it was worth revenging yourself. The woman who had come barging into my kitchen, not so much. Part of me wanted to say: You?

'So how can I help?' I said.

She smiled to herself at that, but didn't immediately reply. She was still looking around the room. The amount of time she took, and the manner in which she took it, made it very clear that this was her show, and she was running it. I was in full fight-or-flight mode, my heart racing and beating so hard I could feel it pulsing in the soles of my feet. I put the glass down because I didn't want her to see my hand shaking when I tried to drink from it.

'How's your mother?' she said.

It was the most helpful thing she could possibly have come out with, because instead of feeling nervous and shaky, I was suddenly furious. I also realised that she had put it all together: who I was, and how my story connected with hers. She had put it together. There was no point stalling or bluffing.

'Why don't you ask her yourself, if you're concerned about her? Because as far as I know, for about thirty-five years you've given ample evidence of the fact that you couldn't give two shits about her.'

If I'd been hoping that coming at her strongly would have an effect, I was disappointed. She gave an amused snort, as if I'd made a witticism. She didn't meet my eye and didn't immediately reply.

'I expect she's fine,' she eventually said. 'She was always tough. People who play the victim usually are, have you noticed? They're survivors. Ruthless. I expect she's been quite a handful as a mother. Sarah certainly wouldn't be shy about putting her own needs first. She was like that when she was young and that's a trait in people that never changes.'

I thought: not a bad character sketch, all things considered, especially since they haven't met since uni. But that's not what I said. What I said was:

'I have no interest in discussing my mother with you. If you have something to say, say it.'

Again, she just smiled, and kept looking around the room. It was as if she was completely in control, and wholly in charge of herself too. Again, anger came to my rescue. I said:

'Otherwise you can just fuck off. I'm busy.'

She started wandering around the kitchen, looking not at me but at the oven, plates, fridge, peering out to the garden, like someone snooping around a house they're being shown by an estate agent – a house they'd already decided not to buy but were checking out from sheer nosiness. In the middle of the table I keep a plate of fruit. The plate was a birthday present from Tony, and it's one of the nicest objects I own. She picked up an orange from the platter and put it back. All of this felt distinctly but deniably over the line in terms of violating my space. She touched Tony's laptop with the tips of her fingers, as if checking it for dust.

'I think I know why you did it,' she said, as much to herself as to me. 'Something about making amends for the past. Some idea of revenge. Vicarious revenge, for something that was never anything to do with you. Doing a thing that your mother could never do for herself. I sort of get it. I'm not saying it isn't stupid, because it is – deeply, tragically stupid. You know that, don't you, that what you did was stupid? I bet you do, even if you haven't quite admitted it to yourself. I expect you started on the idea and then it had a momentum of its own and it was too late and too difficult to stop, even though you knew you should. And now you've done something so sad and shameful that you'll never be able to get over it and you'll never write anything people want to watch or read, ever again. Because things like what you did – they kill the people who did them. People die on the inside. Even the ones who think they are without shame, like you.'

I moved towards the table and stopped across from her. I put my hands on the table and leaned on them.

'It's time for you to go now,' I said. 'You don't know me, you don't have the first faintest clue about me or what I'm like or what I think. We're strangers. I did what I did, it worked, and for the record, I'm glad I did it. Now pretty please, and notice I'm asking nicely, it's time for you to leave.'

'Gladly,' she said. 'If you tell me one thing. I know what you did – you eavesdropped on us. A little spy in our house. Jack loved his gadgets. That bloody House thing. It was something to do with that. It doesn't matter, now. So I'm willing to let the matter drop, as long as you tell me one thing: how you feel about what you did.'

When you're in a fight, an argument, there's sometimes a moment when the balance shifts; a mark is overstepped, or someone shows their hand, or loses control, or says something they shouldn't have. The person who was in the right is now in the wrong, or the person who was pretending to be upset about A lets slip that what's really bothering them is B. This moment was like that. When she said that she wanted to know how I felt, the power dynamic in the room shifted. What came next was up to me; I was now in control.

It's not that I felt myself relax, because my heart was still going at 180 beats per minute. But I did feel on much firmer ground.

'How do I feel?' I said. I looked down, made myself look thoughtful. Took a beat. 'I feel absolutely fantastic, to tell you the truth. I feel like I did exactly what I set out to do. I had a huge hit. I know you think this is all about you, but frankly, that's very much a generational thing. You boomers always think everything is about you. But as far as I'm concerned, you were just a starting point. Raw material. I'm not going to pretend I'm sorry if you feel ill used, or whatever. To be honest, if I were you, I'd just try to get over it. The truth is, you being here is just a speed bump. What happened, happened. As I'm sure you've realised, the only people who know what the marriage in the show was based on are the two of us in this room right now, plus your husband, assuming he's seen it too. Apart from the three of us – nobody knows, nobody cares. It's karma for a shitty thing you did when you were young, and my best advice to you is to just suck it up. Take it on the chin. If I fucked up your marriage, too bad. It couldn't happen to a nicer couple. Now you get on with your life and I'll get on with mine.'

As I said that, I saw her face change. She had seemed clenched, furious, on a mission, with a reined-in energy, a sense that something inside her was deeply pent up. Now she seemed to have collapsed into another state, deeper and less careful. She looked, for the first time since she'd appeared on my doorstep, reckless.

'You don't know, do you?' she said, almost laughing. 'God – it's almost funny.' She gave a mirthless laugh, then another, then a quick bark of real laughter.

'I'd ask to be let in on the joke, but I get the feeling I'm about to be anyway,' I said. In reply, she took her phone out of her handbag and looked at it for a moment, then put it back.

'Jack died,' she said. For a second, I didn't know who she was talking about. When I realised, I felt myself go cold. I thought the absolute worst for a moment – pictured him keeling over with a heart attack when the first episode was broadcast – but she, to give her the single solitary piece of credit she is owed from this entire exchange, did not let me think that for long.

'Before your . . . show went on. Suddenly, one night, no warning. So he never knew what you had done. I suppose that ruins your scheme. Of the two people it was created to hurt, one of them completely missed out on it. It was only half as toxic, half as horrible, as you wanted it to be. Does that make you feel you failed? I do hope so. If you were a different kind of person, I might want you to show some sadness, some empathy, some acknowledgement of just how horrible it was to go through what I did. Grieving, broken, and then your show comes on and leaves me thinking Jack was cheating on me. Take a few true things and mix them in with all these lies. And put in enough private and secret things, things nobody else could possibly know and no one would talk about even to their most intimate friends. Just enough of that to make me locked up with my secret and my loss. What did you think, that it would break us up? Did you picture me and Jack fighting about it, me kicking him out? Is that the worst you imagined? Well, it was so much worse than that, for me anyway.'

It was a good thing that she talked for as long as she did. I had a chance to regroup and to get my face straight. I felt – actually, I'm not sure what I felt. She and her husband had been ideas to me, rather than people; I didn't know them. I knew what they had done to my mother and by extension what they had done to me, and I had eavesdropped on them and made up a story about them and in that sense used them – but that wasn't the same thing as really knowing who they were. It was an idea of a person who had died, rather than a real person. A vivid idea, to me anyway: Jerry in my show was as present to me as this person sitting opposite me right now. I could hear and see him. But that wasn't this woman's husband – it was someone else. The real person hadn't seen *Cheating*. He hadn't been hurt by it, even though that was something I had wanted. He couldn't have been, because he was dead before it was broadcast. Well, so what? Sad for everyone who knew him and especially for his widow, but you know what, it happens.

Also, I knew better than to admit what I had done.

'Sorry for your loss, obviously, but I don't really see what it has to do with me. I'm sure that's a hard thing to hear, but it's true.'

She said nothing to that, just looked at me blankly. The silence began to stretch. She gave another of her barely perceptible grimace smiles.

'Nothing to do with you. You're sure that's how you feel.'

I noticed that without realising it, I had folded my arms. My mouth might be saying one thing but my body language was saying something else.

'It's not so much what I feel, it's what I don't feel,' I said. 'But I repeat: I'm not a monster. I'm sorry for your loss. My mother will be too.' Though as I said that, I was wondering if it was true. She would probably find a way of making it mainly about her. Throw a pity party for herself, with herself in the starring role, or act out a drama around her own sense of loss and bereavement. Or put on an act about a sadness too deep for words or tears. Whatever it was, it could be relied on to be pretty unbearable.

She didn't reply to that. Instead, she took out her phone and pressed the touchscreen a few times before putting it back in her bag.

'I've called a cab,' she said. 'I think we're done here.'

I had the same feeling you get when you're in the dentist's chair and hear the words 'Nearly done'. I had a mad impulse to make small talk; to bring up the weather, ask her where she had bought her coat, ask her if she was planning to go on holiday anywhere interesting. I kept my nerve and managed to keep shtum. Some minutes, perhaps five, passed in complete silence. Five minutes is a long time to spend sitting with a stranger in total silence.

The doorbell rang.

'That'll be your cab,' I said, trying not to sound as happy about it as I felt.

'They don't ring the doorbell any more,' she said.

'Right,' I said, feeling stupid, and reflecting on the fact that I had spent a greater part of this conversation on the back foot than in any I could remember. I went to get the door. It was a delivery, not for us but for the neighbours, and the delivery man was particularly obtuse about trying to refuse my refusal of it. We argued for a few moments and then I lost patience and closed the door in his face. As I did so, the wife, I mean widow, came up in the hallway behind me; she had approached so quickly and quietly that I jumped.

'My cab is arriving. I'm leaving now,' she said. Her manner had shifted register again and she was all business. If she thought I was going to try and talk her out of it, she was going to be disappointed.

'Fine,' I said, letting her past. 'I know you probably don't want to hear this from me, but it's true so I'm going to say it anyway: I am sorry for your loss.'

Was it true? In that exact moment, not really. It was true that I had, to some extent, wanted to mess up her life. But that wasn't the same as wanting somebody dead. Was it?

She stopped in the doorway and looked levelly at me for the last time. She said:

'I don't know if this is something that has occurred to you, but just so you know, I think Jack was probably your father.'

18
PHOEBE

The main thing I thought as she walked off was: you bitch. You fucking bitch.

I was boiling, raging, my mind swerving between lanes, trying to undertake, overtake, outrun its own thoughts. I found myself back in the kitchen, opening and closing the fridge door, then furiously tearing the top off a packet of leaf tea with no recollection of having picked it out of the cupboard. It was one of those times when the adrenaline hits you not before or during a crisis, but afterwards – your body, your fight-or-flight, didn't have the chance to prepare, so it kicks in later instead. I felt like I was on the verge of having a full-blown panic attack.

I thought back to that night. I had known what I wanted to do, in outline, but I didn't have a precise plan. I pretended to be drunk and they, or rather he, Jack, took me in and set me up on the sofa for the night. I barely caught sight of her but I was able to get a good sense of him. He was nice, actually. I hadn't expected that much kindness. I just wanted to get a look-see. I thought I would get into their house and have a look around and take it from there. I was looking for material, really – something to get me started. And maybe if it hadn't fallen out the way it did, I would have done something else, written about something else. But the Wi-Fi codes were right there on the router, and the router was connected to a smart home system and bingo, I was in. The whole thing just laid itself out. I had the idea about the affair straight away: as soon as

I could hear them talking to each other in private, I knew how I was going to do it. The story opened up in front of me. It was too good to resist. In other words, I did what I did for the usual reason people make art, make money, and commit crimes: because I could.

What she had said couldn't be true. It was absolutely the case that I didn't know anything about who my father was, other than that for my mother it had been a casual and immediately regretted rebound thing. (As for the logical consequence of that – the implication that my brother and I, too, were regretted – our mother never quite dispelled the thought. She let that one hang.) It was true that the dates more or less worked, because my mother dropped out of university, after having her life ruined by her so-called friends, at the end of the year, and we were born in the following autumn. But there was no way in hell my mother would have been able to keep to herself a bombshell of this magnitude, a grievance and life-wound of this weaponisable, nuclear scale.

Or would she? Would it work better for her as a nursable, cherished, lifelong grievance? A hidden grudge that she kept like a loathed, beloved pet? A secret that made a desperate situation worse? Something she was planning on keeping to her grave, or better still, to her deathbed – one final last devastating gift for Tristan and me? I had to admit: that would be totally in character.

But it didn't feel right. When I saw Jack that one night, when I was listening to him later – spying on him, if you like, and creating a character based on him – I'm sure that if we had been related I would have sensed something, some click of recognition. And the fact was that I hadn't. Unless wanting to do this, the whole idea of *Cheating*, was in itself that moment of recognition. Oedipus kills the old man at the crossroads because on some unconscious level he knows that the old guy is his father. That's the whole point: the parricide isn't a mistake. It's not a tragedy of randomness, but of intention. He wants to kill his dad. He lies to himself about the fact that he knows what he's done. Maybe I had done something similar.

I tried versions of a conversation in which I went to talk to my mother and came straight out with the question. This story you tell about the person who ruined your life – was that my dad? If it was true, which I didn't think, but if it was, this question would for my mother be the climax of a multi-decade set-up, the final confrontation at the end of the fifth act, the big reveal. She would get to deliver whatever lines she had planned for this moment, strike whatever attitudes she'd been intending to inflict on me. 'I wanted to protect you from the truth.' 'I didn't think you could cope.' 'I didn't want my life's tragedies to overshadow your life.' It would be along those lines. When I started to think about that, it began to seem more possible that she had been keeping the secret for exactly that reason – to stage that scene.

And yet, I say again, in my bones, it didn't feel true. It didn't have the particular weight of truth; the sense of a piece fitting into place.

Let it be admitted that this would have been easier if I had someone to talk to. I was certain, had always been certain, that in doing what I did, I hadn't done anything wrong. I was sure of that; knew it for a fact; would die on that particular hill. But at the same time, there must have been some well-concealed mental gremlin in my head saying something different. I won't call it conscience, because that makes it sound as if the voice was in the right, and I don't think it was. There should be another word for conscience, one that makes it possible to admit that the inner voice telling you to do the 'right thing' is often a bit of a dick.

But the fact was, the real story about how I had conceived of *Cheating*, and the things I had done to make it possible, were still secret, and always had been. The irony was that the only person who knew about it was Kate: which of course had always been the point, that she and Jack would see themselves and their lives and not be able to understand how they were appearing on screen. And then the fun part was she would think that Jack was fucking around on her. A tiny part of me maybe, just maybe, quite liked the idea that it might make them break up; that the thing that had started with my mother being dumped would end with Jack being dumped, thanks to me. An elegant design . . . but not one that I had been able to share with anyone. I hadn't confided in a single soul about what I had done. I hadn't felt able to. I do have friends, but they're not exactly that kind of friend. Work grumbles, boyfriend issues – fine. But this was on a different level.

I had kept the whole thing entirely to myself. Which had been OK by me: there are people who need their hand held and people who don't, and I'm in the second category. Now, in the aftermath of Kate's visit and her horrible suggestion about my biological father, I found myself paying the price for having walked this particular path alone. I just couldn't stop thinking about it, my mind going in circles, looping the loop. How dare she it couldn't be true it might be true how fucking dare she my mother is a nightmare but she couldn't be that much of a nightmare but actually she could how fucking dare she but the thing is it couldn't be true unless but no it's not possible but what if it's true lots of impossible things turn out to be true no no it's not right it can't be but Mum's never wanted to talk about my biological father and that's weird but no not Jack it just couldn't be but what if . . .

And so on. And on. And on. I couldn't work, I couldn't sleep and I couldn't talk to Tony. He could tell something was up and kept asking me if I was OK, which would cause me to snap at him, which would make him go quiet, which would make me want to talk to him even less. I went for long walks, the kind I used to take when I was trying to work, to dislodge an idea or kick-start a stretch at my desk or just to switch off for long enough that it helped me to switch back on. None of it worked. I couldn't step out of myself for long enough to break the whirling, repetitive pattern of my thoughts. I would find myself in a street I didn't recognise, a couple of miles into the walk, and have to get out my phone and look up Google Maps to work out where I was and how to get home. Every day when I went to bed I would think, tonight I'll finally fall asleep and wake up in the morning and I'll have put this behind me. But there was no sleep and no respite and the morning brought no comfort.

After days of this, I cracked, and did something that on some level I knew I shouldn't do: I decided to go and talk to my mother. She smelt a rat straight away, as soon as I rang her to arrange a time to visit.

'What's this about?' she said. People who are exceptionally self-absorbed, and who by definition think everything is about them, have a magical radar for detecting when things really, truly are about them. It must be like being one of those animal species that can hear ultra-high frequencies and get advance notice of earthquakes and volcanic eruptions.

'It's just for a chat, Mum,' I said. 'I haven't seen you for a bit, I thought it'd be nice to come over.' I noticed that dealing with her caused me to tell two lies in two sentences. Without varying her tone, which was exactly the one she would have used to a cold caller trying to sell her double glazing or asking for her bank details, she gave me a time three days later, and hung up.

Not that she would be doing anything for those three days. It's just that because I wanted to meet, she could disoblige me by making me wait.

It was heading into autumn, but still hot. I walked to the bus stop, past the small patch of green space that is half ironically called 'the park'. People were doing that London thing of behaving as if they're not in a big city in the far northern hemisphere on a weekday but instead on Copacabana beach on the weekend, taking all their clothes off and lying down in the park, in between the discarded vapes and the dog shit, not a care in the world. I usually respect their commitment, but on that day I just felt tired, worried, stressed. I knew I had to have this conversation but I couldn't think of any way it would have a positive outcome.

The bus was full and hot. I was wearing a short suede skirt and a skimpy pink top and even so I felt significantly overdressed. The woman in the seat next to me was sweating heavily in an Adidas tracksuit while listening on speaker to a podcast about the importance of visualising your success in order to manifest it.

I got off two stops early and walked the last half mile. To get ready, I had prepared some dialogue, and as I approached my mother's house I ran through my lines. Mum, I know this is a difficult subject, but I hope you understand that . . . Mum, I love you [lie], and I respect [lie] your boundaries [lie – she doesn't have any], but . . . Mum, I know you see the truth that everybody needs to make their own life story make sense [lie].

She opened the door with no greeting and stepped aside to let me in. I fought off an impulse to check the time: I knew it was bang on what we had agreed. She was, bizarrely, wearing an apron, as if I had interrupted her making a mid-afternoon cake, something she had never done in her life. We went through to the kitchen and both sat at the table. She didn't offer me anything to eat or drink.

'I have an appointment later and don't have long. What did you want to talk about?' she said.

I felt myself losing my nerve, and at the same time knew that it was now or never. The prepared lines abandoned me. I took a long slow breath and a long slow exhale.

'Mum, I'm sorry, it's your least favourite subject,' I said. 'I want to talk about my biological father. About who he was.'

I was fully aware that this was equivalent to taking the pin out of a hand grenade and dropping it on the table. The official version was that Tristan and I were conceived in a very brief situationship, a rebound, after my mother dropped out of university. All she had ever said about our father was that he was American. She had not stayed in touch with him, and had never wanted to. She refused to give any further details. The implication was that it had been a one-night stand. No judgement from me. I had seen photos of her as a young woman – she was gorgeous, much better looking than either me or my sibling. She could have had her pick. Pity about being so mad. Mind you, some men like that.

'It's none of your business,' she said. I had been expecting non-cooperation but still . . . I could feel my temper starting to slip away from me.

'Forgive me, and I don't mean to be rude and I also don't want to start a fight, but that is—' I wanted to say objectively insane, but realised, just in time, that I couldn't say that, exactly because it was true – 'unfair. The identity of one of my parents is by definition and in its essence my business. It's about as much my business as anything could possibly be.'

'It was no different from having a sperm donor,' she said, spitting the last two words. 'I brought you into the world, I brought you up. You and your brother. That's all there is to it and I don't want to discuss it any further.'

My mother was, as she hardly ever is, genuinely agitated. She got up and went to her cooker and began fussing with it – turning the hob taps on and off and then bending over to open and close the oven door. A wave of baking smells came into the room. It smelt more like bread than like cake. She had much more of a life with friends and contemporaries than she ever let on to me. The baking must be part of some new persona she was trying out for that audience.

'You're baking now, Mum?' I said, trying to lighten the mood. She ignored me and kept standing, now with her back to the cooker, arms crossed. Sometimes, when you suspect something isn't going to go well, but you feel that you have to go ahead and do it anyway, and it goes just as badly as you'd expected, you feel: well, at least I was prepared for that. And other times, you prepare as thoroughly as you can, and it goes even worse than you thought, and you feel completely horrible about the whole thing. This was one of those times. I had no choice except to press on.

'So here's the thing, Mum,' I said. 'And I say again, I'm sorry to bring this up. I really am. But Kate Hittlestone came to see me.'

My mother changed colour: she flushed. I had never seen her blush, not once. It was alarming, unnatural. Not embarrassment – nothing so trivial. This was rage and loathing. Then she went pale. I thought for a moment she was going to faint. Her face tightened.

'She said that Jack Hittlestone was my father.'

I had tried to be neutral, to be without expectations, about whatever reaction I was going to get. The truth or lack of it, the person I was talking to, were all too volatile to predict. But what happened was she stared at me with a look on her face that I had never seen and that it took me a while to recognise. She was staring at me with unmixed, unmistakable, hatred. In that moment, and maybe not just in that moment, she hated me. I felt a wave of cold pass through my body. She stared at me without speaking for a full minute. And then she said:

'Get out.'

★ ★ ★

I took a black cab home. I felt as if I had suffered a huge defeat and I couldn't explain why.

The whole point of *Cheating* had been to find some form of closure with, and separation from, my mother. And it definitely felt as if I had achieved that – the separation part, at least. Physical separation, anyway. I knew that it would be a long time before I saw her or spoke to her again, if I ever did. It just wasn't supposed to have happened like this. It was meant to be on my terms. My agency, not hers. This didn't feel like it had been that way round. I was overwhelmed with a sense that I had fucked up so badly and also – this was no small part of it – I had no idea what the answer to my question had been. I know it was supposed to be 'no, of course he wasn't your father', but why would there be so much heat around the topic if that was really the case? Rule of life: you only get in real trouble for saying things that are true. So this furious denial was a weird form of confirmation, yes?

The cab ride, travelling in the same direction as the after-work rush hour, took forever. At home, I thrashed around inside my bag for the keys. My head was throbbing with a mixture of stress and dehydration and I could feel my face starting to break out. I wanted to lie down and cry. I wanted to go and stay in a spa for a month. I wanted a shrink, or a confessor, or a partner in crime. I didn't have any of those things, so I would have to settle for what I did have, a twin brother who lived on the other side of the planet. In Sydney – no, actually, that wasn't quite far away enough for him. By now, Tristan would have completed his move to Tasmania. He'd be in that house with the on-point period details and the porch and the Colonial Regency fixtures and the rest of it. There wasn't anyone else I could talk to about Kate and Jack and my mother and 'get out' and the rest. If I had to give the complicated back story of how I had come to write *Cheating*, well, my twin brother would have to put up with that, and if he was going to judge me – which would be wildly unfair – he could get on with it and then we could move on. I couldn't keep all of it to myself any longer.

The only problem was the ten-hour time difference. But there was nothing else for it: I had to talk to someone, that person had to be my brother, and I had to get up at the crack of dawn to do it.

I kept to myself that evening. Tony had homework to mark and he was easy to avoid. I deliberately had an extra couple of glasses of wine. I find that a small, non-emergency hangover reliably wakes me early, with a blood sugar crash jolting me awake around four or five. I sat in front of some crap TV. The evening went according to plan. A wave of sleepiness came over me at about ten, and whereas normally I would have fought it off and stayed up for another couple of hours to avoid waking up in the middle of the night, this time I deliberately gave in. Tony was still at the kitchen table grading papers when I staggered up to bed.

I jolted awake at quarter to five. My mouth was ash-dry and my head was pulsing. It was still dark, but dawn wouldn't be too far away. Tony was next to me, out cold, in a complicated tangle of sheets. His hair was bed-mussy and his stubble was starting to show and I thought, as I often do when I see him sleeping, what a good-looking man he is; a good person too. Not the same as me. I took several deep swigs from the pint glass of water I'd left beside the bed and weaved to the bathroom. I put on my dressing gown and went through to the tiny weird room that I use as my workroom. My most old-lady habit: I keep a kettle there. I used it and stood with my hands cupping a mug of English Breakfast.

I like my workspace. It has a poster of The Beatles, a whiteboard with doodles on it, and – best thing about it – a view out over the small scruffy front garden, and the bit of tarmac where we would park a car if we had one. But the best thing about my room in the early morning is the birdsong. Every dawn, they go hard at it. Through a trick of acoustics, we could barely hear them in our bedroom at the back of the house, but here in the front the chirping, twittering, clattering of four or five different species of birds is as loud as teenagers with a boom box. I stood there and listened and thought, as I always do when I'm standing there in the early morning, that I must properly learn which strain of noise is which. I once looked them up on an app, and though I can't identify the songs, I know what's on the list: blackbird, robin, sparrow, blue tit, thrush, starling. Some people, maybe most people, say that they hear music when they're listening to birdsong. I don't. It's not a chorus, it's reality TV. What I hear is competition, argument, a struggle for supremacy. They're not singing, they're shouting Me! Me! Me!

It was still a little too early to call Tristan. I had decided that the best moment was 6 a.m. my time, 5 p.m. in Hobart. There was more than half an hour to wait. I stood listening to the birds and sipping my tea, and that is what I was doing when I saw the strangest and least comprehensible thing I have ever seen or ever hope to see: three police vans, pulling up to the kerb near our house. Several policemen got out of each van, maybe a dozen in total. They had the air of people trying to make as little noise as possible. My first thought was: what the fuck. My second: one of our neighbours must be growing dope. My third: but why does it look as if they're coming towards our house?

PART FIVE

19
PHOEBE

The night before Tony's trial began, I couldn't sleep. It was the opposite of normal insomnia, where you dread the night slipping away without you getting any rest. I lay and stared at the ceiling and willed the time to go past as slowly as possible, so that the day would never begin. It brought back a memory from childhood, the wish that I'd be able to make time dilate so much that the bad thing, the thing I dreaded, could be pushed off indefinitely – pushed into a future that would never come.

That only seemed to make the clock speed up. Quarter past midnight suddenly was ten past two, then half past three. This night was in a hurry to be over. The only good thing was that Tony, unbelievably, was out cold, flat on his back and snoring softly. It probably helped that he was drinking so much – a beer at six on the dot, and then at least a bottle of wine with dinner, and then a whisky or two afterwards, and then a final beer to finish things off. He looked fine on it, far better than I would have done. I didn't envy him a single thing, apart from that ability to sleep.

I decided to give up at around four. I slid out of bed. Tony, still snuffle-snoring, turned over but did not wake. I put on a dressing gown and went downstairs. When I got to the kitchen, I almost let out a scream: Tristan was already there, sitting at the kitchen table with a hot drink, looking at his phone.

'Jesus, I nearly died of a heart attack,' I said. 'How come you're up? I thought you'd be completely trashed from the flight.'

'Jet lag,' he said. 'My body clock is so trashed, I may never recover. I thought I'd FaceTime Gary and then maybe catch an hour or two sleep before the . . . before we have to head off.'

I went across and gave him a hug. This wasn't something we often did and there was half a beat of hesitation before he started hugging me back. Then he squeezed tighter and tighter still, and I squeezed back – a game we used to play as children. He let go first, and kissed me on the top of my head.

'I won't ask if you're OK,' he said. 'I know it's a stupid question.'

'Good call,' I said. I put the kettle on and leaned with my back against the counter-top. A gesture my mother makes.

'Tony?'

'Still asleep. Thank God. And lucky him.'

'But he doesn't have to do anything today, is that right?'

'Right. He just has to be there.'

Tristan shook his head. He didn't say anything more. He didn't need to. My twin had been great about the whole crisis, right from the beginning, when Tony had first been charged. His combination of incredulity and outrage and moral support was ideally calibrated. He had perfect pitch when it came to saying and doing the right thing. Not just with me, with Tony too – a reminder that Tristan had known Tony before I did. I had got so used to the bitchy, sharp version of my twin that I'd forgotten all about this other side. I had mixed feelings about that: it was good to have Tristan back in my life at a time when I really needed him. At the same time it made me aware of the extent to which, for the previous decade, he had been absent.

When I caught myself thinking this, I reminded myself not to count my blessings. Tristan wouldn't be this present in my life for ever, but he was here now. Just bank that.

'I'm so fucking nervous,' I said. 'And yet there's nothing to be nervous about. I'm not doing anything except being there. And trying to hold it together. That's it. I don't know, it's like, it's school sports day and my kid is in a race, and I'm the one throwing up in the toilet from nerves.'

Tristan said nothing for a moment, just looked at me and nodded. He drank some of his hot drink.

'You don't have anywhere to put it,' he said. 'Lots of feelings, which we both know aren't your favourite things, no offence, and nothing you can do to burn them off, or even distract you. No hurdle to overcome.'

I didn't have much I could say in reply to that. He was right, and we both knew it. And there was something else: the thought that this might only be the start, that the trial would be horrible but what came after could be even worse. Tony's trial was something specific and definite. But the aftermath – I couldn't even guess its shape, its texture, the nature of its days, what the hardest parts of it would be. Tony might be back at home and back at work and the whole thing would be a memory, shrinking in the rear-view mirror. Or it might be the start of something unguessably worse.

★ ★ ★

As for that terrible first day, when Tony was arrested, I still don't know how I managed to get through it. Some parts of it I remember as if they were tattooed on to my brain. With some of it, I remember the feelings I had but nothing else. Some parts I can't recall at all, and only know they happened because they must have. During that initial police raid, I can't recall the specifics of what was said except that somehow, by the force of sheer hysteria, I was able to talk them out of taking my work computer. I did say that everything I did to earn a living was on it, which had the merit of being true. Anyway, for whatever reason, they let me keep my main laptop.

They took everything else. They took my iPad and my old semi-bust (cracked screen) iPad. They took my old computer, sitting in the garage where we stored all the crap we haven't got around to throwing out. They especially took everything belonging to Tony. They took his school laptop, his home laptop, his phones, work and personal and the old burner phone we used when we very very occasionally bought some recreational weed or MDMA. They took every scrap of paper they could find, including an entire filing cabinet full of Tony's stuff.

They had come to arrest Tony, on suspicion of fraud and theft. He was taken away in the back of a police car, about half an hour after the police arrived. He wasn't handcuffed. Maybe the police thought he looked so broken and humiliated that he didn't need to be. Police officers were coming in and out of our house, carrying black plastic bags of our possessions. I'm not normally the kind of person who gives two shits what the neighbours think, but in this case I made an exception: this was something we were never going to get over. I only hoped no one could see Tony with his head down, not even turning to look at me as he was driven away. The last thing I said to him as he got into the car was that I would find a lawyer.

Lawyer. Slight problem, I didn't know any lawyers. But I thought I would know someone who did, and my first call was to Aloysius. The phone rang through to voicemail the first time, so I rang back, and this time he picked up, his voice so clotted and groggy he might have been talking underwater. It took me a moment to realise: it was only a quarter to seven and he'd been asleep. I felt like I had lived a lifetime and a half already that morning. I explained that there had been a terrible mistake, that Tony had been arrested for something he very obviously couldn't possibly have done, and that he – we – needed a lawyer, a solicitor with a speciality in criminal law.

'I'll send you a name,' he said. 'And I'm sorry, it sounds like you're living through a nightmare. Both of you.'

And that was how Hester, who either I or Tony spoke to at least once a day for the next year, came into our life. Our relationship began with a long, panicky voicemail message from me, at half past seven in the morning. By eight she had signed on as our lawyer. She was a brisk, super-practical, attractive lesbian (I assumed), who wore a uniform of black suit and white shirt and with whom I quickly learned never to make jokes or use irony. She was as close to being strictly business as it's possible for a person to be. That was helpful, because anyone more empathetic would have had me regularly checking in with my own feelings, and I didn't want to do that. I just wanted the whole thing to not be happening.

On that first day, before I even met her, Hester went to the police station and sat in on Tony's questioning. In the evening she came to the house. I made tea and we sat in the garden. It was a lovely evening, I remember that: it felt so incongruous to be sitting in the mellow sunlight, listening again to birdsong – the different bird noises of the evening – while discussing the worst thing that had ever happened to anyone I knew. One of Tony's guitars was propped up against the French doors into the garden, and I kept looking over at it and thinking, I wonder if he'll ever play it again? Which was ridiculous, obviously. He wasn't being immediately sent to Devil's Island. But I couldn't shake the feeling that nothing was ever going to be the same.

Hester turned down offers of the tea I'd just made, coffee, alcohol and water. She sat with a yellow pad and was calm and crisp without being blunt. Her manner was as level and neutral as a plumb line. Even so, her voice changed a little as she came to the main issue.

'From the questions that the police were asking,' she said, 'it seems they have reason to think that Tony is involved in the theft of cryptocurrency.'

Even though I knew that was where this had been going, it was very hard to hear. I noticed that she was studying me, while pretending not to. She wanted to see if I was shocked and surprised, or whether I was showing signs that I had known this was coming because I knew Tony was a thief. My reaction did not need me to fake.

'I . . . I just don't know what to say. Something has gone wrong. This is all nonsense. I'm certain of it. I'm as certain of it as I am that you and I are sitting here in my garden.'

Although her expression didn't change, I felt as if something in her shifted slightly. I later came to think that this was the moment she decided that whatever Tony had or hadn't done, I hadn't known anything about it. I know that lawyers defend guilty people all the time, and have to make their peace with it because otherwise they couldn't do their jobs – but I was nonetheless glad that I wasn't in that mental category for Hester. A pathetically small consolation.

The first thing she told me was that if they were going to charge him, it would have to be within twenty-four hours of his arrest. So we would know by lunchtime tomorrow.

The second thing she told me was that in her judgement, having seen many similar cases and judging from the kind of questions the police were asking, it seemed likely Tony would be charged. That was another moment when I felt vertiginous with disbelief. The severity of the charges would depend on what the police found on his computer(s). According to Hester, what the police thought they might have was largely irrelevant: everything depended on what exactly they could prove. And that was an entirely different question, because it could be very difficult to prove that internet activity associated with an IP address was carried out by a specific person. A computer at a specific address having looked at something was easy to prove; a specific person having done so on a specific machine was much harder. If anyone else could have been using an incriminated laptop (say), or the tainted IP address associated with a computer or router, that made it difficult to prove that a particular person had been using the device at the relevant time. If they couldn't prove that it was a specific person, there was no case. It had to be person, time, computer, all three. Colonel Mustard in the library with the lead pipe. This decision belonged to the Crown Prosecution Service, the CPS, and their rule was that they would only proceed with a prosecution if they thought there was a more than fifty per cent chance of winning the case.

My feeling, when Hester explained that, was a surge of relief. Since this was obviously a mistake, it was comforting to know that there was a mechanism whereby the system – which already, even on that first day, felt like a huge miller's wheel, grinding everything in its path – was able to act on the realisation that it was travelling in the wrong direction. Tony would come back from the police station, laughing but shaky and rueful, too, with a funny story about what the senior copper said once they understood that they'd got the wrong person.

Maybe it wouldn't be quite as quick as that. Maybe it would take a few days, or a week or two, or even a few weeks, before the file landed on the desk of someone who could think straight, see straight, and then Hester would get a call and she would call us and that would be an amazing day, a joyous day, the day when we woke up from the horror and realised that it was over, was in the rear-view mirror. We would be able to pick up our old lives again.

Or maybe it would go all the way to the CPS with a recommendation that they go to trial, and some wise old owl of a lawyer would read the papers and read about Tony and think about him and see that this was obviously, flagrantly, plainly a mistake: these things self-evidently could not have been done by this person.

★ ★ ★

For a whole year, there was one colossal topic that never stopped looming over everything that happened. It was a question nobody on the legal side, nobody who knew me, and I myself never explicitly asked. The question was: did he do it? Had I spent the last five years living with someone who stole money and kept the fact from me?

The obvious answer to that was no, not in a million, or a billion, or infinity years. I knew that, knew it for sure. If I had thought that was the case I couldn't have lived with him, loved him, had sex with him, made him my life partner. I knew for sure he was innocent. I had never caught the slightest hint, the faintest glimpse, the tiniest clue to suggest he was willing to break the law and steal other people's property. If anything, one of my issues with Tony was that he was someone who always insisted on colouring inside the lines. He could actually do with being a bit more dangerous, a bit more interesting. Is what I would have said. I was completely certain. Except... was I as certain as I was at the start of the year? I knew it was all wrong, all a mistake, and I was furious at the police and the prosecution for not being able to see the blatantly obvious truth that Tony did not, could not and would not steal. Unless... no. But still, unless... I knew that he really, really wanted to make a go of his music, and that it wasn't happening, and the ability to leave teaching and just go for it full time would be worth a lot to him. The whole point of the little (I thought) dabbling in crypto that he'd done was to make some money so he could leave teaching. But he would never, never steal. Unless . . . no. The fact was, it was impossible to keep the thought entirely out of my head, and once it was in my head, although I was 99.9 per cent certain of Tony's innocence, that wasn't the same as being 100 per cent. That 0.1 per cent made me feel ill.

As for the lawyers – who knew what they thought? The barrister we eventually hired was like a surgeon who was going to take out a tumour. She had a specific job to do. Not a pleasant job, and very much not a job that you could offer to some rando you bumped into on the street, but a job she had been trained for and was good at. Asking her what she really thought about Tony would have been like asking that surgeon what they thought about the character and personality of the body they were operating on. The answer would have been: what's that got to do with me?

I did wonder whether it would have been different if she had the same visceral sense of Tony's innocence that I did – whether her work would have come with a degree of heat, an additional intensity and sense of personal involvement. She had as much emotion as a mechanic called out to change a car tyre. If she had thought he was innocent, maybe her vibe would be different. Or maybe that's just who she was and how she was. She had been our solicitor's choice – I couldn't have found a criminal barrister to save my life, I wouldn't have known where to begin – and I have to admit that in the early stages of meeting her I had moments of wondering if she was a mistake. She was about the same age as Tony and me, which I thought might be too young; I think I had a picture in my head of someone more world-weary, more cynical. On some level I maybe also thought: your job is going to be to make the jury like you, but how are you going to be able to do that if you can't make me like you?

As for Hester, that was trickier. She walked with us all through the process, right from that bizarre and terrible first morning of Tony's arrest. I was there too, for all of it, whether I wanted to be or not. I wasn't in on the police interrogations, obviously, but apart from them I don't think I missed a single conversation that Tony had with any of the relevant professionals. The reason for that was simple: Tony asked me to be there.

'About half of it is a blur,' he said, after meeting Hester on that first day. 'She says things and for some of it I'm right there in the room, but for a lot of it I'm just nodding and it's a blur. I need you there to keep track. One of us has to have their head straight and I can tell you right now it's not going to be me.'

I ended up by making a close study of Hester. Her zero-affect approach never wavered. I never knew what she felt, or indeed if she felt anything. Tony and I were outraged at everything. She never was, and did not pretend to be. When we expostulated and got angry, or sank down into sadness, she did not join us. Our most basic response, to much of what he went through, was that we couldn't believe it: 'I just don't believe it!' was almost a mantra. 'This can't be happening!' Hester always believed it. She never had the slightest doubt that it was happening.

Despite that, because Hester was the person who had to lay options out in front of us, I ended up with more sense of what she was thinking and how her mind worked. If Tony had been guilty, and had an interest in minimising his sentence, he would need to know how that played out. There were two crucial meetings, and the first of them was about six months into the horror. We were in Hester's office, in Fulham. It was a converted residential building in a side street, close enough to the Fulham Road for the traffic to be a constant background noise. This was the end of winter and the room was both overheated by radiators and draughty from the gusts of air that came in through the just-opened window. Her male secretary, an enormous clean-cut young man who looked like a rugby player and seemed out of scale with the building and the office, put down a tray of tea and biscuits, and left us to it.

'The heat can't be turned down, it's on or off, sorry,' she said. 'We vote on it.'

I waved it away, de nada. Tony wasn't listening.

By this point, it was clear that the case was not going away. A date was booked for the plea hearing. It's the moment at which you're given the choice of a trial or a guilty plea. Hester never said, 'if you're guilty, what you could do is . . .' What she did was to spell out the options, with the formula, 'what clients sometimes do is . . .' The shorthand version of what people did was to prepare for a guilty plea by offering to cooperate with the authorities. They would prepare to express deep and convincing remorse. All of this, taken together, would in the case of

middle-class defendant

clean record

reasonable judge

add up to a suspended sentence. That was all-important: the sentencing guidelines were complicated and there was a big range of options depending on degree of planning and amount of harm done. He was alleged to have stolen a little over a quarter of a million pounds. In context, I didn't know whether that was a little or a lot. The minimum he could get was a conditional discharge, which we had been told was unlikely, and the maximum was seven years, which we had been told was also unlikely. For Tony, all of this would mean that he never worked in a school ever again.

In the face of Tony's furious assertions that none of this was in any way relevant to him, Hester immediately backed off, holding her hands up, implying that this, obviously, wasn't pertinent for a case such as his. She also let slip a giveaway word, when she talked about Tony as a defendant who 'professes' his innocence. Tony immediately flared up, and she apologised, promptly and with energy, but in that moment I think I saw what she really thought. Tony was just another man professing his innocence, too stubborn or too much in denial to take the best deal she could get for him.

I think of myself as a fairly cynical person. At that moment I got a glimpse of a cynicism, or a realism, much more profound. Hester actually didn't care what he had done. She had no view about that, and didn't need one. This was just how the game was played.

The question of a guilty plea came up only once more. This time it was with the trial date set, and only weeks away. We were at the barrister's chambers in Lincoln's Inn. In another context it would have been interesting to see the Inn, to get the vibe, try and get a feel for what sound people call the 'room tone'. Instead, what I mainly felt was how much of a disadvantage we were at, going through this life crisis in the hands of people for whom it was just another workday, just another job. For us, it was the worst thing that had ever happened. For them, it was Tuesday. The barrister was wearing a trouser suit and a beautiful dark-blue silk shirt, the kind of just-right outfit that can only be put together by someone who spends a lot of time thinking about and shopping for her clothes. I thought she might be a fun person to know in civilian life.

It was a shared office, sorry, 'chambers', but the barrister she shared it with had made himself scarce for the meeting. I gathered that this was a standard arrangement. I could see a stack of files and papers higgledy-piggledy on his desk, each of them in a bulging brown folder with a ribbon around it – I remember thinking, aha, so that's why they call them 'briefs'.

The barrister was so subtle that I didn't notice how she steered us towards the question of a guilty plea. Perhaps she and the solicitor between them agreed on an approach. Or perhaps they didn't need to, because they had danced this particular dance so many times. She talked for a while about what the discovery process had revealed, and what evidence the prosecution was going to bring to court.

'This is the point at which the client sometimes begins to think about taking the other route,' she said.

I thought: what on God's green earth does that mean? The whole point of this process is that we have no choices. Exactly nothing is up to us. Then I realised. Tony did too. There were a few moments of uncomfortable silence. Then Tony snapped out of his reverie or funk or blow on the head or whatever it had been.

'I'm not pleading guilty,' he said. His voice was shaking. 'I need you to understand something,' he said to the barrister. 'This goes to you too,' he added to Hester. 'I am innocent. I know you're used to dealing with people who say that they didn't do what they're accused of doing. You're probably sick of hearing it and have got used to the idea that most of the people who claim to be innocent are lying. But in my case I truly am innocent. I AM INNOCENT. Get that into your heads. I didn't steal any bitcoin. I never have and never would. I have no idea what happened to get it on my computer, but whatever it was, it was nothing to do with me. I don't care what the pragmatic stuff is about how to plead. There's no chance that I'm pleading guilty. Understand? No chance. I didn't do it and I'm not going to say that I did. I don't want to discuss it any more and please don't suggest it again.' The two lawyers looked at each other and after a few seconds the barrister said, 'All right then.'

That year was like a long corridor, heading to somewhere you desperately didn't want to go. Every few yards down the corridor there was a doorway, and we knew, we just knew for certain, that one of these doorways would open as we came to it, and we would step through, and the terrible thing would be over, and we would no longer be heading to the place where only bad things could happen. We would be free.

But that didn't happen. None of the doors opened. We walked all the way down that long corridor, for a year, and at the end of it, waiting all that time, waiting patiently, waiting expectantly, was West London Crown Court.

20
PHOEBE

When the judge comes into the courtroom, nobody calls out 'all rise', and nobody stands up. The judge does not bang a gavel. Lawyers do not jump up and shout 'objection!' The judge doesn't say 'overruled' and 'sustained'. The judge doesn't ask 'how do you plead, guilty or not guilty?' A court clerk has already done that, at a separate hearing. Court is not like TV. The drama is not obvious, is not laid out in front of you. Even if you are intimately involved, it is not dramatic. What it is instead is intense. We were in court for three days and it was the longest, most intense, most exhausting three days of my life.

So it wasn't like TV; but it was deeply shocking to see Tony in the dock. I was in the front row of the public gallery, next to Tristan. Tony's parents hadn't come, because they couldn't bear to. Both of them had heart problems and there was a non-zero chance the stress of being in court would kill them. There were a few random people sitting at the back of the court. I tried not to think about who they were: I hoped they weren't journalists. What they mainly looked like was people who had wandered into the court to spectate because they had nothing better to do. Apart from them, the only people in the room were the participants. The judge was up on the bench. A clerk sat in front of her. A verbatim reporter sat to one side. The lawyers were in the well of the court. The dock was on the left, the jury box on the right. Tony sat in the dock next to a dock officer, an athletic young Black man who looked as if he quite liked the idea of Tony making a run for it, just so he could catch him.

It should have helped that this was not my first time at the courthouse. As soon as I heard its name mentioned, I began to have nightmares about West London Crown Court. In some of them a crowd was standing around outside, with banners and placards, yelling and chanting, and I had to push my way through them, sometimes with Tony and sometimes not. In another recurring dream I was trapped inside the courthouse and knew that I had to force my way out through the inflamed, furious, screaming crowd. Their faces came close and I couldn't hear exactly what they were saying – and that was part of the horror, the fact that I couldn't make out what it was they were yelling, so I didn't even know what the Bad Thing was supposed to be. In these dreams it wasn't Tony who was on trial but me, and I knew that I had done nothing wrong but I was full of dread and guilt anyway. That was a thought that would come to me in the nightmare, that it made no sense to be feeling so ashamed and guilty when I hadn't actually done anything; when I didn't even know what I was supposed to have done. The fear and guilt were the only things that were clear and real.

I decided that even if West London Crown Court was as bad as I dreamt, it would help to see the reality; so after months of these dreams/nightmares focused on the place, I took an Uber there to look at it. I didn't tell Tony, or anyone else. I didn't want him to know how frightened I was. I didn't have a clear mental picture of the court, other than that of somewhere tall and broad, formidable, grand, Gothic, imposing.

The reality? That part of West London turned out to be a classic London suburb, street after street of ugly semi-detached houses with hardly any signs of life, certainly not of street life. As for the courthouse itself, if I had to sum it up in one word, it would be 'municipal'. An ugly two-storey red-brick building with a one-storey entrance area that could have been a school reception, or the annexe to a church hall. My imagined crowds of family, friends, interested parties, journalists, were all absent. It didn't feel as if anything dramatic had ever happened there, or ever would. It didn't feel like a place people went to for the most important, and often worst, experiences of their lives. Inside the building, the municipal vibe continued. There was a depressing café where the food was served in plastic containers with plastic cutlery, presumably so that no one could use any of it as a weapon.

I came back from that trip hoping that having seen the reality would help my bad dreams. It didn't work. I kept having the nightmares. The only difference is that they were set in a more accurate version of the court. In the dreams, it was still me on trial. I still woke up yelling, or covered in sweat. For that whole year I had the nightmare at least twice a week. And now it was time for a different kind of nightmare.

The trial began with a certain amount of procedural muttering around the lawyers. While that was going on, I had a good stare at the jury. I was looking for signs of empathy, or wisdom, or an understanding of the gravity of the occasion. What I saw instead was a fairly scruffy mix of typical Londoners, the kind you'd see in any Tube carriage. Nobody had dressed for the occasion. One young male juror looked barely old enough to vote and one old lady looked eighty at least. There were seven men and five women, which I took as a good sign – the men might be more open to the idea that a couple of wrong clicks on a dodgy website or in a spam email could have you ending up in the dock.

I tried to get a read on the judge. I couldn't. She was a woman in her fifties. Her accent was pure Received Pronunciation – a BBC newsreader from the time when they weren't supposed to be from anywhere. If her wig and robe were supposed to erase signs of individual character and make it look as if she was a role and not a person, they were doing their job.

The most distinctive-looking person in the room was Tony. He looked like what he was, a handsome man who had accidentally lost an extra stone and was now possessed of a haggard, emaciated beauty – the kind of beauty that certain kinds of young junkies can have, but more tormented. If you were putting on a passion play and looking for someone to cast as Christ, you would stop right there and say: use that guy.

The preliminaries came to an end and the prosecution barrister got up to make his opening speech. Hester had warned us about what was going to happen: this was the moment when the full case was laid out. The rest of the prosecution case was the evidence that supports this story. The speech was intended to be devastating for the defence. I knew all that. And yet I wasn't prepared for just how horrible it was to have the case stated so clearly and comprehensively and, I had to admit, very reluctantly, so well. The prosecution barrister was a man in his late forties who had a tired, irritable air. He could easily have been a sleep-deprived parent, or been riding a Red Bull rush while fighting off a hangover. Unfortunately, in the context of the court, his bad humour was an effective tool. He made it seem as if Tony and the things he had done were the reason for his irritability – that this disgusting man and his revolting crimes were the reason why he, a decent man with an unpleasant job, was carrying this anger; that it was the disgusting duty of dealing with crooks and thieves that burdened him, and by implication the jury. It was sneaky and subtle and played on the fact that not a single person involved in this process wanted to be here.

And that was just his manner. The story he had to tell made it so, so much worse. According to the prosecution, Tony's computer had irrefutable evidence of his having stolen login credentials to three people's cryptocurrency accounts, and then having used the logins to move money to his own account. There was metadata showing when this had happened. It had taken place over a period of months. Analysis of the computer showed that it was only Tony who could have been logged into his account at the time logins were stolen and then the bitcoin was moved, because the files were protected by biometrics linked only to the owner of the computer. There was no ambiguity or complexity around the fact that he and he alone could have committed the fraud and theft. The gist was simple: two hundred and thirty-nine thousand pounds' worth of bitcoin that used to be in other people's accounts were now in his account. The only way it could have got there was if he had stolen it. The prosecutor sat down. I didn't look at the jury to see their reaction – I couldn't bear to – but I did look across at Tony. His head was down. I willed him to look up and meet my eye so I could try and communicate that I was here for him. He didn't. I had never seen him so hopeless and broken.

Tony's barrister stood up. My nerves did not settle. In the weeks before the trial I had moments of wondering how well she would do in court: she didn't have the rough and tumble, knockabout manner I had for some reason been expecting – too many courtroom TV dramas, probably. But now that she was speaking in court, I saw why Hester had recommended her. The fact that the prosecutor was a grumpy older man and the defence was an attractive younger woman was part of it. If she did not think Tony was guilty, maybe it gave some jurors permission to think the same. The story she told, about how easy it was to click on corrupt links, about how mistakes could be made, about which of us hasn't had things on their computer that they didn't knowingly put there – I could see how some jurors might find this convincing. Tony didn't need all twelve of them to believe him, he only needed three; and he didn't need them to be sure, he just needed them to think that the prosecution case wasn't as certain as they said. Three out of twelve. Reasonable doubt. She said this calmly and empathetically and this style of delivery, too, I could see was a tool designed to give the jury permission to see things her way. I'm reasonable, and this is how it seems to me. You also are reasonable, and as reasonable people I invite you to see things as I do. That was the implicit message. I could see how it might work. I could also see that it was Tony's only chance.

The barrister said that there was evidence – stressing that word, which was clever, the idea being that they say they have evidence, but so do we – of a campaign of harassment and stalking directed against 'Tony and his partner'. Some sort of vendetta might be behind the appearance on Tony's computer of material that he knew nothing about. There was no way to prove that's why it was there; equally, there was no way to prove it wasn't. I was biased, because I knew that what she was saying was true, but I did also think, we have a chance here. She doesn't need to prove it, she just needs to get three of them to think it was possible. One of the male and one of the female jurors seemed to be listening closely to what she was saying about internet harassment. Excellent!

The judge told everyone that we were breaking for lunch. Tony was led out of the dock and came to join us. I asked him if he was OK and he shrugged in a way that I knew meant: could be worse. I felt, for the first time since the morning the police had come to our house, a glimmer of hope – a possible route out of this. Our barrister and solicitor went off together to talk. Tony and Tristan and I went to the café, and it was microwaved baked potatoes and beans with a side order of tentative optimism all round. I hadn't allowed myself to think much, or at all, about what it would be like if/when Tony was acquitted and this was all over. Now, I allowed myself to peek at the possibility, like a kid leaning around a wall to sneak a look during a game of hide-and-seek. It felt good.

After lunch, the prosecution began to lay out its case in detail. The prosecutor called a computer expert to the witness box. The expert was a clipped, precise, youngish man with a clipped, precise beard and the air of having done this many times before. The prosecutor recited a list of the expert's credentials and he deigned to agree with them. He couldn't quite hide how pleased he was with his own cleverness, which I hoped might work less well with the jury than he thought. He explained how the metadata matched Tony's laptop to the thefts. He was asked how certain he was about this and he said he was completely certain. He was asked about the threshold for reasonable doubt, and he said that there couldn't be any. Tristan, ordinarily a world-class fidgeter, was sitting completely still, radiating tension and the desire to be somewhere, anywhere else. I couldn't blame him.

The expert's testimony went on for most of the afternoon. I stared down at my feet, or snuck glances at my brother, or at Tony, who seemed more and more haggard, or the judge, whose professional unreadability never wobbled. The details about what the police had found mounted up, and got heavier and heavier. It felt as if a pile of stones, a cairn, was being piled on top of Tony's chances of acquittal. At the end of the expert's testimony, our barrister got up and tried to cast some note of uncertainty around what he had said. The one thing that might have done some damage to the prosecution story was when she asked the witness if he could think of a single occasion on which he had ever been wrong, and he said that he couldn't. In another context, making him look like an overconfident twat might have been effective. After the jury had seen what they had seen, the chance of it cutting through was zero.

Finally, the afternoon came to an end. Tristan and I waited in the car while Tony talked to his barrister. Tristan had offered to do the driving, which was a relief, because I was too shaky. We didn't talk on the way home. Tony went straight to the fridge and poured a huge glass of white wine, which he took upstairs with him as he went to shower and change. Tristan and I looked at each other.

'Well, that was a day,' he eventually said. I didn't disagree. And the fact was, the least enjoyable part of it hadn't happened yet. I took out my phone and waggled it at my brother, then gestured towards the garden. He rolled his eyes and nodded. I stepped outside, did some breathing exercises, and made the call.

'Phoebe. I've been desperate,' said my mother. 'How is poor Tony? I've been thinking of him all day. That poor lovely man.'

★ ★ ★

We had thought that the prosecution case would take up all of the second day, but that was wrong. There was more evidence along the same lines as day one, from two additional experts, with both barristers largely repeating their act. Then, not long after lunch, the prosecution barrister wrapped up. Now Tony was going to have to give evidence.

Putting him in the witness box had been a difficult decision. Something I learned, in the course of preparing for the trial: the defence only puts the defendant in the box if they have no choice. The whole point of being 'innocent until proven guilty' is that you stand there in the dock as an innocent person. You don't have to give an account of yourself and your actions; the state has to do that. You shoot holes in their version. Shoot enough holes, and the defence's work is done. If you can't do that, you need to do something extra, and give your own account of what happened. The level of risk goes up dramatically. If you look shifty or untruthful or your version of events doesn't sound convincing, you might just bury yourself.

All this was conveyed to us very clearly but with a degree of indirection. Hester didn't actually come out and say 'if you look guilty we'll have to make you testify', but the gist was plain. The message: if we had to call Tony to give evidence, we would know that the trial was going badly.

On the second morning, Tony told me that the decision had been made. He was standing in the bathroom, brushing his teeth, when he pseudo-nonchalantly gave me the news. Apparently, the barrister had made it clear on Monday evening that Tony was going to have to testify. That was what they had been talking about while Tristan and I waited in the car. It was one of the reasons he had been so silent the previous evening. I now knew what that quietness had been. It was the same thing he used to do in the week or so before the start of term, when he would start talking less, go into himself, and mentally prepare.

He shrugged. 'She said it was a close call, and there were two ways of doing it and we shouldn't panic. But on balance, she thought it was a good idea to put me on the stand.'

Not true. But even as a person who makes a point of calling people on their bullshit – to a fault – I knew better than to say so. What this meant was that in the opinion of the relevant professional, it was more likely than not that Tony was going to be found guilty.

21
PHOEBE

It was Tony's decision. But as a result of that choice, the first person into the witness box was me.

'Do you swear to tell the truth, the whole truth, and nothing but the truth?'

The whole truth. There's a thought. Starting with my mother, and my childhood, and my work, and my getting into Jack's house and getting access to his password and his smart home set-up, and all the things I heard and learned, and how I used that, and *Cheating*, and my first taste of proper success, and how I had started to feel about Tony, and then the weird stuff that had begun to happen, and Kate coming and telling me that Jack had died, and learning that he might be my father, and how I felt both completely chewed up by it while also feeling nothing at all, and how relations with my mother had been broken off, which is what I had always wanted, and yet at the same time it felt like a disaster, and then how Tony had been arrested and how I was 99.9 per cent sure he was innocent but how tormenting that 0.1 per cent was, and how much I resented being up here in the witness box but how I also knew I had no choice, and how all this had brought my mother back into my life, constantly singing the praises of St Tony and talking about how worried she was and how he was the only thing she could think about and poor poor Tony and how unfair it was – take all those things together and the answer was no. I definitely wasn't going to tell the whole truth. But what I was going to do was try to answer the questions and give our version of the narrative. Our competing story.

Tony's barrister was standing in the well of the court, looking up at me and smiling – which was not something I'd ever seen her do before. Her manner was warm, empathetic. It said that we women know how to stick together through hard times. She was projecting a vibe that she liked me, which to be honest, I don't think she did. At least, if she did, she'd never given the slightest hint of it. I suppose the idea was that the more of a good person I seemed, the less likely it was that Tony was a bad one.

'Tell me about the events of last September,' she said. I knew this was coming but even so it took me a minute. Soho Farmhouse.

'The pizzas,' I said.

We took it from there. The pizzas, the white goods, the negative stuff about me online, the school stuff about Tony. The questions were gently served and I did my best to make what had happened sound as disorienting as it had actually been. How well did I do? No idea. It was like being on stage in front of an audience who were forbidden to respond – who weren't allowed to laugh or cry or clap or boo, so the actors had no way of telling whether they were managing to get the story across, or whether they were slowly and horribly dying.

It went by fast. That would have been a relief, if it hadn't been for the fact that the thing I was dreading most was what was going to happen next: the cross-examination. The prosecution barrister did the very off-putting thing of seeming as if he wasn't listening at all to my evidence. He didn't once look at me but kept his head down, apparently taking notes. I was braced for a kicking. I also knew that a middle-aged man bullying a younger woman is not a good look, and that he would need to be careful if he wanted to avoid coming across as a massive dick. If he did that, it would be unpleasant for me but might help Tony.

The prosecutor got up and looked at me. He had his usual air of barely suppressed irritation. The courtroom felt even more airless than usual. I was expecting him to go through everything I had said line by line and nuance by nuance; to be put through the wringer. But what he did was so much worse. He only asked two questions.

'Did your television programme have any bad reviews in the newspapers?'

It was so far out of left field that my brain short-circuited.

'Er . . . well . . . depends what you mean by bad . . . "mixed" maybe . . . not that anybody cares what the *Mail* or *Express* say . . . and I got the *Times* guy who never likes anything . . . I mean lots of them loved it, but you never get a full set of raves . . . that's just not how it works . . . you only ever remember the bad bits, true, but . . .'

I can only describe what I did as wittering on. I had been nervous. Now, on top of that, I felt embarrassed – even, to be honest, a little humiliated. As I was talking, I realised that the subtext was to imply that the online hate campaign was no different from what some professional critics had said, and I started to try and address that point, but that just made me witter more. I sounded as if I couldn't tell the difference between somebody not liking something I had written and a hate crime. He let me dig myself into that particular hole, and did not ask a follow-up question. It was excruciating. I finally was able to force myself to stop talking. He let the silence hang for a while and then he said:

'Do you and the defendant ever argue?'

'No, we're the perfect couple,' I snapped back. And he just looked at me, and I realised that now the person who looked irritable was me. I was also doing an excellent impersonation of somebody who was brittle, and slightly volatile, and unlikely to tell the full truth about what happened in my relationship. Again, he just let what I had said float in front of the jury, and then he said, 'No further questions.'

I left the witness box and went back to where I had been sitting in the gallery. Tristan squeezed my arm. I know he meant well, but it was that thing where someone is doing their best to reassure you but all that makes you think is that you need to be reassured because you've just massively fucked up. I risked a glance at Tony but he was looking straight down. It was fully as bad as I had thought.

There were three character witnesses after me: the headmistress and head of department from Tony's current school, and the headmaster from his last school. They said nice things about him and were convincing, at least to me. The prosecution didn't bother to cross-examine them or challenge their version. During their testimony, the prosecutor made it obvious that he wasn't paying any attention. He was writing on a yellow legal pad, pantomiming the fact that as far as he was concerned all this character evidence was irrelevant – the issue isn't whether or not the defendant is capable of seeming a nice bloke and good teacher, most of the time. That's not relevant. The issue is whether he stole bitcoin. The fact is that he did and we can prove it.

That was the end of the second day. The judge adjourned and said that the defendant would testify in the morning, and then the defence and the prosecution would make their concluding statements. Then she would give her summing up, and after that it would be time for the jury to consider their verdict. As he got up to leave the court, Tristan and I turned to each other. We didn't speak. There are moments with a twin when you know for certain what the other is thinking. My look said: Tony is going to prison. His look said: I know.

22
KATE

It was an unseasonably warm late autumn morning, and the South Bank was busy with a mix of tourists, parents with pre-school-age children, and the general surf of people mysteriously free in London in the middle of the week. I was walking along the side of the Thames with Conor, heading from Waterloo Bridge towards the London Eye. Conor was eating a pistachio ice cream from a cone. He was wearing a very subtle light wool Italian suit with a rich purple shirt and a pocket square; also boat shoes with no socks. I was going on a prison visit later that day and dressed accordingly. The inmates don't like it if you are either too smart or too casual, so I was wearing a businesslike but not too severe mix of black trousers, dark-blue jacket and silk shirt, with a printed scarf Jack bought for me in Paris knotted around my neck. Conor and I made an unusual couple and I could see people sneaking glances as they went past, wondering what the story was.

'I mean, it's perfectly obvious that Jack wasn't her father,' I said to Conor, 'and if she'd thought about it for half a second she'd have known that couldn't possibly be true. That mad-woman Sarah would never have left us alone for a minute if she'd been pregnant by Jack. It would have been Medea on amphetamines. I hadn't planned to say it, but it just came out in the moment. An inspired improvisation. You should have seen her face. I think if I'd actually shoved a knife into her she'd have looked less shocked.'

Conor's response to that was to take a slow, thoughtful lick of his ice cream. I waited for him to add a comment, but he didn't.

'I think it helped, though,' I went on. 'Apart from being fun in itself. I'm absolutely certain that was what she was thinking about when I left, and not the fact that I'd been alone inside for a couple of minutes while she was wrangling with you over the delivery. It's that thing you were talking about, which I have to admit I understood in theory but wasn't sure how to make it work in practice – misdirection is the key. To, what do you call it, social engineering?'

Conor nodded. 'Social engineering.'

'It reminded me of when I used to go shoplifting, in my distant youth. That's all misdirection too. All I can say is, I understand how people get a taste for these things. It's like what magicians do, sleight of hand, except with people and their feelings. Very clever. And of course, it's the same rule as it is with magic – never show them how it's done.'

I was smiling, but Conor was looking serious, at least insofar as that is possible for a man in a beautifully cut suit eating an ice cream on a sunny day. We came to the area where people set up tables covered in second-hand books, and I stopped for a moment to browse. Jack used to love the bouquinistes in Paris, along the side of the Seine, and even though he didn't read French he always made a point of picking up at least one or two books, usually French versions of things he had already read, or, occasionally, picture books. He would then spend the rest of the day complaining about how wildly inconvenient they were to lug around with him, until I finally told him to stop moaning and shut up.

Daphne said that she could tell when I was thinking about Jack, from the look on my face. Perhaps Conor could do the same thing. He said:

'Did it help? With missing Jack, getting over him. Did it help, what you did?'

'Yes, I think so. I mean, I didn't think it was going to magically make everything better. Obviously. But it gave me something to focus on other than grief. Anger is more fun than grief. And revenge is better still.'

'And that's what it felt like?' said Conor. 'Revenge? I know that's what it was supposed to feel like. But that's no guarantee.'

'Oh, Conor, that's so sweet, are you worried for me?' I said. 'Concerned for my immortal soul?' This was unfair of me, but he had been brought up Christian and it was an accepted part of our relationship that I occasionally teased him about it. 'We both know perfectly well you took exactly as much revenge as you wanted to. Or is it OK for you to take your revenge because you're a man?'

He didn't like that. He frowned and made a batting-away gesture with his ice cream cone.

'I mean it,' he said. 'It was a lot, what you did. A lot.'

For a moment I thought about saying, 'not what I did, what we did'. From Conor's manner, that would have been a mistake. Also, in truth, it wouldn't really have been fair. Conor had helped me – more than helped me, he had made what I had done possible. Without him, I wouldn't have known where to begin. But the desire to do it had all come from me. I was the motive force. I was both the driver and the engine. That would make him, what, the conductor?

It began the same day I had the revelation at my therapist's – my former therapist's. I suddenly saw that Phoebe must have eavesdropped on me and Jack and had used the proceeds of that eavesdropping, details from our intimate life, to make her little show. The clue was in the fact that the characters' speech was close to things we had said, indeed was sometimes verbatim. But the look was often wrong. She could hear us but not see us. All the input was auditory. How could that be possible? As soon as I framed the thought, the answer came to me: she had hacked Jack's smart home set-up. I couldn't work out exactly how she had done what she did but as it was later explained to me, there might have been any number of routes – it wasn't necessarily that difficult or technical. It didn't matter; what mattered was what was going to happen next.

The first thing I did when I got home was to go on the internet and do the opposite of what I had been doing. Previously, I had been in the ostrich position, trying and failing to hide from references to *Cheating* and its author. Now a switch had been thrown: I wanted to know everything about it and Phoebe Mull. I went online and read everything I could find. For two days, I barely moved from the computer. Interviews, reviews, internet chatter, social media chatter, everything. I watched the show in one burst, taking notes. The revelation wasn't obvious; it came to me in the form of an absence. She liked her image, which was spiky and cool and self-invented and filled with the deep, oblivious complacency of her generation. But the giveaway was that she never talked about her background or antecedents or where she was from. She had taken care to have no past. That interested me. Eventually, I saw a chance remark on a discussion board about someone who said they had known her before she changed her surname – and it gave her former name and then, all of a sudden, the whole story became clear. Phoebe Mull was Sarah Hadling's daughter. Of course she was.

When I realised that, everything made sense. She hated Jack and me. She had probably been brought up by a madwoman constantly telling her how we had ruined her life. How I had stolen the life that was supposed to be hers. She would blame us for everything bad that had ever happened to her mother and to her. And then she became a TV writer and was casting around for a story and found one that could scratch a lifelong itch for revenge.

The thing about revenge, though, is that you give what you get. At least, I do. Take from me and I will take from you. You will come off worse. The thing she had tried to take from me was my happiness. So that's what I decided to take from her. I thought about how I might do it, and I came up with a few ideas, and then I called Conor.

He had been amused, especially at first.

'What you're talking about is fucking with her,' he said, over coffee at his silly members' club in Soho. 'Fucking with her on an epic, unprecedented scale.'

'Yes.'

'Doing to her what she did to you.'

'Yes.'

'Ruining her life.'

'Yes.'

He brooded on that for a minute. I could tell that he needed more of a push. It was time to go all in.

'You've said that I saved your life,' I said. 'If you mean that, if you ever meant that, I'm asking you for this in recompense. It's the only thing I've ever asked you for, and I'll never ask you for anything else.'

'Let me think about it,' said Conor, signalling for the bill. 'I can't pretend that I don't understand. I'll get back to you.'

The idea of starting with deliveries came from him. The idea of beginning an online campaign against her came from me, but he knew how to execute it and how to create and coordinate the botnet. He was quite certain that none of this would be traceable. There was a division of labour: I wrote the negative commentary, gossip, and hostile chit-chat about Phoebe's work. Conor read it through, and made changes where he thought they were necessary. At the start, these were mainly about making my prose less syntactically and grammatically correct. I soon got the hang of that and I picked up some slang too, and before long Conor could post and repost what I had written without editing.

The idea of moving to focus on Tony came from me. The execution came from me too. I had begun to pick up hints that Conor was thinking I had gone far enough; that embarrassing and inconveniencing Phoebe was an end in itself. Perhaps he thought of it as a grief project, a way of me getting out of my own head and reconnecting with the world – a bizarre version of processing loss. He did not understand how I felt about what she had tried to take from me, and how determined I was to take from her in return. I didn't tell him when I started posting rumours about Tony at school. When he realised – he never told me how – he came to see me at home, and we talked it through.

'I'm just not sure, Kate, it's not like he's done anything to you. Except live with that woman.'

'You don't know that, Conor,' I said in return. 'He might have been in on it all along. He might have been egging her on.'

Conor made a face. He wasn't buying it. By now, I knew what I wanted; it had come to me when I had first thought of going after Phoebe's partner. But I could tell that Conor would need to be walked carefully to get to where I needed him to go.

'This was an attempt to destroy me. To destroy my marriage. What do you think would have happened to me and Jack when that show came out? What do you think it felt like when I heard that dialogue, heard Jack saying to his mistress the things he only ever said to me? Have you ever felt a humiliation like that?'

This was manipulative and sneaky of me, because I knew the answer to my question was yes – the thing Conor had minded most about his time in prison was the humiliation of it, the loss of respect. Self-respect included. I felt a surging sense that I was going to get what I knew he could give me.

'When people get divorced, they say there's this terrible thing that happens that nobody warns you about. You have this stack, this folder, of happy memories from the marriage. Even bad marriages have some. Marriages that had long good stretches leave you with trunkloads. You can take comfort in those memories when times are hard. But then when you get divorced, it's as if you lose access to them. Like forgetting a password. You know they're there but they are no use to you. That's what she tried to do to me – she tried to take away my past. She almost took Jack away a second time, after I had already lost him. So that's why I'm going after her happiness, and I'm not going to stop until I've done to her what she tried to do to me.'

Conor gave a tentative nod. I could tell this had got through to him. He got up and went and looked out of the window. There were building noises coming from the street – the beeping and clattering of a bin lorry reversing and being loaded. I let him take his time. He turned back to me.

'There's something I could do. Something really serious. Unleash a weapon, basically.'

I nodded. This was what I had been hoping for. I didn't interrupt.

'I've had my doubts. I have to admit there were times when I regretted saying that. But . . . the thing is, you saved my life. I've always said that and it's true. So I think, if this is what you're asking, I have to give it to you. All you need is five seconds to plug a USB drive into a computer, and the software will do the rest. It creates a footprint online, and loads stuff on to the computer. As I say, it's a weapon. I made it to get back at Ambrose. Which in the event I didn't do. But you can only use it once, and you can't un-use it.

No take-backs. You need to be sure.'

We looked at each other. I held out my hand. I wondered, for a moment, if I had horrified him. Conor took his time, and I watched him make up his mind. He put his hand in his pocket and took out a thumb drive and palmed it to me. He almost flinched as he did so.

'Five seconds?'

He nodded. 'Stick it in, count five elephants, it's done. The difficult part is gaining physical access to someone's computer. You might need help with that. But the hacking, this does it for you.'

★ ★ ★

And now, on the South Bank, we had come to the end of something. I could tell there was a speech he wanted to make, a conclusion he wanted to deliver, a severance. And that was fine with me. I could have made him say it, but out of gratitude – a gratitude I deeply and sincerely felt – I let him off.

'I know you feel I went too far,' I said to Conor. 'And I understand. I don't hold that against you and I don't expect you to pretend you don't have your feelings. So what I'm going to do is release you. I saved your life, according to you. Well, now you have saved mine. We're even. We don't have to see each other any more. Jack always used to say, people should let things come to an end, when they reach an end. That's what this is.'

Was I hurt to see a moment of relief in Conor's eyes? Maybe a little. But I had expected it. And I meant what I said. He had done enough. To be frank, I also found his twinges of conscience, if that is what this could be called, tiresome. I wasn't interested in his regrets and his second thoughts. He sighed and shrugged.

'Thank you,' he said. 'And goodbye. I hope you find peace.'

I laughed. I said,

'Of course. I already have. Goodbye, Conor.'

'What's so funny?'

'Nothing. An in-joke. Thank you again. I mean it, about saving my life.'

He walked away. It really was a truly remarkable suit.

I was still smiling, thinking of something else Jack used to say. When people involved in a bitter conflict talk about wanting peace, what they mean is they want victory. In any case, it was now time to take a taxi to Wandsworth prison.

23
KATE

When I went back to my prison visiting work, I found that, in my absence, I had magically been promoted. Nobody explained this to me, either the fact or the reasoning behind it; it was just that I was now in a supervisory role. It was the opposite of that French saying that *'les absents ont toujours tort'*, the absent are always in the wrong. In this case, seniority had been bestowed on me. The new job involved monitoring other visitors, designing rotas, and performing initial interviews and assessments. It suited me. I had more responsibility but also more autonomy.

I had allowed an hour to get to Wandsworth, which only takes half an hour by cab, but I wanted a margin for error. Happily for me, a cab was waiting right there on the rank close to County Hall. There was a tiny beat of surprise when I told the cabby to take me to Wandsworth prison; that often happens, and I always enjoy it. It had been hot on the South Bank, but once the journey was under way, air moving through the cab made it much more pleasant. I like that sense that autumn is hitting a peak but you can feel the winter in the offing. I go through cycles of loving London and hating it. I was in one of my more positive phases. I had things to keep me busy; I was going on holiday with Daphne later in the month, walking in the Pyrenees, which would have been a huge surprise to the person I was two years ago, but I was really looking forward to it. I missed Jack multiple times a day, and sometimes multiple times an hour. But I was able to function. And I felt that I had done something about my grief; I had taken steps.

Prisons are cruel places, all of them, but I often think there is something especially cruel about the location of Wandsworth, so close to the centre of one of the world's great cities, and also so close to the green spaces of the Common. Travelling there, you go: London, flash of green, prison. I've never asked any of my charges whether they feel the closeness of the trees and grass and space – what could they possibly say: 'yes, and it makes everything so much worse'? But it also makes it one of the better ones to visit, because you are in an agreeable part of town on the way in, and you're in an agreeable part of town the second you come out.

The cab driver dropped me in the first visitors' car park. I could tell that he had been bursting to ask what business took me to the prison but hadn't quite been able to summon up the nerve, in case my reasons were disastrously personal. I was in a magnanimous mood. After telling him to add ten per cent for the tip, I said:

'Prison visiting.'

He laughed. 'I thought you might be interviewing for a job as the new governor.'

That made me smile. I could imagine what Jack would say, something along the lines of 'he's probably in the market for a new dominatrix'.

They know me in reception, though that doesn't prevent formalities around identification and taking custody of my phone. The senior guard who's usually on duty is one of those decreasingly common but very welcome British types with an inviolable rule about opening all interactions with small talk about the weather. I showed him my passport and he pretended to look at it for half a second.

'Bit hotter today.'

'Yes, though it's already starting to ease off. I always think that when the afternoon begins to be cooler than the morning, winter isn't far away.'

'Hotter again tomorrow though, according to the forecast.'

'Let's hope so. I'm not quite ready for my winter coat.'

He passed my handbag and jacket and tote bag of paperwork into the scanner and gestured me through the metal detector. I stepped through and collected my stuff.

'I'm well aware I'm a little early, George. I'll go and sit in the waiting room.'

He made a small bow as I left. Really, I must have been giving off the most extraordinary pheromones that day, to judge by the effect I was having on men more or less my age.

The waiting room was one of those public spaces in which the misery has accumulated so long and so densely that it feels as if it is smeared on all the surfaces. Prison waiting rooms, hospital waiting rooms, the room outside the room in which the person with authority is busy doing something else. These are the rooms where people wait for bad news, where nothing ever happens on time, where you know you're going to leave sadder than you were when you arrived. You can't see the built-up misery but you can feel it, and once you know it's there all you can do is think about wiping or washing it off. Three women were already sitting there waiting at separate tables. A mother, a wife and a girlfriend, if I had to guess, returning characters in the reliable rep company of prison waiting rooms. The mother was about the same age as me; she caught my eye and nodded. The girlfriend, who was jiggling her leg and staring up at the roof, visibly struggling with the absence of her phone, could easily have still been in school.

The sight of her made me think of Jack. 'When people talk about the great criminals of world history, nobody ever mentions Tammy

Wynette. But has any work of art, in any medium anywhere, ever done more damage than the single line "stand by your man"?'

I took out my notepad and papers and pretended to look at them; in reality, I knew why I was there and to whom I would be talking, and what today's running order would be. I had one initial assessment and three check-ins with inmates whose regular visitor was on holiday. But the main order of business was my first appointment. He was the reason I was here.

One of the younger warders came into the waiting room and called to me.

'Mrs H? We're ready for you.'

I smiled, got up, and followed him as he buzzed me out of the room into a corridor, and then buzzed me through to the meeting room. He went away and I sat myself up at the desk. Two minutes later he came back with the person I had come there to meet. The guard stood in the corner, which is protocol for the first meeting with a new inmate, until the visitor has signed off on feeling safe. This guard, a gym monster like quite a few of the twenty-something wardens, was so pumped up that he could barely fold his arms over each other. If you were nervous, he would have been a good person to have on your side.

I wasn't nervous. Not at all.

Prison breaks many men, and here this inmate was, looking inches shorter and years older than I knew him to be. Good-looking, the profile of his partner had said, though you would be forgiven for not thinking so now. His hair was greasy, his skin was pallid, and he had the evasive, avoidant body language of a man much further into his sentence. Ah well, nobody ever said doing time was supposed to be easy.

The truth was, with the first sight of him and the first ten seconds in his company, I had everything I needed – everything I had come for. But I take my charity work seriously, and there were formalities to be gone through. I introduced myself and explained who I was and what I was there for. Position and permission is what they teach us: explain who we are and then ask if we can do what we're supposed to do.

'Can I just check your name and details and so on?'

'Tony Mull,' he said. 'I'm doing two years for something I didn't do.'

I took a moment to give him time to supply the details, but they were not forthcoming. That's something that happens and we're trained not to see it as a problem, especially in the early stages of incarceration. Prisoners can't rehabilitate until they face reality, and that takes time, but guess what, they have plenty of time. So where's the rush?

'Theft,' I said. 'Two years. You're ten days in.'

'For something I didn't do,' he said again. The words might be defiant but nothing else about him was. I admired that he was sticking to his truth and thought, but obviously didn't say, good for you. I looked over at the jacked young guard, whose face had the classic set, hardened look of a warden sick of dealing with criminals and their lies. It's not easy, being our society's lowest form of life.

'So how are you feeling, Tony? How has your first week and a bit been?'

He looked a little wild at that – as if it was the stupidest question he had ever heard. Which of course it was, considered as a serious question, and not just as a prompt to get him to talk. I did a good job, I think, of acting as if I was waiting for an answer. In truth, I was just looking at him and making the most of the moment. I knew, as he did not, that I would not be back. One of my concerns, before coming to the prison that day, was that I would be overcome with feelings that I didn't want: that I might be swamped with remorse, say, or that I might have a version of church giggles, a totally inappropriate wish to burst out with confidences and tell him everything that had happened, everything that I had done, all that had gone on between me and Jack and Phoebe, and the real reason why he was in there.

I didn't feel any of that. All I had was a curiosity that I couldn't call mild – it was a strong curiosity, as strong as any I had ever felt – but which had been very quickly and completely sated by the simple fact of meeting him. I could see that I had done what I wanted to do. I was happy for me.

'I don't want to talk about it,' he eventually said.

I went through some of the routine follow-up manoeuvres we are trained to adopt, in an attempt to establish first empathy and then some connection, on which subsequent visits could build. Of course, I wasn't actually doing that – I was thinking back to the reason he was here, the time I had gone to visit Phoebe at her house, with Conor's USB drive in my pocket.

I had thought it was going to be a difficult choice. To do or not to do. But it wasn't difficult, not at all. The things I had done up to that point had not been commensurate with the harm that had been done to me. Phoebe's plan had failed, because I had seen through her. But on this point, English law and I agreed: the outcome didn't matter, only the intention. And her intention had been murderous.

When I gave her an opportunity to show remorse or grief or empathy or basic human decency, by telling her about Jack's death, she chose not to. Her response to me was as cold as it could have been. And part of me was pleased. I could do either too little or too much and she took away the choice; she forced me to do too much. The decision was as easy as the action itself. My only worry was that it wouldn't work.

It was frustrating to have missed what actually happened; it was disappointing not to have been there, an invisible observer right there in the room. I could guess more or less what it had been like, but that wasn't the same as being there and hearing the heat and panic in their voices. I also wished that I could have been at the trial, but it was just too risky.

My evidence for how it worked was now sitting across an unsteady prison table. It made me feel warm to think about the effect this would be having on Phoebe. I had to discipline my thinking, because I might smile, and Tony would detect something wrong. Not that that would matter; but I wanted to make sure he didn't remember me and had no reason to mention me to Phoebe when she visited. On some level, I regretted that. In an ideal world, she would realise what I had done, and realise also that there wasn't anything she could do about it. That would be more painful for her. But you can't have everything.

I kept going through the questionnaire and he kept dissociating. There was nothing about the exchange that was significantly different from any of the other times I had visited a prisoner for an initial assessment. This would be the last time we would ever meet.

The half hour came to an end. I gave the guard a look and he gave one back.

'That's all we have time for,' I said to Tony. 'Regular visits will begin after I file the assessment. That should be in a week or so.'

He was so numb that he didn't understand this was a dismissal. The guard came over to him and signalled for him to stand up. When he did, he stayed there for a moment staring at me. For the first time in the entire conversation, I felt he was fully emotionally present.

'You don't understand,' he said, or gasped, or cried – a sound I still sometimes remember and think about. 'I am innocent.'

I looked at the guard and flicked my eyes sideways to the door. He read my cue and took the prisoner by the arm and began leading him out of the room. I smiled at Tony.

I said, 'Everyone in here is innocent.'